HOME MOVIES

HOME MOVIES

RAY ROBERTSON

CORMORANT
BOOKS

The publisher gratefully acknowledges the support of the
Canada Council, the Ontario Arts Council, and the
Department of Canadian Heritage.

Cover design by Bill Douglas @ The Bang.
Printed and bound in Canada.

Cormorant Books Inc.
RR 1
Dunvegan, Ontario
K0C 1J0

Canadian Cataloguing in Publication Data
Robertson, Ray, 1966-
Home Movies : a novel
ISBN 1-896951-02-3
I. Title
PS8585.O3219H65 1997 C813'.54 C97-900310-5
PR9199.3.R532H65 1997

Mother
Father
Mara

All my people are larger bodies than mine,
quiet, with voices gentle and
meaningless like the voices of sleeping birds.
                                    —James Agee
                                    Knoxville: Summer, 1915

For as long as he could remember, snowstorms had been his heroes. . . .

Hockey practice wasn't until six-thirty, and the alarm wouldn't go off for another forty-five minutes, but up and out of bed for an intended hurried-down-the-hall-and-back pee he caught by ear alone the howl and wind-whip sounding of the season's first blizzard. The small, frozen incoherent bathroom windowpane next to the toilet showed him outside nothing; didn't have to. Just listen to that thing. . . .

Thirteen years old and Chuck Berry innocent, on the heels of his feet he duck-walked down the chilled tiled hallway floor, first past the closed bedroom door of his grandparents, then that of his mother, barefooted flesh relaxing only upon hitting living-room heavy shag shore. He approached the big picture window that overlooked the front yard and street and pulled to each side of him the heavy green winter curtains his grandmother every October hung. Like some pubescent winter king set on apprais-ing his empire from above, he stepped forward into the rayon sanctuary. The hair on his legs and arms stood immediately straight up, but he did not register cold.

In spite of the new inches of it everywhere, he couldn't, as he never could, see from his early morning perch the tidy lines of steady angled snow as depicted on the American television pro-grams he watched. Only the streetlight on the front lawn of the neighbour's house across the road offered confirmation of the night's activity: a thousand (they taught him at school each unique) snowflakes frenzying under the overhanging light's yellow spot of glow, a petri dish of hysteria. Further, a surer sign: auditory affidavit in the even testimony of steady winded roar and windowpane occasional tick tick (pause) tick, the latter the irregular but manifest rhythm of the intermittent tiny meteor of snowflake turned to sleet-shot colliding with windowpane.

In the middle of the front lawn half a foot of his hockey net poked above the night's new white covering, intersecting elbow of red crossbar and goal-post the only evidence of last night's before-bedtime world. The cars parked in all the driveways along the street were enormous snow sculptures of impenetrable abstract design. Neat rows of Wednesday-morning garbage cans survived the night as whipped-cream–topped cylinders of no apparent purpose. A streetful of doomed attempts at lawn-ornamented individualism was gently but utterly erased by only a few hours of night-time steady falling. The hockey stick with which he hadn't scored the winning goal on a breakaway in the last seconds of overtime was two feet under. Everything was lost of function, was not itself, was nothing; being nothing, everything could be anything, could be perfect. Possibility flushed him altogether; no faulty plaster job around the base of the windowpane could admit a draft big enough to extinguish.

Several minutes of this.

Then, pleased with the progress of his kingdom, as close to content as could be, he gave a quick last survey outside, spun around in place, broke through the hanging wall of curtain, and beat it like hell back down the hallway to his bedroom, shivering in his underwear and T-shirt the entire way. He slid into bed and pulled up tight to his chin the covers, waiting for the serene bawl of wind outside his bedroom window to affect as he knew it could.

But someone was in the bathroom — probably his grandfather getting up early for work — and flushed the toilet. An explosion of soiled water shot through the pipes of the house, this quickly followed up by successive piped-water acts of sucking, then expulsion. Five minutes later the radiator's clanking began. An ill-tempered orangutan loaded up on whisky and armed with a monkey wrench came to mind. And stayed there.

Under the blankets he listened to the steady metal banging of pipes until the alarm beeped off and he knew it was time to get up.

PART ONE

1

He hoped the receptionist would never call out his name; felt very comfortable, in fact, just where he was. Thumbing the afternoon away through the stack of fashion magazines at his end-table side, he would sample the occasional rub-on cologne, search out familiar body parts and faces, and see just how summer's new look was shaping up. Then, perhaps, in time, a kindly grey-haired janitor (head resting easily on liver-spotted folded hands and standing-straight-up broom) would shoo him home at day's end, gentle knowledge and a goodnight and good luck to you in all you do, son, his. But he wasn't the one who had insisted upon this appointment. Eight messages on my machine in three days, he reflected, two of them from Devanchuck himself; not just to get me in here to explain how lucky he feels to have me on the label. Rejection, clearly, he thought, without much surprise. But, James wondered, how could he have decided so quickly? He had only dropped the tape off less than a week ago.

Too soon, then, the door he was waiting on opened, and out came the rhythm section to Colour Wheel, an eight-man reggae act steadily gaining popularity on the local club scene. James wasn't exactly straight on the band's particular brand of liberation politics, but he did have it from a good pillow-talk source that Devanchuck — owner, president, and actual overseer of the small Toronto-based label Willie Pee Musics, which both they and James shared — was planning on investing a significant portion of that fall's advertising budget into pushing the band's new disc, tentatively going by the working title *Dance Until You Be Free (Songs for a New World Order)*. James's newest work wasn't, as far as the company was concerned, going by the name of anything. He put down that month's *Flare* on the end-table and rose from his seat, moving towards Devanchuck's open door. Hurry up and face the music, he thought, thinking, also: Not a bad title for an album. But whose?

"I'll let you know when Mr. Devanchuck is ready to see you, Mr. Thompson." Francine, Devanchuck's secretary, did not tolerate unannounced visitors; became downright ornery, actually, at the very prospect.

"Well, it looks like he's finished up with—"

Standing, leaning forward, hands flat on her desk, "I'll be sure to let you know when he's ready to see you, Mr. Thompson," she said.

"I think I'll just—"

"I said I'll let you know when he's ready for you."

James continued his creep towards Devanchuck's door, nodding at the three exiting Rastafarians.

"Man," the tall one in the middle answered. James thought he recognized him as the bass player. The air that passed between them was sweet and warm. James smiled, pleased by the thought that someone was able to pass a middle-of-the-afternoon business meeting ripped out of his gourd.

"I'll let you know! I said I'll let you know!"

James could hear Francine picking up the phone, punching hard at numbers. Insult to injury, he closed the office door behind him with a heel-kick of his cowboy boot.

Before he could accept Devanchuck's offered hand, the intercom came on. "Mr. Devanchuck?"

"Just a sec, will you, James? Grab a seat there." Devanchuck gestured to the cushioned swivel chair on the other side of the desk. "Yeees?" He answered as if he was expecting bad news.

"I'm sorry to have to bother you with this sort of thing, Mr. Devanchuck, but it seems that Mr. Thompson didn't hear me when I informed him that I would let him know as soon as, and not before, you were ready to receive him."

"Oh, that's all right, Francine. All in the family, right?"
"Sir?" Pause.
"Yes?" Pause.
"I mean; what?"
"Okay, then. Appreciate it if you could just hold the fort out there for a little while, Francine. No calls or crazies, allrightee? Got to talk a little C&W with our boy James here." He gave James a quick wink.
"Well, if that's the way you want things to operate, sir, fine. Just understand that I did inform Mr. Thompson that I would notify him when you were ready for him. Please be aware of that fact." Over and out.

Like many not old yet but not young any more either, whose job it was to supply the daily grease to the bureaucracy of Toronto's substantial arts community, Francine knew for certain, if she knew one thing, that she wasn't a secretary; a musician, a muralist, a mobilist, a performance artist working primarily with media images of female oppression juxtaposed with found objects of fast-food waste — these, certainly. And just this past month, an experimental novelist. But a secretary? As a consequence, it was almost a matter of pride that she couldn't type, wouldn't take dictation, frequently was late in getting cheques mailed out to the artists on the company's roster, and often closed down the office hours early when Devanchuck was out of town. Only for the reception-room watch-dog routine did she for some reason show anything beyond suffering and indulgent boredom. Why Devanchuck hadn't fired her long ago was a mystery to anyone having anything to do with the label. James suspected long-term monkey business.

Devanchuck looked at the now silent black communication box on his desk, for an instant not Devanchuck any more; someone capable, that is, of sitting still for thirty seconds without talking or using karate-chop hand gestures to make absolutely clear what, at pivotal conversational moments, he rarely failed to refer to as "the rub".

Physically, he wasn't much of anything; medium every-thing, and, on bad days, not even that.

Spell broken, Devanchuck leaned back in his chair, smiling, entwined hands behind his head revealing sweat spots the size of softballs under the arms of his white Christian Dior. Pointing with his chin in the direction of the closed door, he asked, "You know the boys, don't you, James?"

"Colour Wheel? No, can't say that I do."

"Get to, James. Get to know them. This World Music thing is hot right now — very hot. The future of our business. Absolutely. Consider it an investment in your own musical future to keep your nose close to the trail of what could be the next big thing. And believe you me, James, rhythm is the next big thing. Rhythm."

Across the large mahogany desk that separated them, James offered the considered nod and pursed-lip smile usually reserved for the likes of vacuum-cleaner salesmen prideful of being able to clean up the mess they've just made on your floor. "Well, I appreciate the advice, Mr. Devanchuck, but it's not really—"

"Not really your thing. I hear you. And I respect you for the strength of your musical convictions. Really." A sharp slice of the atmosphere announced that the topic was finished. "You get a chance to catch the Jays' game last night?"

"No," James said, "actually we were playing last night. Trying to keep the name alive on the street, you know."

"Right, right. Too bad. Hell of a game. Darn Gaston left the starter in too long again, though. Think he'd have learned by now to know when his guy was out of juice. Same basic principle in running a business, you understand. Sure. Stay too long with a dead arm, and boom!" Emphatic right-hand slashes began to fly in front of Devanchuck's face. "Before you know it, the other guy's hit a grand slam and you go from sitting in the dugout with your name stitched on your back to sweeping peanut shells off the stadium floor and having to buy a ticket if you want to get into the park." Lesson over, Devanchuck's folded hands fell back into his lap. "They ended up winning it in the eleventh, though. And hey, all said and done, that's all that matters, right?"

"Right," James said. Which was worse? Beeper-belted Toronto businessman fat-ass ensconced in corporation-purchased Blue Jays box-seats who, since the Jays' first World Series victory, could not stop using baseball metaphors to illustrate each of life's many-to-be-learned lessons? Or this particular Toronto businessman with Willie-Pee-purchased Blue Jays box-seat tickets, an ever-widening underside, and this particularly insipid baseball metaphor for life? Close call always goes to the lard butt sitting in front of you.

"Look, you're an intelligent man, James, so I'll spare you the company claptrap about how glad we are to have you with the label and how pleased we've been with your work for us so far and how here's hoping we can continue with this mutually beneficial relationship and blah blah blah." Each blah was a chop: chop, chop, chop.

"I appreciate that, Mr. Devanchuck."

"But James, here's the rub." Devanchuck leaned forward in his chair, tasselled Bardolinos softening his landing. "When I bought this label back in '83, you wouldn't believe the junk I was contractually locked into. Unbelievable. Really. Thirty-five-year-old schoolteacher punk rockers, computerized dance music troupes going by the name of various French Philosophes, Christian heavy-metal acts throwing New Testaments and "I've Seen Him" T-shirts into the audience. No shortage of artists, that's for sure — and understand here that I use that term purely descriptively and not in any evaluatory sense. But do you know the one thing we were lacking? Do you?" Invisible blocks of wood crashed beneath his hand.

James raised open palms and shook his head.

"Integrity, James. Integrity. I wanted to be proud to

say that I ran a record label that didn't cater to the lowest commercial barometer, didn't just give the people what they wanted but — and here's the rub, my friend — gave them what they *needed*. Absolutely." Regarding the glorious genealogy of Willie Pee Musics, James was no innocent; more than a couple of times, around the open bar at company Christmas parties, he had heard variations on this very same speech. He nodded along anyway, chin in hand, one leg crossed over the other, waiting for the real "rub".

"So I cleaned house," Devanchuck continued. "Hunted out and signed up young, committed musicians like yourself. Talented and sincere individuals of all musical persuasions and interests who — the only thing I ever demanded — put the music first and personal ambition second. And in return, I like to think that we as a label also always put the music first and the pursuit of the almighty buck in its rightful place as a distant second."

Why, James wondered, were rich people the only ones who threw around expressions like the "almighty buck"?

"But to everything there is a season, James. That's in the Bible and Pete Seeger too. It's long and boring and too technical to go into, but with all these cutbacks and the government putting the bite on every small business to tighten its belt — that and, well, some family legal difficulties I'm not actually able to discuss with anyone outside the tribe, you understand — an album's worth of country-and-western songs without words to go along with them is not something Willie Pee Musics would be able at this particular moment in time to subsidize. And frankly, James, that's what would happen if we went ahead with this idea of yours. Subsidization."

"Did you at least listen to the tape I dropped off?"

"Didn't have to. Once Francine told me what we were dealing with, well, that's when we started trying to get ahold of you. Hard man to reach, you are. The life of a musician, I guess," he said, winking again. "I envy your

Bohemian prerogative. Reminds me of my old Yorkville days."

James tried on a smile that would have made a good before-photo for a laxative product. He uncrossed his legs, boots flat on the floor now, and looked through Devanchuck's sixth-floor window at the Toronto day passing by. Grey governmental offices and insurance and banking buildings punctured the cloudscape. In the distance he could see the CN Tower looking bored with itself. Tourists rode up and down the elevator all day long.

"Look, James, I've never been a man to tell another man how to do his job and I'll be darned if I'm going to start now. But ask yourself this question, will you? When was the last time you heard a country instrumental on the radio? Any instrumental, for that matter? I mean, stop me if I'm way off base here, but isn't the whole appeal of the country-and-western song the cry-in-your-beer-and-sing-along-with-the-jukebox deal?"

Before James could answer, "Hell," Devanchuck continued, "you wouldn't even need a video for what you're proposing to do now, would you? And let's be honest. Even the smallest label such as our own is prey to how many plays its artists' videos get each day on the old boob-tube. Sign of the times. Age of the image. Illiterate culture. All of that. Read your McLuhan, for goodness' sake. He's one of ours, you know. An honest-to-goodness Canuck with a real world-class intellect. Taught at the university not ten minutes from where we're sitting right now. Not every Tom, Dick, and Harry is aware of that fact. Anyway, gotta change with the times, James, or the times will change you. Simple fact of. . . ." He waved away the incomplete thought with his chopping hand. "But hey, don't get me wrong. I don't like the direction the business is taking any more than you do. Heck, I remember following Ian and Sylvia around the country on their North American tour in '71. Or was it '72? Anyway, we were just kids. Little younger than yourself, of course, but we were young and happy and maybe just a little bit foolish, too, but we—"

"So what's the deal here, Mr. Devanchuck? Are you telling me you're letting me go?"

"Not by any stretch of the imagination, James, not at all. As you know, we signed a two-record deal with you with an option for a third back in 1989. You've given us two records, we've been happy with those records, and we've been glad to put out and promote those two records. Win-win situation for both of us, right? Okay. It's just that I think we've been more than a little bit patient with you in waiting for that third album for some time now. Two years and four months since your last release, actually. And I think the time is ripe for a new James Thompson album. Very ripe. And for the past year or so I have tried very hard, but without much success, to impress upon you the importance of getting a new James Thompson project done and out there, this only because of the absolute necessity of staying alive in your audience's mind. Because we both know what comes after ripe, don't we, James?"

James: upturned palms and raised eyebrows.

Devanchuck: "Rotten."

"And what's wrong with *Queen Street Rag* as my third album?" James asked. He felt as he imagined a defence lawyer with an admittedly guilty client must: doomed in his pleading, utterly indifferent to his cause.

"James, Willie Pee Musics is simply not interested at this point in time in an all-instrumental album. Nothing personal. Wouldn't matter if it was rock, reggae, or folk music. Heck, the only two jazz musicians we're carrying right now are both women singers, for goodness' sake. You know, the Billie Holiday thing, the torch-song-type unit. Just the way it is. Anyway, I'm willing to put this error of judgement on your part out of mind if you are. We'll just write it off as a musical experiment that didn't quite pan out. But now it's time to get back down to business. To work. What we need to see you do is put some of those typically Thompsonesque lyrics of yours to that music you've already got. You know what I'm talking about. Small-town Saturday nights. Eccentric local sorts — the lonely-uncle-on-his-farm bit was always one of my personal favourites, by the way. The blow of the factory whistle at closing time. Reckless young couples discovering love in the timeless back seat of the old Ford. All the stuff we've grown to love and respect you for. And heck, the job's already half done, isn't it?"

"Sorry?"

"Half done. The job is already half done. The music's already written, right? So you just need the other half. The words."

Words, James thought. Sure: All I need are the words.

"I've never been a big advice-giver, James, but I'm gonna go out on a limb here because I know how secure you are — as an artist, I mean — and that you won't take this the wrong way. Now, I'm not saying that you haven't got a stashful of new lyrics ready and waiting to go, or that this instrumental thing of yours wasn't a bona fide effort. But let's say you don't and it wasn't, okay? Let's just say. In that case, may I suggest a trip back home? I mean, what is it, a couple hours south of here?"

"Three and a half, actually."

"Three and a half hours. A hop, skip, and a jump. You go, you soak up the sights and sounds, write an album's worth of lyrics, and everybody's happy."

"How often do you get back home, Mr. Devanchuck?" James said. It was more an accusation than a question.

"Well, Toronto is my home. I guess I'm always home then, aren't I?"

"Lucky you," James said.

Devanchuck offered an affirmative nod and grin, stood up, walked around his desk, and put a hand on the shoulder of the protocol-pushed-up and rising James, guiding the younger man out of his office and almost entirely out of the waiting-room. Francine looked up from the book she was reading and smiled at him. James glared back.

"Three things, James," Devanchuck said. "Do me a favour and keep them in mind, will you? Okay. First, Willie Pee Musics believes in you. As an artist. Do not ever doubt this. Second, never forget your audience. They're the ones who really sign your paycheque, not me. Simple and clichéd, I know, but true. And third, deliver to me an album's worth of real songs — the kind with words to them — four months from now, by the first week of September, or we terminate our working relationship. Allrightee? That's my boy." He lifted his hand from James's shoulder and gave him a goodbye pat on the back that felt like a push, sending him on his way out of the office.

"Oh, and James?"

James turned around. Francine was still smiling.

"What's your take on this infield-fly rule thing? I mean, just what the heck is the deal there? Is it a rule, or isn't it?"

James left the door open, wide open, behind him.

2

Eating sidewalk, miles of it, it seemed, in quick clicking cowboy-boot steps through this neighbourhood then that, Every set of eyes is a potential lover tonight, he thought: Queen Street enchanteds chattering out of late-show foreign film double features; myopic bookstore beauties drifting amidst open-binned remainders, peripheral glances fitful for kinder, cleaner, Canadianized Jack Kerouacs; even the muted furore of barfront-felt, overamplified rock and roll — sole music for the brain stem — right in one ear and not out the other until stepped out finally in irresistibly metered, boot-footed steps.

For seven blocks he clenched a quarter in the palm of his right hand, the push in the pit of his stomach — the origin of all no-good notions — audiblizing: something, anything, but not just nothing. Every phone booth along the way was an invitation to initiate salacious oblivion; every open-air café a too-easy excuse for escapist imbecility. He permitted, even encouraged, the city to divert his mind from what it should have been on, but was successful only in covering a lot of ground.

As James continued into his second hour of walking, his brain finally fell into the groove of reflection the situation at hand demanded. Devanchuck's September ultimatum seemed too much information at the moment to process, however, so instead he pondered that faceless collective that supposedly signed his royalty cheque each month.

James figured the majority of his audience to be about a forty-five percent each way even split between authentic small-towners such as he had once been, and confirmed big-city citizens (most of these from Toronto) like he had now become. The former, resentful of having to miss out on so many of the soul-stirring things they were sure were going on without them in the big town, were thrilled to hear in James's music their own lives made to add up to something more than the dull sum of their parts; James of late had come to refer to this portion of his listenership as the longing-for-what-is-not pile. The latter, not finding in the big city the absolute sense of personal fulfilment they felt entitled to as inhabitants thereof, managed to persuade themselves that in the kind of small town James depicted in his songs something like true self-realization and completeness of Being might yet be possible; these James dubbed the nostalgia-for-what-never-was pile. Only to the remaining ten percent of his audience did he at present feel any genuine sense of connection.

These were individuals of an entirely different demographic from the normal country crowd. Most were longhairs James's age or younger, more likely to spark a spliff than down a forty-ouncer, more apt to wear tie-dye than a string tie, more familiar with Smashing Pumpkins and Pearl Jam than Merle Haggard or Hank Williams. Some city-born, others subway-migrated from one of Toronto's outlying suburbs, this small but faithful segment of the city's Generation X found in the figure of James their very own country slacker.

For one thing, there was the way James and his band executed live their chosen musical genre in as unadorned and image-free a fashion as the most alternative of the alternative bands in town. The Paddocks could and did rock out on occasion. How far was it, after all, from "The Race Is On" to "Get It On (Bang a Gong)" when all you wanted at last call was a dance-floor full of feet having as good a time as they could? But this missed the point; the straight-ahead, no-bullshit approach to playing that James insisted upon was just as appreciated when the steel guitar solo-moaned on a slow number as when the electric guitars made their encore appearance. No-frills delivery was un-deniably in, and James's was one of the few country-and-western acts on the Toronto club scene that did not com-promise purity of execution for cross-over radio possibil-ity. Country grunge; James had credibility.

There was also the not insignificant fact that neither James nor any of The Paddocks looked like a country mu-sician. If not quite as hip as the younger segment of their audience, James and his bandmates at least did not fit the stereotypical picker image, T-shirts and blue jeans being about as rustic as any one of them ever got, James's cow-boy boots the only pointed pair in the band. James, Smitty, the steel-guitarist, and Scott B., the bass player, all wore their hair unkempt, collar-length long, the drummer, Freddie Webby, a burly, transplanted American mid-west-ern Zen/Bud Light zealot with a rock-and-roll background but an impeccable sense of brush-stroke, country-waltz rhythms, going the distance with a goatee, nose ring, and a blond mane hanging halfway down his back. The word on the street and in the hipper zines distributed around town said that James and the boys were the genuine article, and James in particular was singled out for his country visionary talents. An excerpt from *Glue Shot: A Music and Cultural Monthly (Volume #1, Number #2)* :

> *James Thompson wants to bring country-and-western music to a generation for too long raised on the musical gospel of distraction in the name of the Holy Lord Noise and Emotional Numbness. Thompson wants to show the punks and the rockers and the head bangers and whoever else might be listening that country music played as it should be played — and as Thompson and his band The Paddocks play it: with honesty, energy, and emotion — is a musical form for all people, and not just an anthem for ignorant rednecks. Make no mistake, though — it is less what Thompson's songs say than the artful, heartfelt way that he and his band musically say them that convinces. A revolution fought with a fiddle bow: this is James Thompson's unique musical cross to bear.*

He found himself turning onto Bloor Street just off Spadina. It was, by now, a jacket-cool but pleasant all the same mid-May early evening. He pushed open the door to the Niagara Tavern and took his regular spot by the front window. A steady parade of Bloor Street passers-by kept him light on his mind, the indeterminable nature of who was coming and who was going and for just what reasons never disappointing for its contemplative effect.

For James (not the first; not likely the last) Toronto was all of the things you simply could not get or be at home, the reason so many of its three and a half million quit where they came from so they could be here instead and do and see and say: This is my city. I'm from Toronto. This is where

I'm from.

Good bookstores, record stores; beautiful, intelligent women; all-night, everything-on-the-menu-all-the-time diners; green-treed and streetlight-lit wonderfully lonesome midnight streets; clanking streetcar rides (Sunday afternoon hung over, right to the end of the line, then right back where you started from, recovered); three newspapers, each with an above-average sports section; Chinatown, Little Italy, Little Portugal; Kensington Market on Saturday afternoons; dripping eavestroughs in darkened, after-dinner fall; the deep August hum of air-conditioned-alive renovated Victorians, ROOM and SHARED KITCHEN and BATH signs fluttering in paint-peeling but still regal wooded windows; a city, then — a City. And, for James, even more than these other things, an allowing and even occasionally encouraging place to do what, of everything else he did, the thing he liked to do best: make and play the music, country-and-western music, that occupied his mind and other important body parts a good portion of every day's day and night.

But if, as the big book says, you can't go home again, it's as equally true that you can't entirely leave home, either. So for James, for the most part, the Niagara and not, for instance, the Holy Ravioli or the Decameron, situated along considerably more fashionable Queen Street West.

At each of these other two, it was true, a CD jukebox stocked full of good jazz, classic country, and the best of all the good new rock, the waiters and waitresses alike with their tied-back dyed black hair and pallid cheekbones, charming for their failed-model sighs and work-world disdain whenever forced to cease flirting with the equally attractive clientele and actually take an order from a customer simply wanting to order food. But, on nights such as this one, James desirous of only a quiet place to ponder the how and why of picking up the pieces of his life: "Wheel of Fortune" on the Niagara's television set suspended above the salad bar, and Rebecca, his waitress, an overworked mother of three trying to manage a five-day-a-week split-shift schedule, collect the alimony on time from her jerk of an ex-husband, keep on the wagon and out of trouble her occasional boyfriend (and Niagara cook), Leo, and still find the time to give her kids something like a decent home life.

Surrounding James, the other side of Toronto scattered itself at greasy-skinned red-and-white checked tables identical to his: lower-division civil servants, the checkout girls and stock boys from the supermarket across the street, a loud liquid-supper contingent of after-work postal carriers. No one but the staff knew him here. Better yet, for a little while, at least, he neither knew nor had to know (for professional reasons or otherwise) anyone else either. For almost as long as he had called Toronto home, the Niagara had always meant the Indispensable S's Three: solitude, soup, sanctuary.

"Menu, James?"

"Nah. Just a cup of tea with lemon and . . . what kind of soup you got tonight?"

"Same as we had all day, dear, chicken vegetable."

"That'll do. Any chance we can get that thing turned down?"

"Now, how many times do we have to go through this, dear? You know dinnertime around here means 'Wheel of Fortune' time."

"No harm in asking."

"No, there never is, at that. You want today's papers?"

"That'd be all right, yeah, thanks." He waited for his food and drink and newspaper and stared out of the restaurant's large plate-glass window.

A tattered Native American in dirty white sneakers and a logo-less red baseball hat panhandled a college-age couple moving quick and looking nowhere but straight ahead. Walking backwards, begging, the man fixed his attention on the male face of the couple, burned-out bulbs of dark eyes never letting the other go, yet never successful in making contact, either. Persistence finally paying profit, the woman took some change from the handbag hanging over her shoulder and handed it in haste to her partner which he then dropped in the man's reaching-out palm. The native stopped walking, tottering slightly where he stood. He stared down at the silver coins in his still out-stretched hand as if clueless how they, or even the hand at the end of his arm, had gotten there. When James had ar-rived in the city five years before, "Indian" hadn't been a bad word. Things had been much simpler then.

Devanchuck still in his ears, Real songs, he reminded himself. Thompsonesque songs. The kind with words to them. That was the question. For too long now, though, not, to James, a particularly interesting question. And this not quite the proper attitude for a working musician, es-pecially one who didn't want to have to sell his next re-lease out of the trunk of his bass player's car. So: to the source: Datum.

James's hometown had served his career well enough as the origin of two albums' worth of just the sort of small-town celebratory lyrics Devanchuck was now demanding. The majority of these James had written in a fourteen-month burst during his first couple of years in Toronto. Sleeping on the floors, couches, and sometimes even beds of new friends and lovers, looking for kindred country souls while jamming around town on open-stage nights and in the kitchens of all-night parties, James had enjoyed for the first time the fruits of a three-hundred-mile per-spective, the time and distance that allowed him to shoot in one enormous, since-adolescence-swelling wad of words the accumulated selected mysteries of the small-town spot of a wet spot he called, to whoever bothered to ask, "Back home." By the time he had met The Paddocks and landed a three-record contract with Devanchuck and Willie Pee Musics, he had had his own Toronto bed to sleep in, and a steadily unshakeable sense that he had never lived any-where else.

That by the time he and The Paddocks had become a working band and were busy touring his first record James could get more excited about exposing the younger, rock-and-roll portion of his audience to Loretta Lynn and Jimmie Rodgers covers in one set, then challenging their country connotations in the next with numbers like his own Hendrixian "Voodoo Child Waltz" — these, rather than soulfully exploring the place his first record, *Hometown, My Town*, took its name and inspiration from — was not the problem it would become later. He was twenty-two at the time of the release of the first album and just beginning to really learn about all the glorious things he could make happen in a smoke-filled room full of complete strangers. Factoring in life on the road, women who didn't expect you to call them next week, and a young man's capacity for excess, it was not a period of great reflection.

Six years after he had left home, and another album later, Datum, to James, had become not much more than an infrequently in-the-flesh visited place whose primary importance lay in its once-upon-a-time benefaction of the by now blurry people and predicaments from which the majority of his original songs so long ago it seemed to him had sprung (three or four falling in and/or out of love songs per record excepted). Datum was no longer his muse. Datum had become a place. Datum had become a fact. Datum: a two-syllable word without referents pointing ethereally elsewhere.

And this just would not do. Not in terms of a band anxious to record and tour (a band ready to work). Not in terms of a record company grown tired of his repeated cries of artistic somnambulism (a record company ready to sell). Not in terms of the majority of his public, eager for another James Thompson album (a public ready to purchase). And certainly not in terms of himself (a singer ready to sing his very own songs).

If Datum was by now an admittedly dim spot of illumination, James knew, nonetheless, that it was still the only light he had to go by. If fairly certain that Toronto was where henceforth his ten-gallon hat would be hung, James also knew that the city could never come to replace Datum as the place from which generous and authentic offerings of songed peopled-pie must necessarily get cut. Like Joyce dutifully collecting his Dublin gibberish so many miles and years away from home, James knew Datum was the only game he could honestly expect to play to win. Problem was, he really had nothing to say. Not a goddamn thing.

And if pressed by professional or self-induced personal prods of reflection for an explanation for his lyrical barrenness, the answer was inevitably the same: a classic case of the difficulty that often exists when one attempts to too forcefully get past intimate appearances to the actual song-story ideas themselves. Absolutely.

He chalked up his first burst of song-story words in part, then, to the gainful distance his move to Toronto had provided, the worthwhile way in which all of the poetically pregnant Datum things he had carried with him for so long finally came to be seen in the properly clear light of the lamp of objective perspective that shines ceaselessly the thing-in-itself. The old Platonic peek-a-boo, certainly. And about this, he knew a couple of things.

Impressed as hell, James had been, encountering *Plato for Beginners* in the Datum Public Library on a self-searching metaphysical mission at age seventeen; a genuine relief for a budding small-town country-and-western chronicler (and lifetime resident of same small town) to find musty-book confirmation that oftentimes the things we perceive in this world are imperfect imitations of a more perfect original form. Translated: If life (understood here as Datum) sometimes seemed like a place people were born in, ran around in, made more like themselves in, and died in, just stand back and scratch a little bit deeper and you were sure to find what James had all along been after: the ballad, the yarn, the tale, the myth. Simply put, what James had begun to refer to as *real life*.

And being of a mind (like most minds) that sees such a significant idea much better out of the mouth of a particular person in a particular place at a particular time, James's mind eventually claimed Joyce's *Portrait of the Artist As a Young Man* (James's for ever adored Moocow book) as the perfect Platonic embodiment of artistic deliverance from mere running, making, and dying (regardless of Dublin or Datum doing). Double identification, in fact, in that James, life-line early-on invested in a manifestly foreign musical craft (American, after all, in origin and evolution) could empathize entirely with Stephen Dedalus's purposeful self-exile and necessary state of aesthetic expatriation.

Not unusual, then, in this period of fresh Dedalusian identification for the teenaged James to more than once call out on unposted postcards to his patron saint, Stephen of Secular Hope, at times of overwhelming everydayness. The response was invariably silent, but the ready and provided ear to his own restless noise was every time eminently satisfactory all the same.

Lately, however, Plato just seemed like little more than a real nice Idea, and epiphanies — of the Joycean sort or otherwise — were about as rare as a strong showing of the Canadian dollar. Six years and two albums into his career, James had accumulated so much time and distance between himself and his home base of inspiration that he should have been able to see his way to a lifetime's worth of songs, or a double album, at the very least. Instead, he could barely see a thing. Or even remember, for that matter, anything worth seeing.

Further, and more troublesome still: deeper than any official explanation he gave to himself or others, James had come to increasingly wonder whether the insipid lyrical blankness he encountered of late each time he turned his thoughts homeward was less a question of him being unable to poetically distance himself from Datum, and more a question of Datum itself being basically insipid and blank; this, a question, of course, easily answered in either the affirmative or negative with a deliberate, song-writing sojourn to Datum. James, however, rarely seemed to make it back home.

Rebecca returned and set down his tea and soup, took a minute on her feet. "Missed you guys last night over at Restless Winds. Sign outside said it was the last show you're doing for a while."

"Yeah, well, it might be for a bit longer than a while, too." James picked the slice of lemon up off his saucer and squeezed it into his tea.

"You and The Paddocks aren't breaking up, now, are you? You know you promised me that if I ever decided to get smart and give Leo his walking papers you'd introduce me to that good-looking pedal steel fellow you got there, Smitty What's-his-name."

"No, no, we're not breaking up. Just . . . taking a little rest," James said.

"Thinking of taking a holiday, are you? Planning on making it back home for a while, maybe?"

"That would seem to be the popular decision."

"Well, good for you," Rebecca said, pulling silverware, a napkin, and two packages of crackers out of her serving-apron, setting them down on either side of the steaming bowl of soup. "I'd love to get back to Alberta for a spell. Can't remember the last time I saw my sister. Said you were from down near Windsor, didn't you? Forget the exact name of the place."

"Sometimes I wish I could forget it too," he said. Or remember it a whole lot better.

"Now, now, don't be like that. Do you some good to get out of this rat race for a while and visit with your family. Besides, give all the women in town a nice vacation too."

James smiled into his teacup.

"And like they say, dear," Rebecca continued, "we've

all gotta come from somewhere. It's where you end up that counts." The postal workers had gathered up their dirty-grey mailbags and were noisily trying to figure out at the cash register who had had the extra bottle of Molson Golden. "Get you your paper after I take care of this crew."

"Sure. No hurry," he said. At the table directly across from him, a red-toqued pensioner working on a mug of draft beer studied the line on tomorrow's horse races, in the process exposing the front page of *The Globe and Mail's* sports section. James took a first, cautious sip of his tea.

The Stanley Cup playoffs began in three days but, looking at the old man's paper, James noted only an off-day report on Guzman's throwing arm, a preview of the Jays' upcoming homestand against the A's, and another Royal Commission into illegal doping and track-and-field athletes. Turning into more of a damn baseball town every minute, he thought. He forced himself to look away from the headlines.

Out of the restaurant window he spotted a photocopied flyer for last night's show flapping against a telephone pole, the gathering evening wind working hard at breaking it free from its two remaining staples. He quickly looked away from it too, and saw by the clock hanging over the TV that it was nearly nine-thirty and he was late. He spooned at his soup, drank his tea, and looked up at the spinning wheel on the television often enough to know that he wasn't where he should have been.

3

He would have liked the time alone the walk over would have provided, but was already an hour overdue. He paid his bill at the register, thanked Rebecca, and counted himself lucky to just catch the bus. On board, he found he didn't have a token, cursed his rotten luck, and dropped two loonies in the box, fifty cents more than the fare demanded. He rode as far as Dundas Street.

The party was a going-away gathering for Smitty put together by his girlfriend, Annie. The address James had been given led him by foot from the bus stop to the sort of place he would have never of his own choice frequented. Close to the Skydome, in the restaurant district, Mr. Humps and Bumps was an overpriced restaurant by day and an overheated dance club for restless professionals by night. Five-hundred-dollar leather jackets were the principal code of after-work alienation. Foreign films and who was fucking who were discussed with equal intensity between trots to the dance floor, bathroom, and bar.

James made his way through the revolving glass door to the place and identified himself to the pony-tailed teenager working the door. The boy checked his name off a list, stamped the back of his hand, and gave him three tickets, each worth one free domestic beer. Dim lights, thick smoke, and loud dance music momentarily stunned him. He moved towards the bar, hoping to be ticketless before he ran into anyone from the band. No one in the group, James especially, had really expected the label to buy the idea of the all-instrumental album. The meeting with Devanchuck had been little more than a foregone occasion in failure, at best a chance to buy some more time. James's recent decision that The Paddocks should lie low for a few months, in the hope that perhaps the time off would recharge his creative batteries as nothing else for the past couple years had been able to, was not a popular decision among the boys.

Smitty had taken the decision not to spend the summer playing the hardest. Only thirty-one but the elder of the group, he had child support, alimony, and a girlfriend who liked to spend the majority of her time (and much of Smitty's money) at whatever happened to be the club of the minute, the more condescending the doorman, the more appealing the saloon. Smitty simply could not afford a summer of not touring. He had decided that the only way he could stay ahead in the inactive interim was to spend a significant portion of the summer as a deckhand on a fishing boat. Smitty had made James aware of the fact that the hours he would be spending working on the ship were going to be incredible, the work itself backbreaking, and the company not at all congruous to a steel-guitar player with a handlebar moustache and a taste for good cocaine and late nights. James had been made aware of this fact.

He saw Smitty and Annie sitting by themselves at a corner table. Before he had a chance to slink away, they saw him. Smitty waved him over. James gave a little half-wave and took a long pull at his beer as he walked around the edge of the dance floor. Annie got up just as James reached the table.

"Glad you could make it, James," she said.

"Evening, Annie. Figured the least I could do was come by and see what kind of finger-food you were serving." He nodded at Smitty.

"Cut that shit out, both of you," Smitty said. "Make it three tequilas, Ann, and take your time, okay? I want to have a word with the leader of the pack here."

James slid into the chair next to his steel-player and surveyed the scene on the dance floor in front of them. A tight pack of bodies gesticulated mutely in the semi-dark, each dancer more anxious than the next to appear utterly indifferent to the shared commotion going on, a collective passivity of emotion offset by a floor full of contorting arms, rubber necks, and bobbing heads, an entire people drowning in a pool of ennui. Monads with attitudes, James thought. He finished his beer in three deep, uninterrupted swallows. He hoped Annie in spite of her with them would hurry her return with the tequila. "Your girlfriend can sure throw a hell of a disco," he said.

"Give it a rest, all right? I'm sick of you two playing cat and dog every time you're in the same room together. This shit gives me a headache too, but people like to dance at these sorts of things, so what are you going to do? You can't play Hank Williams all the time, right?"

"Why not?" James asked.

Smitty looked at his boss, then shook his head. "And the sad thing is, you're not trying to be funny, either."

James picked up Smitty's beer from the table and took a drink. He looked out at the dancers again.

"Have my beer, James. I was only drinking it."

"Thanks," James said. "You're a pal, you know that?"

"Sure I am. I also need to get something cleared up with you before your old pal here ships out tomorrow with Captain Highliner and the rest of the crew."

"Shoot."

Looking at the dancers himself, Smitty took a pause, then began. "You've got to understand that this fishing deal is just a one-shot thing. I can pay a few bills and maybe even clean myself up a little bit out there, but I can't afford to wait out this dry spell of yours, or whatever the hell it is you want to call it, for ever. None of us can."

"That's not news, Smit. Hell, I'll miss playing live more than you, for Christ's sake. But I think everything will be all right by the time you get back if I just hang around town and take it easy and really concentrate on—"

"No, James, you can't. . . ." He turned in his seat and looked James in the eye. "No," he said.

"No what?"

"No, everything is not going to be all right. Not if you stay in Toronto. I know you. Shit, I give you two weeks before you're so sick of going through the same head games you've been going through since Devanchuck put the squeeze on you for a new album a year and a half ago that to save yourself you'll *have* to start playing solo somewhere. I'll come back in August smelling like a fucking tuna to find out you were playing for tips at the Canada Tavern all summer. No, it won't work. You know as well as I do that the only way left is for you to go back home and try to—"

"We've been through this, Smitty," James said, "and I told you I'd think about it. In a month or so, if things aren't going as well as I expect, a decision will get made. And it'll be my decision. Not yours or the band's or Devanchuck's or anybody else's. Mine." He finished Smitty's beer, and placed the empty bottle on the table with a slow carefulness intended to make clear the finality of his words.

Neither said anything for nearly an entire pounding song-length. Finally, Smitty spoke. "You know where Webby and Scott are tonight?"

"I figured I'd be seeing their ugly mugs around here once the bars closed down. Why?"

"Webby and Scott are in Brantford tonight. At an audition. An audition for a Grand Funk Railroad tribute band."

Expressionless, James looked at Smitty, then broke into a wide smile. "Get the fuck outta here," he said.

"There was a quarter-page ad in *NOW* yesterday. Some promoter from Detroit is putting together a rock-and-roll revival show of bands from the early seventies. Webby called him up, and he says the guy is promising four hundred and fifty bucks a week, plus room and board and a thousand-dollar bonus when the thing wraps up at the end of July. And that's American coin, too. That's like, what? Six hundred or something Canadian per week?"

James stared out at the shaking bodies in front of him and slowly shook his head. "That's cold, man. Real cold. I thought we all had an understanding. I thought we had something between us."

"James—"

He turned to Smitty. "You wouldn't pull something like this, would you, Smit? You wouldn't stab me in the back, would you?"

"Nobody stabbed you in the back, James. Christ, you can get romantic sometimes, you know that? They have bills to pay, that's all. You think either of them is actually looking forward to supplying the rhythm section to a twenty-five-minute jam of 'We're an American Band'? It's about money, that's all. Money."

"I don't buy that, Smitty. I thought we all agreed that, no matter what happened, nobody — for sincerity's sake, for the sincerity of the band's sake — would play with anyone else as long as you guys were my band."

"Screw sincerity, this is about cash. You're doing okay with the royalties from your albums — that and the fact you live like a bum — but the rest of us have got real lives to live and real bills to go along with them. Hell, the only reason I'm not in Brantford tonight is because Iron Butterfly and Blue Cheer didn't use steel-players. You've got to be realistic, James. It's a business too, you know."

"So what's the deal? Are you saying I should start looking for a new rhythm section? Maybe a new steel-player, while I'm at it?"

"Cut the melodramatics. Neither of us is drunk enough for that. And nobody's jumping off the good ship *Paddock*, either. But you have to admit the sonofabitch *has* been on dry land for an awful long time now. Long enough that something has to be done."

James looked away from the dancers and down at the floor between his cowboy boots.

"Look, James, I don't know where the big deal in you going home comes from, but whatever the hell it is, you've got to push it aside and go back and get down some damn words. Go back and get the job done, and you're home in three weeks — a month, tops. Home in Toronto, I mean."

James looked up.

"It's the only way, James."

Annie returned with the tequila, set a brimming shot glass of clear liquid in front of each of them, and sat down. "You owe me thirteen dollars, Smitty."

"Thirteen dollars for three fucking shots of tequila?"

"Three seventy-five each and I tipped the bartender. Is there a problem with that?"

"No. No problem," he said. "Let's just hurry up and toast something. I have a ship to catch in the morning, and a limited amount of time to go about forgetting it."

Each picked up a tequila. Backsides of hands salted, lemon slices at the ready, no one made a move. Seeing that neither her boyfriend nor James was about to say anything, Annie spoke up. "To a good summer."

"To a good summer," Smitty repeated.

"Sure," James said. "To a good summer."

All around: lick, shoot, suck.

Setting his glass down, looking at Smitty, "I'll think about it," James said.

4

Middle-of-the-night departures are seldom schemed decisions. Mostly they just happen, like getting arrested, or developing a rash. Subway rumbling done for the night, stumbling home alone after Smitty's party, James found himself on the sidewalk in front of the glass-windowed front of the downtown Greyhound depot, staring at an enormous advertisement for the provincial lottery: YOU CAN'T WIN IF YOU DON'T PLAY! Even inebriated, it pained him to have to admit how often life imitates advertising. He stood and stared at the thing until his fingertips began to hurt a bit and he realized he was cold.

There was no line-up inside, and he bought a one-way ticket for the next bus leaving for Datum. James had come to associate travelling by Greyhound with a death in the family, the infrequent trips he had made back to Datum since leaving home had been, almost without exception, for this reason. He reminded himself that there were exceptions to every rule. He patted the ticket in the pocket of his T-shirt and told himself he was doing the right thing.

Catching a taxi to his apartment, he was back at the terminal twenty-five minutes later with his guitar and a bulging, ill-packed knapsack (including: *The Portable James Joyce*; notebook and pen; *Farther Along: The Best of the Flying Burrito Brothers* and *More Big, Big Hits of Tammy Wynette* cassettes; address book; prescription bottle half full of Dexedrine tablets; *Official National Hockey League Record and Rule Book*; four condoms; several extra guitar strings; IF YOU DON'T LIKE HANK WILLIAMS YOU CAN KISS MY ASS boxer shorts — a gift from the band; six guitar picks; and clothes). He had an hour to kill before his 2:15 bus left and he knew a Chinese speakeasy in the area. He stuffed the knapsack into a fifty-cent locker and took the guitar along with him.

Duncan Lee's served authentic Chinese food from noon on, and low-quality liquor in white teacups after hours. James sat at a table near the back, with his guitar in its case sitting upright across from him. After a perfunctory glance at the menu, a young oriental male who spoke perfect English appeared.

"What can I get you?"

"Glad you asked. Bourbon. And keep them coming, okay?"

"You're the boss. Anything to eat?" They liked it at Duncan Lee's if you had something on your table to go along with your little white cup of illegal liquor.

"No. I'm fine, thanks."

"Sure you are," the waiter said, heading for the kitchen.

"One more thing?"

The waiter did not turn around or answer, just stopped walking and waited where he stood.

"No more for me if I ask if I can play the piano over there."

"You play the piano?" the waiter asked, turning around.

"No," James said. "No, I don't."

5

He came back home just the way he wanted: slightly drunk, and in the dark.

Cornfields, campsites, Crown land, and, as he got closer, plastics and car-parts companies sliding by, in a seat by himself at the back of the bus he posed to himself in good philosophical fashion the question of what of Datum was indubitable. From this he would begin looking. For songs. Real songs. The kind with words to them.

This, he knew: he was born James Morris Thompson, the only child of a man and a woman who, as far as he knew, their whole lives long never gave a thought to living anywhere else but the place they were born, the place he was born, too — Datum, Ontario, Canada.

Too, he knew: a medium-sized town in what only people from around there called The Great South West, Datum was distinguished as being, aside from Oshawa and Windsor, the biggest Canadian manufacturer of automobile parts to American car-makers. Most of the men worked for the automobile plant, South Western Ontario Steel Works, the rest mainly for the city in various service-sector capacities. All other forms of employment were suspect.

He also knew: his father, James "Jimmy" Thompson, had been a shop worker like his brother, Buckly, and their father, Morris Thompson, before them. But before he, James the younger, emerged from the woman who would one day be his mother, he was one parent short, the result of a freak accident involving his father, a heavy wind coming off Lake Erie, and an orange-lacquered transmission suspended for advertising purposes from a single silver chain over the entrance to Beverly's Auto Repair.

And here things got a little bit fuzzy. And not, as he would have preferred, because of the brain-blotting effect of the five teacups of watered-down bourbon ingested at Duncan Lee's.

The thing was this: no one had ever been able to sufficiently assuage James's befuddlement as to why a man married not even six hours, and on his way to Niagara Falls with his new bride for a three-day honeymoon, could not wait until his return home to see about the new line of transmissions that Mickey Beverly was supposedly offering, for a limited time only, at near-wholesale prices, to anyone carrying a South Western union card. James to this day had much difficulty believing that any man — no matter how fine the machinery or how extraordinary the deal — ever needed a transmission that bad. He also had a real problem digesting the accepted wisdom that said his father's death could be simply and directly attributed to a heavy piece of machinery falling on his head. This seemed too crude an explanation to James, even for a town like Datum.

6

Up on one elbow, he rubbed his eyes and tried to focus. Having slept in his clothes, he thought vaguely of a shower. He wondered if the water had been turned off. All his Uncle Buckly had said over the phone the night before was that the people who had bought James's grandparents' house wouldn't be taking it over until the end of the summer, and that he was sure it would be fine if James stayed in the basement until July or so and watched over the place for them — cutting the lawn, pruning the bushes, that sort of thing. His uncle had made him promise not to bother the neighbours with any loud music. James had assured him from the pay phone outside Duncan Lee's that he was looking forward to a quiet and productive visit home, and not to worry.

Finding the faucets still flowing, James decided against a shower and settled instead upon a vigorous splashing of cold water on the face. He gathered up some loose change spilled onto the fold-out bed on which he had slept and moved towards the almost noontime light at the top of the stairs. Although his eyes were gradually becoming adjusted to the darkness, the basement was nearly completely black and he ripped a small piece of skin off his forehead on the way up the steps, knocking against a magazine picture of his grandmother's favourite Toronto Maple Leaf — an eight-by-ten colour action photo of Johnny Bower she had gotten signed and framed years before James was born.

Yep, this is it, he thought, sitting on the bottom step of the stairs, dabbing at the blood with his handkerchief: I'm home, all right. Here less than twelve hours and my head hurts and I'm already hating the Maple Leafs.

Think of the stories, though, he told himself — admonished himself, in fact. Mother, father, uncle, friend: all are heavy on the vine ready for the kind of C&W poetic harvesting only I can give them. I've done it before and have the albums to prove it. I'll do it again and have a new album to show for it.

This little bit dutifully said in his head, his spirits were lifted considerably. His forehead, however, still hurt like a sonofabitch.

7

Genuine imitation some-name-in-French-he-couldn't-pronounce sunglasses stopping most of the potential damage afternoon sunlight has been known to inflict upon weaker constitutions than his, James walked pleasantly, without purpose. The grass could have used a cutting and the hedges were a bit on the shaggy side, but it was, after all, his first full day in town, so he decided to put off whatever had to be done until tomorrow. Besides, tomorrow was Saturday, a quintessential yard-upkeep day. Eating wasn't an option, at least for the time being, so the only question that remained was where to show his face first.

The nursing home where his mother was now living was the logical choice. But what about the woman he had been receiving charmingly erotic (if at times slightly nebulous) letters from over the past few months, who lived in Datum and always signed her letters "I Can See for Miles and Miles, Melissa"? On second thought, he decided, better skip that particular tryst until some lyrical headway gets made. And Christ, wouldn't M.C. be pissed off if he found out I hadn't looked him up first sober light? In the end, though, he found himself walking without deliberation in the direction of his Uncle Buckly's place, an old converted farmhouse on the outskirts of Datum, near the cornfields, away from the factory.

On the way over he kept his eye open for a mailbox to drop in a postcard he had written on the bus ride home but hadn't had a chance to send off yet. At a gas station near that indefinite point in every small town where the town ends and the countryside begins, he found one. He stood by the side of the empty dirt road and looked over what he had written.

> *Dear S.,*
> *How goes the battle? Been a long time. A hell of a long time. Keeping clear of home, fatherland, and church, I hope. That's my boy.*
> *On my way back home to Datum, myself. No, no emergency. No one sick that I know of. Just a little epiphany-hunting trip. Hoping that the view up close will be a little bit better than it has been way up high. Wish me luck. The pot has been awful empty lately.*
> *Yours in silence, exile, and cunning,*
> *J.*

James smiled, dropped the thing in, and continued on his walking way.

8

During the time that, by slow inches, James, as a child, was a getting-older young person, Datum benefited like a lot of other small but heavily industrialized southern Ontario towns from its close proximity to the American border. Everyone, it seemed, had to have a brand-new car or truck to call his own. Everyone too, it seemed, had just enough left over in the pocket on payday Friday to put down just enough of a down-payment to get just the vehicle he wanted. Mid-sixties to late seventies, South Western clanked and banged all year round, day and night, all in a wonderfully impossible attempt to supply the U.S. workers with enough of some of the less important parts needed to put together the vehicles that the Americans would then ship back up north in finished form for sticker-price sale. The short end of the stick; any fool could see that. But at close to eleven dollars an hour, your average grade-ten-educated guy on the assembly line wasn't bitching all that loud. Enough shiny stuff lying around the house and parked in the driveway to shut up — if he knew what was good for him, anyway — even the most fervent Toronto-transferred *Datum Daily News* Canadian nationalist columnist.

For the most part, then, nobody in Datum went wanting. A few, however, did more than a little bit of yearning. James, it could be said, was one of those yearning ones.

When, naturally, James as a young man had begun to ask questions about his mother and what life was like when she was his age, and what his father was like at his age, and what and what and what, people would try to remember some important dates, tell him this and that, and encourage him to go outside and play street hockey.

Not satisfied with mostly correctly recollected birthdays and polite incidental remembrances — or with his mother's patient TV-staring and occasional humming

silence — James became increasingly interested in genealogy, pedigree, history: in short — the Past. So, for instance:

"Grandpa, did you ever fight in the war?"

"Nope."

"How come?"

"Too young for the first one, too old for the second
one."

"Oh." Head back down to high-school homework
spread out all over the kitchen table. "Too bad," James said.

Knifing margarine abundant onto two pieces of hot
toast, "Too bad?" his grandfather said. "You daft, boy?
Don't they teach you in those books of yours that war is
hell?"

"I guess so."

"I guess so is right," his grandfather said, with a look
that, on the face of a different man, might have been considered contemplative (a man in the movies, perhaps:
close-up of an aged Henry Fonda in well-worn cardigan
and wire-rimmed spectacles, taken in just the right slant
of afternoon light pouring through the curtainless kitchen
window behind his head), but which here disclosed plain
pause before the resumption of speaking and buttering.
"Besides, got my job at South Western on account of the
Second World War and most of the regulars going over-
seas, and most of them not coming back home. Went from
making a straight fifty-five a week as a goddamn milk-
man — twelve hours a day, every day, half a day on Saturday — to making a buck seventy-five an hour with all the
overtime you could handle at time and a half."

"Oh."

"Yes sir, me boy," he said, slicing his two pieces of toast
on top of one another in half, "that was good timing for
the Thompsons, that war was. Damn good timing."

About this time, James's grandfather discovered a notebook on the bathroom hamper entitled *The Thompsons: A
History*, written in James's handwriting. And while decent
though not great grades at school were expected of a young

person among medium to good families in Datum, overtly intellectual curiosity was frowned upon, akin to a young boy caught playing with dolls, or a teenage girl who could throw a baseball better than her brothers. The error of the ways of the young was always quietly but firmly pointed out. James's grandfather got his son Buckly on the telephone, and asked him to please have a few words with his nephew about priorities — Uncle Buckly, not James's mother.

James's mother had been an orphan at birth, raised in a foster home headed up by the local religious big shot, the Very Reverend Lester G. Hazel, and his wife, whom no one knew as anything but Mrs. Lester G. Hazel. The Hazels dead in an automobile accident three months previous to their daughter's ill-starred marriage, it was decided soon after James's father's funeral that Margaret would stay permanently with her dead husband's parents. This, after a brief period at Datum General Hospital where the expert opinion declared that, for whatever reason, never really of what might be called a strong emotional disposition to begin with, the brutal dissolution of Margaret's hours-old marriage was the final blow to an already fragile mind. It was determined that nothing could be done for Margaret medically and that henceforth she should be kept away from any more bad things happening to her.

James's grandparents had taken to Margaret, a quiet girl old-fashionedly polite around her elders, right from the moment she and their son had begun dating. But because they were nearly fifty when they took on the task of caring for Margaret and providing, soon after, a home for the infant James, it was the Thompsons' other child, Buckly, a year older than James's father, who became the closest thing James ever had to a real parental figure.

At the time of James's birth Buckly was just starting his third full year at South Western, living in a cheap bachelor apartment downtown, and putting away nearly all the money he brought in every week for a down payment on a dilapidated abandoned farm outside Datum city limits. None of the Thompsons had farmed since the family first emigrated from Scotland in the early 1800s, but Buckly was a hard worker and visited his parents weekly, so no one ever bothered to question the downright eccentricity of a blood-line automobile worker dreaming of being a gentleman farmer.

Buckly used the occasion of his father's alarmed, historically hysterical phone call about the notebook to take James out for his first beer in a bar, the bar being the Duke of Connaught Bar and Grill. More restaurant than bar, more a daytime eating place than a nighttime drinking place, the same withered, mug-of-beer faces (out of style suit jacketed and scuffed black Oxfords below) nonetheless let you know while you downed your tuna-fish on whole wheat that other forms of fuel consumed here could do the trick just fine too. Most of the men who frequented the place lived in small rooms in large pigeon-painted buildings still a decade away from being demolished to make way for the downtown mall. The majority of them survived on some sort of pension or government income, a few others God knows how, all of them somehow managing to move through their days with a minimum of broken hips and a good deal of afternoon napping, each ending up nearly every early evening at the Duke for his vegetable soup and Saltines, maybe a grilled cheese sandwich if the appetite was there, and the first of many glasses of draft beer. Although his uncle spent a large part of his time at the Duke — mainly to watch baseball, since he didn't own a TV — James never knew him to drink alcohol. The waitress brought over a ginger ale for Buckly before he and James had even sat down. Buckly paid for the pop and ordered a Labatt Blue for his nephew.

James had been drinking beer (along with the occasional quick pull from a friend of a friend's mickey of Southern Comfort or cherry whisky) before school dances at friends' houses when their parents were out for the evening, and in parked cars on bored Saturday nights, for a couple of years, so the beer itself was not a brand-new thing. Still, he attempted to sip at the brew set down in front of him as casually as possible, not wanting the other drinkers in the bar to think it was his underaged-first in a licensed establishment. A lot like sex, he thought.

His uncle started right in.

"I want you to quit bothering people with all these goddamn questions about the Hazels and your mom and your dad too," he said, stirring his drink around to get at the ice cubes at the bottom of the already nearly empty glass. "You're getting to that age where you think if you know about things that happened before, you'll know what the hell's going on now. Well, forget it, pal. I know it has to be hard on you sometimes, seeing all your friends at school having a mom and dad and all that, but that just isn't the way it is for you. Your grandma and grandpa are good people — take good care of you, believe me — probably better than half the parents half their age, drinkin' and screwin' the next-door neighbour every chance they get."

His uncle signalled to the waiter for two more of what they were having, although James wasn't half done with his first beer.

"So just can the wide-eyed wonder thing for now, all right? Be better for both of us. Do you realize I had a woman at my house when your grandfather called me up to ask me to talk to you? You have any idea what that kind of thing does in terms of mood and such at a time like that? Devastating. Both of us be better off if you quit this history business."

"C'mon, Uncle Buckly," James said, "look at what I'm working with here. For starters, I've got a ghost father killed by a falling engine who nobody seems to remember anything about—"

"Transmission," his uncle corrected him.

"Okay, transmission. But why the secrecy? Why can't

anybody tell me anything about the man? He was my father, wasn't he?"

"He *is* your father, for Christ's sake. And what secrecy? What do you want to know? What haven't I told you that you've ever asked me about?"

"For starters, more than just that he was a tough hockey player with a bad right knee. More than he had a good sense of humour. More than he could drive better drunk than sober. More than he was well liked by almost everybody he knew. More than the same stuff everybody else knows."

"Jesus, James, what is it you're after? That *was* Jimmy. He was my brother and we got along as good as any brothers do, I guess, but about all I can say is, all those things are true. He *was* a mean sonofabitch with a hockey stick. Ever tell you about the time we were playing Wallaceburg and he slashed their big guy, Lawrence, I think his name was, right across the—"

"Goddamn it," James said, surprised, as all youths are, the first time they curse in front of the grownups and get away with it, "that's just the kind of stuff I don't want to hear. What I'm talking about is something entirely different, something deeper than that kind of thing. What I'm talking about is the very Being of Dad, the very . . . forget it. Just forget it."

James resigned himself painfully to the fact that his uncle, though a great guy with the tall tale, knew absolutely nothing of ontological truths. But how could he? Uncle Buckly read nothing but the sports page. James himself had only learned a month before what the word meant, Will Durant and his *Story of Philosophy* (and specifically Chapter Six, "Plato and His Theory of Forms") supplying the first real metaphysical relief he had yet to receive for his growing sense that there just had to be more to it all than just what it appeared there seemed to be. Insufficiently secure suspended transmissions were, increasingly, simply not cause enough.

"Okay," his uncle said, after enough silence had passed between them for each to nearly finish his second beverage, "here's the deal. I've got something — and don't ask me what it is because that isn't important right now — that'll maybe help you get at I guess what it is you're after."

James swallowed the last of his beer quickly, nearly yelling, "What is it?"

"For Christ's sake, I told you not to worry about—"

"Okay, okay," James said. "What's the deal?"

"I'm not telling you what it is because I don't want you wrapping your mind around something that just don't at this point matter one spit."

"What do you mean?"

"I promise to give you this thing — and I'm not even saying for sure it'll help you get what you're after, but it might — but you gotta wait until you're twenty-five, that's all I ask. Then I'll give you something that might help take care of all these damn what-happened-in-the-past questions. I don't want you to have it right now because you're the sort that'll end up making a full-time job out of a nice memory. No way for a sixteen-year-old boy to carry on. Just wait until you're twenty-five, let's say. In the meantime, think about hockey or pussy or cars or something. And quit leaving your goddamn personal obsessions in the crapper. One day you'll find your grandfather dead in there on the linoleum with your manifesto stuck under his nose."

"Okay," James said, glad (whether because of the promise of the Thing or the two quick beers, he couldn't be sure) that his Uncle Buckly was his uncle and not somebody else's.

"One question, though," he said.

"Shoot," his uncle replied, sucking on the cubes in his ginger ale.

"Why twenty-five? Why not twenty-one or even nineteen? I won't be a kid when I'm that old, either."

"I don't know. Twenty-five just popped into my head, for Christ's sake. Goddamn it, James, has there gotta be rhyme and reason for everything? Huh? Does there?"

9

James made it to his uncle's house in a little less than an hour, a nice walk along the country-road way made even nicer by the pleasantly composing effect the exercise had on his intoxicant-irritated nervous system and stomach. He made a point of keeping an eye open for any evocative atmosphere he might see along the way.

If downtown Datum could be said to be plagued by an ugliness of excess — convenience stores, mini-malls, fast-food emporiums, and used-car lots leaving absolutely nothing to the imagination — the rural perimeter of town, while not exactly beautiful, at least lacked a plenitude of eyesores. Primarily, numerous variations on a theme of this: a small barn about a hundred yards behind a small house, both right in front of a small field, the nearest neighbour maybe a quarter of a mile away. Not much to either anger or inspire.

Buckly's place was the anomaly of the concession: no barn (torn down almost immediately upon point of purchase to make room for an enormous vegetable garden); no field (sold to V. Smith and Sons, the nearest neighbour, at a small profit that went directly towards the mortgage); and no anything that would lead anyone living within Datum city limits to believe that anyone who didn't have to live out here, so far from the new mall and all the other good stuff in town, would.

Since 1971, however, Buckly had lived out here by himself, neither a resident of town nor a farmer like his neighbours. Making his living on the double-digit hourly wage he earned at South Western as a fifteen-year-plus man, he depended for his thriving on, first, tending to the various needs the vegetables in his garden in their abundance demanded, and, second, the silence that occurred without exception on summer nights a little after dinnertime, when he would sit, one leg crossed over the other, in a shabby green lawnchair, with the Detroit Tigers game on an at-his-feet AM radio, sipping weak iced tea and enjoying the closest thing a person born and raised in the suburbs can feasibly have to a oneness with the elements. Not a philosophical desire to smooch with nature put Buckly most nights out there, though, big whooshing trees he could not have identified if his life depended on it providing quiet breathing sounds all around capable of calming even the most maniacal of heart and head. Neither something fine and higher, either, like a reclusive need inspired by a troubling desire to think or scribble or shout aloud in his own hovelled privacy; no, none of these things at all.

To no end of irritation to Buckly, however, a man who had over the years grown to feel very strongly that life needed no added ingredients mixed into its telling, something along these lines in the musically lyrical lines of his nephew, James.

When James's first full-length recording came out, in the summer of '89, he immediately shipped it to his uncle in the most travel-friendly form possible, cassette. A record man through and through, Buckly had to take the thing with him to work in order to hear it. He knew that the ten or fifteen university boys the company hired every June to fill in for some of the vacationing regulars on the afternoon shift brought in a boom-box every night to go along with their stashed six-packs and washroom-rolled joints. Buckly didn't anticipate any problem in securing some playing time for his nephew's tape.

Of course, Buckly's younger fellow workers were simply MTV-stoned noise-mongers with no use for country-and-western music, even if composed by a home-grown player. But if Buckly was quiet and reserved to the point of occasional rudeness (except at his 8:15 suppertimes, sharing the sports section with James's old friend M.C., the only person at the plant he considered worth even waxing mindlessly about the weather with), he was nonetheless respected by the boys as somebody who, in a pinch, would cover the next guy's ass when the line really got rolling. As well, despite his greying temples, the word among the college kids was that Buckly Thompson was the kind of man you didn't want to fuck around with. Period. An unpleasant incident early in the summer — involving a slightly stoned philosophy major bent on referring to Buckly, not especially affectionately, as "Gramps", and the latter's steel-toed work boot — guaranteed this. The boy's operation was described by Buckly's foreman as "minor".

Uncharacteristic of Buckly, a notorious clock-watcher regretful of every moment he was at work and not in his beloved backyard, he showed up fifteen minutes early one day, hoping to listen to at least one side of James's album before the long-hair riff-raff began to file in. He had heard through the assembly line grapevine that the boy who supplied the stereo every night — referred to only as Shithead by the others — was always dropped off at the gates of South Western by a white Camaro half an hour before their shift was supposed to report for work. When Buckly arrived at the plant, there, predictably, was Shithead, sitting on a bunch of bundled-up, yet to be used car springs, waiting for the rest of the guys to show up.

Buckly nodded at the boy's surprised expression as he pushed without asking James's tape into the machine and hit the play button. He sat on a pile of springs near Shithead and looked straight ahead, waiting for the music.

After suffering through the irritating, high-pitched electronic whistle at the beginning of the tape that announced, as best Buckly could figure, that the music was about to start and you'd better stop whatever you were doing and get ready to listen, the opening number jumped out, a jaunty instrumental he identified from the back of the tape cover as "Husky Dog Breakdown". Buckly smiled. Pleasant, of course — an airy little soft-core bluegrass number employing James's acoustic guitar, a fiddle, and steel guitar. But more than that. Scraps of years-old images played in Buckly's head of James as a boy washing Buckly's old Pontiac under the big weeping willow out at the farm on weekends to make a little extra spending money. Buckly laughed. He'd heard this melody a million times if he'd heard it once, James whistling away, keeping time with his bare feet in the soapy water to the same tune over and over again, as busy with the tune as he was with washing the car.

Buckly was enjoying himself, just sitting and listening and pleased with being the kind of surrogate father who had managed to have a hand in turning out what had turned out to be a pretty decent human being with a damn fine ear for melody, as well. All those Flatt and Scruggs albums lying around the house all those years probably didn't hurt either, he almost laughed to himself.

Then, goodbye "Husky Dog Breakdown" and the opening verse of selection number two, "Uncle's Place":

> *Who knows why he sits alone on his land*
> *Taking in his time, him his own man?*
> *What mystery inside uncle lives in the night*
> *Won't let him live with the others*
> *In the easy daylight?*

Buckly didn't wait for the song to finish.

"Okay," he said, jumping up from his steel seat, "here

we go." Pushing stop, eject, then putting the tape into the breast pocket of his T-shirt, he sighed hard at the waste of a damn fine tune — spirited pedal-steel playing throughout — looking at the grey concrete floor for an answer to the question he had asked himself for years: Why can't the boy be happy with things just the way they are?

What he saw when he finally looked up from his thoughts, though, was not an answer, but only Shithead. Aware of the older man's obvious unhappiness, and worrying that he might be steel-boot casualty number two, Shithead, by way of a shameless attempt at appeasement, managed only "I liked the music. Especially the one with words to it."

Buckly would have preferred a confrontation — was actually very much in the mood to use his fists and/or feet — but only registered some feeble words uttered by a useless little snivelling prick sitting on a bunch of greasy car springs.

"What the hell is that boy thinking sometimes?" Buckly asked, not needing a reply, only an audience for his complaint. "I just don't like people all that much! I just want to be left alone! Where the hell's the fucking 'mystery inside uncle' in that?"

James crossed his uncle's unadorned front lawn and approached the familiar front door. Climbing the plain cement step that served as the sole welcome mat, he realized with some annoyance that he had nothing to show for his walk, had registered no particularly evocative landscape. He promptly reassured himself that it was still early in the game. Very early. Plenty of time to be evoked yet, he thought. I shall be evoked.

A knock. An answer.

"So. You're here. Just like you said you'd be."

"Yep."

"So. Whadoyou know for sure?"

"Not much," James said.

"Well, that makes two of us."

I've missed this, James thought.

"Gotta go get some perishables, but gotta be back here by no later than 3:15 because I gotta be at work at four. It's 1:15 right now."

"Mind if I tag along?" James asked

"Hell, no. Let me get my keys and chequebook and let's go."

Sitting together for the first time in years in the '67 Buick Skylark of James's perpetual shotgun-riding youth, they idled at a red light in front of the Canadian Tire outlet on what everyone in his family had always referred to as "the other side of town", that being the part of town housing the handful of people who didn't dirty their hands for a living — doctors, lawyers, dentists, et cetera. ("Not working people, honey," his grandmother, good wife to a good union man, had instructed him early on.) The light turned green, and Buckly shifted into first.

Buckly, as usual, in addition to the vehicle's motion, controlled the radio as well. He didn't have a tape deck, so, between odd nods at the road and at James recounting recent Toronto/music business history, he searched the dial for a song that would not enrage. James was usually so busy playing music now that he rarely listened to anything but himself. The radio seemed to have metamorphosed in his absence into a continuous beer commercial with occasional time-outs for oldies and classic rock. He found it difficult to determine when the commercials ended and the music began. His uncle snapped the knob to off after three or four fruitless trips across the dial. Also along for the trip, Al, Buckly's black Labrador retriever, nodded quietly, full belly stretched flat out across the car's back seat, unaffected.

"So. What's new?" James said. Between his first two albums, he had managed to squeeze out three songs from the substance of his uncle's life. Time for an update.

"Man and woman came to the door of the house the

other day. Introduced themselves as Mister and Missus So-and-so. Said they were with some church and asked me if I wanted to be born again. I told them I've had a hard enough time dealing with the one life I've got and, Christ no, I sure as hell don't have the strength to go through all this bullshit a second time. They didn't like that. Didn't even offer me any of their free literature." Buckly smiled.

One more time: "But how are *you*, Uncle Buckly? I mean, how are things? With your life, I mean."

Buckly shot his nephew an annoyed glance across the front seat of the car. Both hands on the steering wheel, the pinkie on his right hand pointing to the local drivers' examination building, he said, "Ever tell you about Ollie Smith used to work there?"

"No, I don't think you ever did."

"Okay, here we go. Ollie Smith was an alcoholic of the pretty bad variety. I know people will tell you an alcoholic can have problems with the stuff this or that way, but Ollie just plain got drunk every day. Lived a few houses down from us on Bark Street in the forties.

"Sometimes us kids would be out carrying on and coming in at, say, three in the morning, and we'd see old Ollie on his front porch with just the streetlights for light and he in his rocking chair on, say, a Wednesday night in the middle of summer, with a big bowl of hot soup in his lap and his dog, Trout, at his feet lapping up a little bowl of chocolate milk that was bad for him but tasted real good, I would imagine. Shall I continue?"

"Sure. What's with the soup?" James said. Almost intuitively he knew this was the question he was supposed to ask.

"Okay, well, you see, Ollie'd come home good and late and drunk on those nights and his wife, Olivia — funny isn't it? His name Ollie, her name Olivia? — anyway, Olivia would have hot split-pea soup waiting on the stove for him. He was supposed to eat the soup on the front porch and sober up a bit and then come in the house. No sooner. Olivia tolerated Ollie's drinking just fine, as much as anyone can tolerate someone who's an everyday drinker, but no scenes or slobbering in the house. That was actually the rule, I swear: no scenes or slobbering in the house. Even had a little note made up to that effect stuck to their fridge with a magnet. A banana, I believe."

"A banana?" James asked.

"A banana magnet," his uncle replied crossly. "Shall I continue or are we through?" he asked, not very sincerely, but with the impatience found in many natural orators who like to think they can walk away from an unappreciative crowd.

"Sure," James said, "sure," knowing his uncle was incapable of not finishing a story, but wanting to appear appreciatively expectant all the same.

"Okay, so like I say, there would be Ollie rocking soft in his chair with that bowl of pea soup put together by his wife in his lap, and it being late July, let's say, and the wind nice and warm through that big maple tree that used to stand on his front lawn, and he as happy as a pig in you-know-what with a fine Royal Tavern buzz in his head and that dog of his drinking the chocolate milk that Ollie would always bring home whenever he'd been out carousing." His uncle stopped; the story was over. He turned his attention back to the road.

James beamed. This was it, he thought. Exactly the kind of thing I've been starving for. He could just hear the frisky little banjo-powered number that had been kicking around his head for the last half-year as the soundtrack to this new Datum tale. What would he call it? "Ollie's Night Out"? "Trout's Sweet Treat"? Very Thompsonesque, if he said so himself. Damn, he thought, wish I had my guitar with me right now.

"Ollie still kicking around, Uncle Buckly?" he asked. Hell, he thought, that's what I'm here for, isn't it? A bit of hometown anecdotal research? If the old boy was still alive, he'd take over a six-pack, shoot the shit for an hour or so, and see if there weren't any more Ollie Smith bits to be soaked up.

Buckly, adjusting the AM dial in an ultimately vain attempt to get last night's late baseball scores from the coast, drove without speaking for a good thirty seconds. Finally, idling at a red light near their destination — the only grocery store in town that stocked Buckly's favourite U.S. import, Michigan-made Vernors soda pop — he looked his nephew directly in the eye.

"Nah, died about ten years ago, I believe."

Damn, James thought. "Buried out at Freeman Port Cemetery?" he asked.

"Nah, up near Kingston somewhere."

"Kingston? What was he buried up there for? He move up there in his old age?"

"Move, hell — he was doing time up there."

"I don't get it."

"Caught him offering little boys five-dollar bills to let him touch them you know where. After they'd busted him, the police found out he'd been doing it for the better part of twenty-five years. And getting away with it, too."

James shrank, all of him. Nothing but platitudes sprang from his mouth. "His poor wife. What a shock. It must have been a horrible . . . shock."

"Shock, hell, she went away when he did. Turns out she was the one giving him the money."

"Ah, come on, Uncle Buckly, really . . ." James nearly pleaded.

"No shit. And guess what the paper said she gave at the trial as the reason for her helping old Ollie out ?"

No response from the passenger side.

"And I'm quoting from the newspaper here, so you know it's got to be true: 'Got the miserable sonofabitch out of the tavern once in a while, didn't it?' Jesus H. Christ, huh?" Buckly wasn't laughing, but James could tell that his uncle wasn't unamused, either.

"I ask you, James: Who but the human race could have said something like that? Who but, huh?"

Smarting from the acquisition of what was definitely not going to be the source material for the world's first pedophiliac country-and-western song (even if he could manage to write the words for it), James kept quiet, pretending his best to be interested in the numerous new minimalls that seemed to have sprung up on the Datum landscape since his last time home, sixteen months before, for his grandfather's funeral. Buckly was silent as well, manoeuvring the car in predatory circles around the grocery store lot in an attempt to find a parking space that wasn't designated for the disabled. ("Where the hell *are* all these disableds? You ever see one of them shopping? I sure as hell haven't.") He finally spotted a space and pulled the Skylark in.

James rolled up his window and sat surveying the sea of deserted shopping carts that surrounded the car. "You know, I think I'll pass on the shopping if you don't mind. I could probably use the walk back."

"Suit yourself," Buckly said, shutting off the engine and rolling up his window.

"I'll give you a call Sunday when the Wheels are back in town. Playing Tilbury, I think I saw in the paper," James said.

"Right," Buckly replied, pen in mouth, attempting a quick, pre-shopping trip balancing act of his chequebook.

"Right," James said. He opened the car door and put one cowboy boot on the blacktop.

"James," Buckly said.

"Yes?" James almost yelped. Something. Anything. Not just—

"Don't slam the door, will you? Damn thing's rattling like a sonofabitch and I don't have a clue what the hell's the problem. Plan on looking at it maybe tomorrow, if I can find a damn minute."

James closed the door to the Buick as if in slow motion,

then walked through the parking lot towards the intersection. Of course, he would go see his mother. Now he was in the mood.

10

A few months after moving in with the Thompsons, the newly widowed Margaret drew her mother-in-law aside and told her in a slightly embarrassed tone that she had decided to stop taking lunch with her and Mr. Thompson because she was starting to get fat in the stomach, and she had never ever been fat there before and she didn't want to start being fat there now.

James's grandmother had sat Margaret down on the living-room couch, sighed, and patiently told her, old hand resting on young, about how she was going to get much fatter over the next little while, but soon enough she and her and Mr. Thompson would go to the hospital and have a doctor make Margaret thin and beautiful again, and never again would Margaret have to be fat for as long as she lived.

Towards James — whose upbringing his grandparents took on as their self-appointed task — his mother showed, throughout his childhood and right up until he left home for Toronto to seek country-and-western self-fulfilment at age nineteen, the same simple sweetness she showed all those who lived in the house, though little else. He was, along with James's grandparents, simply one more nice person in the nice little house they all lived in. Margaret stayed in her bedroom a good portion of the time — her late husband's childhood bedroom, in fact — watching TV from sign-on to sign-off and helping out with the house-work whenever the mood struck her. To the teenaged James, his mother resembled nothing more than a kind of Canuck Laura Wakefield on lithium, a mostly silent, often smiling small-town belle always having to look just *so*, though mercifully lacking the famous southerner's trou-bling nervousness.

During his term as a full-time Datum denizen, James sometimes liked to think that throughout all her quiet years his mother somehow managed to know something no one else did, just as now he periodically liked to imagine that every foaming street person he ran across in Toronto was privy to a wisdom that the clean-clothed and well fed could not possibly possess. Mostly, though, he encountered only the shivering famished. Ditto — though of course in a dif-ferent way — his mother. Like a lot of great thinkers and country-and-western singers, however, James was never one to give in too easily to the easy tyranny of facts.

It was the first time James had seen his mother anywhere but in his grandparents' home. He had been forced to leave immediately after attending his grandfather's funeral for an eastern Canadian and northern Maine bar-tour booked months in advance. Buckly had taken care of all the de-tails of his mother's necessary relocation (James's grand-mother having passed away shortly after he had moved to Toronto), soon after the funeral sending an explanatory letter in his typical no-nonsense style to the Newfound-land box number James had left behind. The letter said, in effect, that his mother was fine so not to worry, and that he had managed to get the first six months of her lease at the nursing home at last year's rate by agreeing to take, as is, the only unfurnished room in the place.

For several years after he left Datum, James had made it a priority to send his mother monthly postcards of To-ronto landmarks and points of interest, with a casual hello and don't-forget-me sentiments scribbled on the back. He had no reason to expect otherwise, but the consistent silence of the object of his postings nonetheless disheartened him as the years added on. He became a less and less diligent correspondent. His increasingly infrequent efforts did not appear to be noticed.

"So, Margaret, how have you been?" James asked. Early on, it had been decided by his grandparents that, to avoid painful confusion and possibly even worse, James would call his mother by her first name.

"Fine. And you?" she answered, a little impatiently.

It was early afternoon, and his mother, watching wrestling on an oversized TV that seemed to occupy a good quarter of her room, appeared a little put out by this familiar stranger interrupting her viewing schedule. The TV guide sat on a nightstand to the left of her bed, open to that day's listings. She had had one of the attendants underline in red all of the shows she wanted to be sure she didn't miss.

The room was outfitted with furniture collected from the Thompson home, and decorated with trappings that Buckly, the executor of his parents' wills, thought his sister-in-law would appreciate being surrounded with in her new abode. So, for example, Margaret's mother-in-law's extensive collection of Toronto Maple Leaf knick-knacks (miniature hockey sticks and cereal-box hockey cards predominating) had found their way onto nearly every flat surface in the room. Margaret herself had never been one for hockey. The back and forth, non-linear flow of the game never seemed to hold her attention for very long. Regardless, Mrs. Thompson had instructed Margaret, that if anyone should ask her, her favourite team was the Toronto Maple Leafs — not having an NHL team to call your own in Datum being equal to not having an opinion in matters of federal politics in larger, more urbane centres. From an early age, James had been a devoted Detroit Red Wings fan.

His mother hadn't looked at James directly yet, except to accept thankfully, even greedily, his basketed offering of candies, fruit, and Coca-Cola. Far from the constant fretting over her svelte figure of so many years before, Margaret, now just six and a half months short of her fifty-third birthday, had become a connoisseur of all things edible.

"I'm fine, and you?" James said. Realizing he had already asked this, he quickly changed the subject. "What are you watching?"

Over the years, the television programs his mother was interested in had formed the foundation of most of their conversations. For a while James had held to a theory that secretly his mother believed she mentally controlled the events that occurred on the screen in front of her. He had had no reason to think this, but the notion had pleased him greatly.

"James, I'm watching wrestling. You can see that."

"Right. And, uh, how do you like, um, the residence?"

Upon checking in to visit, James had been instructed by the slightly butch nurse at the front desk that under no circumstances was the term "nursing home" to be used in front of any of the residents. Apparently, some of the more sensitive among them found the expression disturbing.

"It's a nursing home, James. It's good. Plenty to eat at 11:45 for lunch and 5:30 for supper. Get a snack in the evening, too. Not much for breakfast. Good-for-you things, mostly. Don't like that kind of thing much. Can watch television all I want, though. Not like living with the Thompsons. Always wanted me to go outside and sit on a lawnchair in the sun. Don't much care for the sun. Like wrestling, though."

She turned up the volume on the remote and had another of the chocolates James had brought with him.

James knew what happened next. Nothing but the dinner bell would draw his mother out of her TV drone for hours, the specific action on the screen not nearly as important as the mere continuation of motion and noise coming from the box. He rose from the chair beside the bed, knowing, like an animal sensing entrapment, that cutting short the visit might diminish his impending dark mood as well. He gave his mother a short hug and quick kiss and closed the door to her small room behind him as he left.

Exiting the nursing home through a back door leading to the parking lot, James fumbled for his sunglasses, squinting at the shock of all-of-a-sudden sunlight. He called up the opening verse of "Darkly, His Widow", a song about his mother from his first album, but made it only as far as the second verse. He began to hum the melody of the chorus instead. The plain but pleasant three-chord acoustic guitar progression that anchored the song cheered him slightly. Pretty, isn't it, he thought. Maybe a quick beer at the Duke first, and then get down to some serious song-writing business. Could start with Uncle Buckly. Or Mum. Or—

"Hey."

"Hey," James answered. He didn't know the woman sitting on the hood of the car parked closest to the nursing home's back door, but answering her hey with his seemed the only proper thing to do.

"Visiting somebody you know?" she asked, pointing the toe of her right black cowboy boot in the direction of the nursing home.

"Yeah, uh, a friend," James said, aware that he was lying but not sure why.

"Uh-huh."

"Yep."

"Uh-huh," she repeated, this time a little slower. Tube top and blue-jean cut-offs to go along with the boots, she looked like a juvenile delinquent who had slept her way onto Hee Haw.

As a musician James had dealt with his fair share of adoring young women wearing practically nothing, but this was different. This was Datum. Beauty parlours and bobbysocks were not yet things to be laughed at on late-night black-and-white television reruns.

"And you are . . . ," he said, voice trailing off, hoping somehow for the blanks to be filled in.

"And I am . . . ," she said, slowly sliding off the hood, the tube top riding up over her pierced belly button. She stood in front of the car with her hands on her hips. Smiling, she slowly looked herself up and down as if to say, This is who I am, you idiot; do you like who I am?

"Um, I'm sorry. Should I know who you are?" James asked.

"Oh, cowboy," she said, shaking her head but at the same time smiling. "You're just like your songs, aren't you?"

She took him by the hand and led him across the parking lot to her pickup truck. As she unlocked the passenger door for him to get in, James right away noticed, mixed up with some yellow parking tickets and his latest cassette, *Saturday Night Serenade*, the pistol on the dashboard. He climbed right in anyway.

11

Bourbon, he thought; I must have drunk bourbon. His eyes the feel the sound of old phonograph records, he judged by the light making its way through the basement curtains that it probably wasn't morning any more. He tried to sit up, but the sledgehammer to his head encouraged him to lie back down. Bourbon, he thought; I must have drunk bourbon.

Memory arriving in the slow chunks it does after a long night of abuse, he remembered leaving the nursing home and riding around the back roads of town sharing the afternoon and a pint of Old Crow with the woman from the parking lot. Her name, of course, was Melissa, she of the fan letters.

Like James, she was a basement dweller, since age sixteen occupying for "privacy's sake" the lower regions of her parents' house, a renovated Victorian near Datum's older downtown core, a house once belonging to Datum's first mayor. Her father was a trial lawyer who occasionally took her along on business trips to Toronto. For this, she said, she would always be thankful, "The cosmopolitan exposure to, I don't have to tell you, a just wonderful city like TO" helping to offset in great part the "wastelandic effects of growing up in, I don't need to tell you this either, a little shithole of a little town like Datum." Her mother headed up Datum Mental Health and was a significant partner in the city's first and only vegetarian restaurant. "Oh sure," she said, "sweet people, but hopelessly bourgeois through and through all the same."

Nineteen years old and just graduated from Datum Collegiate Institute, the same high school James had attended, she was spending the summer in Datum waiting for an elderly uncle on her mother's side to die so she could collect what she figured to be a small but still significant inheritance, move to Toronto, and concentrate on her poetry. She counted Baudelaire, the early D.H. Lawrence, and Patsy Cline among her major influences.

After the sun and most of the Crow had gone down, they had ditched the pickup at her parents' house. M.C.'s wife, Jeanie, worked as a waitress at the Duke, his usual Datum place of alcoholic consumption, and James was sure he didn't want his reunion with either her or M.C. to take place under present conditions. So, already three-quarters in the bag, they something like walked downtown to Michael's.

In spite of the not insubstantial amount of alcohol ingested over the preceding hours, James felt a little uncomfortable sitting amidst the usual Friday-night Michael's crowd — unmarried factory workers and middle-aged bachelor farmhands in town for a big night out — while directly across from him sat a barely turned nineteen-year-old, shoulder-length-black-haired beauty discussing, with little regard for conversational discretion, the intricacies of *The Flowers of Evil* and Owen Bradley's unfortunate saccharine production touch on some of Patsy's latter records, all the while periodically ordering more drinks from the bartender by holding up her draft glass and yelling across the packed room, "Hey! Buddy! Four more of these when you're finished whatever you're busy at right now!" This, and the way she walked bouncing braless to the washroom at the back of the bar every so often, put James a little on guard. She always came back, though, and, fairly confident no riot was imminent, James tried to enjoy his beer.

Keeping the jukebox alive all evening with what seemed like a small fortune in quarters, she matched James beer for beer and told him, she said, nearly everything he needed to know about herself if they were going to spend the summer together as lovers and possibly even more. Among other things: she liked it best when the man was on the bottom, but wasn't opposed to occasionally taking it from behind, either. She wanted to write her opus ("A sort of modern cowboy thing, the world's first existential-urban Western composed in verse, really") before she turned twenty-one, but knew there was no real big hurry. She had never been big on boyfriends before, but was sure she would have no problem being monogamous if she managed to find the right person. She owned both of James's records and thought he had the potential to be Canada's own George Jones if he kept himself open to constructive criticism offered by those in the know, like herself, and avoided, for the most part, hard drugs. Also, she thought she had had enough to drink and wondered if James had as well, and didn't he want to come home and make love with her right now? Her parents were very liberal, she said. They were used to guys spending the night.

James remembered completing the act satisfactorily enough, if not downright athletically, given the amount of booze in his system (tongues like the hands of overworked Chinese translators to the deaf; body-part pistons lubed well and working), and then, sometime after, in the cool of easy breathing and loose-limb stretching, falling asleep to the sounds of his own music playing faintly on the boom-box sitting on the night table beside her bed.

He also remembered, if hazily, how just before nodding off Melissa had asked him various unanswered questions regarding his lineage and why — he thought this was what she had said — why he didn't simply call a spade a spade, because that too can be a beautiful thing, you know? He also thought he had dreamt a little, but nothing that upon awakening made any sense.

12

Upon reasoned reflection, James was not entirely comfortable with the prospect of spending his very important myth-digging trip home waking up very feasibly too often much too leukaemia-like hung over in (embarrassingly, there was no other word for it) that hot little *thang* of last night's warm love-sack.

Being a card-carrying member, however, of that branch of country-and-western song-writing that says a bad thing suffered by the body or brain right now isn't necessarily such a bad thing if down the road something of a more permanent nature is delivered (what the uninitiated typically refer to as a "hurtin' song"), the temptation — professional, not to mention purely physical — was obvious. And she did like her beer. And not just as an easy path to girl-giddy drunkenness, either; more: the actual beer taste of it, the actual beer act of consumption of it — in fact, the whole splendid hops thing of it. He liked that in a woman. Still, there were things to do and get done, motivation of a manifestly practical sort behind his being in town. So no, none of that, he decided. Not for a while, anyway.

He thought about cutting the grass, or maybe just watering the flowers out back, but found himself wandering downtown instead, the walk hopefully helping to dissolve the nastier effects of his hangover not yet taken off by his sleeping in the excess of noon; the main idea, however, being that a haircut might not be the worst move he could right now make. Something about a stranger's professionally caring indifference all around the sides of your head and up the back of your neck usually able to supply the simple grounding that religion or proper manners had provided to occasionally directionless young men of another, more civilized time.

He had almost made it as far as the barber shop when his uncle's Skylark pulled up beside him. Oblivious to half a King Street full of Saturday afternoon slowed-down honking drivers, Buckly crawled the Buick alongside his nephew walking on the sidewalk, one arm hanging out the driver's side window, the other resting easily on the wheel.

"Haven't got but a minute, so here we go. Your birthday is right around the corner, isn't it?"

"Monday."

"Monday. Right. And you'll be how old?

"Twenty-five." The held-up honkers were by now strangely rhythmic in their anger, a symphony of metallic burping aggravation.

"How old?"

"Twenty-five!" James shouted above the clamour.

"Twenty-five. All right. In that case I got something for you."

James looked at the stalled line of blaring cars, then back at his uncle. "Okay?" he said. "Right?"

"How soon they forget," Buckly said, pulling his arm back in the window, the car picking up speed. "I'll see you around, birthday boy."

James ducked inside the Trend Den, a half-dozen single-finger salutes and sustained, indignant beeps from the street announcing his arrival. The entirety of the shop looked up to see what kind of person could inspire such a sour greeting. He closed the tinkling door behind him and took his place among the waiting-their-turn old men and magazines, and looked down between his feet. A gleaming black-and-white checkerboard floor assured him he was in the right place.

CFPO, The Great Big Voice of the Great South West, Datum's AM and only radio station, supplied a steady flow of that musical half-breed called "New Country", a form of music distinguished by its fusing of the worst elements of both country and soft rock. Just over the top of a dominating string section, a thin electric guitar, and a nearly inaudible fiddle (violin?), a "hard-living mama who's broken a few hearts" described how tonight she was going to "put on her high-heel shoes and tight fittin' jeans" and "turn a few heads at the old K-Mart," the whole thing kept sprightly moving along by an up-tempo, 4/4 rhythm supplied by a perfect electronic drumbeat. The others in the barber shop — both the genuinely red-necked older ones in overalls and baseball caps, in town for their once-a-month buzz, and the medium to older ones who worked in the factories and offices in town and just wanted a little thinning out of the front, back, and sides (leave the part where it is, please) — tapped along tempered feet to one song after another, the same even rhythm of their moving shoes never varying with the changing tunes.

James surprised himself by being a little put out by the fact that none of the men seemed to recognize him. Back in Toronto he prided himself on not being remotely concerned with anything so silly as street-clothes visibility. Of course, back in Toronto he could count on someone asking him to confirm his identity at least once a week. He was disappointed in himself for his honest longing to affirm that he was who he was.

He waited his turn and attempted to lose himself in the magazine he had chosen from the strewn selection, holding it up, as did all the others, folded as wide open as it would allow in front of his face. All the magazines were of the same real-man variety: *Carnivore Hunter's Monthly*, *Bow and Arrow Digest*, *Outdoor Life Illustrated*. He selected the only one that had a woman on the cover, albeit a woman in a string bikini sitting backwards on a powerful motorcycle holding, in one hand, a fourteen-inch pike by the gills, and in the other, what appeared to be the instrument used to catch the prize. Underneath the picture were, in bold black print, the lines WIN THIS ROD! DETAILS INSIDE! James skimmed as slowly as his fingers would allow, trying to imagine the life of a professional duck caller, as well as what kind of man ordered hair transplant treatments from a mail order company with a Kalamazoo, Michigan, PO box number at the back of a hunting magazine. He ignored with vigour the sign that hung over barber-shop chair number one:

HAIR MUST BE CLEAN
IF IT IS TO BE CUT.
NO EXCEPTIONS!

Ignoring with vigour, he flipped, and waited his turn.

Rubbing his hand up and down the back of the new stubble now the back of his neck, James exited the Trend Den seven dollars poorer but, in spite of the CFPO musical damage endured, purposefully refreshed. He would haunt the haunts, massage his muse, and finally get his songwriting act into gear. A slow start was all he had suffered, he told himself, not negative confirmation of one damn thing. He said it again: Not negative confirmation of one damn thing.

And then James was seen. Somebody had saw. Pinky, I think, has seen me, James saw for himself. And, Christ, I really need that, don't I? Just when I'm getting back on track, I really need that. Like a fucking hernia, I need that.

Then: Okay, you got me, James conceded, slumping forward slightly in his walking, as if somehow psychically shot. Do your best hello, he told himself. Go on and get it over with. Do your best surprised. Pinky crossed the street and James offered over his hand.

"Pinky."

"Jimmy Thompson."

Fingers-through-fingers hands clasped in front of him, black-haired lily-white arms resting comfortably on his belly as he spoke, Jeffrey Pinkereskie was a fat man at ease with his own flab. Even as a public-school classmate of his, James could never recall Pinky showing the usual kind of childhood insecurities normally guaranteed to (along with stutterers and kids needing thick glasses) children for whom the term "pudgy" or "big-boned" was considered kind. Quite the opposite. Unexceptional to an extent remarkable, Pinky had always worn his considerable weight like an expensive new coat, his nose-in-the-air airs and big-belly hall-monitor strutting way allowing him the opportunity to exhibit an acute sense of unearned arrogance.

A grade-twelve graduate without honours (like James

himself, the first high-school graduate in his family's history), Pinky had failed the Datum police entrance exam so many times they finally just told him, "Ah well, don't worry about it, son, not really hiring right now anyway. Hear the Fire Department's looking for a few good men, though, whydontcha head on over there?" Instead, he had ended up as a part-time security guard working all the hours the other, more experienced guards didn't want. Eventually, after eating more shit than any man with even half a conscience in good conscience should, the company rewarded him with a full-time gig as head man in charge of security over at the new downtown mall, Northern Maples. He thrived on the increased responsibilities the job offered. Never had one man extracted as much joy from a list of tasks that included, among others, security-officer-coffee-break sentry and washroom-safety-maintenance-and-patrol inspection, than one Jeffrey Pinkereskie. Also: he smoked cheap cigars continuously, had never, to James's knowledge, been with a woman, and still lived with his mother in his childhood home over in the east end.

"So I hear Jimmy Thompson is making a bit of a name for himself up there in Tee-ron-ta," Pinky said. He lit up a fresh cigar, uncrossed then recrossed his arms across his belly, and sucked at the stogie until it glowed a deep orange, awaiting James's reply.

"Getting by, Pinky, you know — getting by. Actually, I'm on my way over to, uh—"

"Not what I hear," *suck suck suck*, he said, ignoring James's answer, "not what I hear at all. What I hear is, Mr. Thompson's making hisself a pretty little penny up there in Tee-ron-ta town, that's what I hear." *Suck suck suck.*

At this, nauseous anger began to rise up in the pit of James's stomach. And not just because he wasn't making a pretty little penny up there in Tee-ron-ta town, either.

In truth, despite his two records doing more or less okay for fairly traditional country music on a small, independent label — about twelve thousand copies sold all told — this, and the fact that he and The Paddocks played in and around town pretty regularly, with even an occasional southern sojourn to a northern American border town, the reality of the matter was that it was damn hard to make a living (manage, that is, to get by without having to work a day job) by simply playing good, honest country-and-western music in a city like Toronto that, despite being, twang-wise, *the* Canadian place to be dollar-wise by virtue of sheer club-going and plastic-buying numbers, could never quite decide from month to month if it was European cultivated or New York chic. Like a lot of imported American cultural goods, country music was viewed by most Torontonians as, yes, not without its own Yankee frontier charm, but, of course, hopelessly unsophisticated in a primarily white-male, patriarchal, not to mention inherently misogynist and musically rudimentary sort of way. At present, Third World hip hop was the culturally rarefied portion of the city's passion: a million and a half university-educated white people desperately trying to convince one another that respect for different value systems and cultural practices (particularly the so-called "primitive") could be most liberally demonstrated by dressing up in brightly coloured handmade hats, beads, and vests, and unrhythmically embarrassing the hell out of themselves on sweaty, overpriced dance floors.

Still, it was not for a lack of incoming funds that James flinched as he did at this moment. Rather, because (steady now, it's only Pinky you're talking to, remember? What did you expect, artistic empathy?) money wasn't the point of the music he made, was it?

"Whadoyou make doing that music biz thing up there anyway if you don't mind me askin'. Forty, fifty grand a year?"

James's stomach tightened, both fists, too.

"What's a fella" *suck suck suck* "of your Garth Brooks type cal-e-bar bring in per year, you think? Before taxes, I mean. One, two, three mill per year?" *Suck suck suck.* "Not bad for a little song and dance once in a while, eh?"

The midday May heat, mixed up with just a touch of humidity, worked together with Pinky's mere presence to soil what had been, until just a few minutes before, the best damn seven-dollar haircut/soul-refresher available without a prescription in Datum. Back in Toronto, tonight — Saturday night — was open-stage night and dollar-fifty long-necks at Restless Winds; afterward, greasy finger food and musician gossip at Spooky Doo's until dawn (and maybe, if each felt up to it, the blonde waitress with the nose-ring and water-bed who never failed to make the best Spanish omelette afterward for breakfast). Instead: Pinky. And all that that implied.

What am I doing here Who am I kidding How did I ever . . . ? Then, the Thing, he thought; that's the thing Uncle Buckly was talking about. The thing for my twenty-fifth birthday. Dominos of memory crashed backward to his uncle's once-upon-a-time barroom promise, not quite, but nearly making Pinky disappear.

Maybe there, James considered, maybe there in the Thing just the break I've been waiting for.

"Well, good on you, then, Mr. Thompson," Pinky said, "good on you. Sounds to me like you're makin' yourself a pretty little penny up there in Tee-ron-ta town." *Suck suck suck.* "Did I happen to mention that I'm head of security now over at the new mall we got in town — Northern Maples? Yeah" — continuing to suck as he spoke, not noticing that James was not noticing — "got me a staff of three men working under me over there at the moment. Basically, our function at this juncture is to—"

Here, something along the lines of a cheap miracle on an almost muggy May Datum day: the St. Clair West #416 bus that made its way more or less past James's grandparents' house hissed to a stop directly in front of them. The door accordioned open and James, leaving Pinky in mid-sentence, stepped up into the bus.

Falling into the seat nearest him — a single-seater

immediately behind the driver — he peered out of the tinted window to see Pinky squinting up at the bus, calmly attempting to relight his cigar. James slouched down and looked straight ahead.

Disease, he told himself; he can't just be a symptom. Disease. Gotta be. He slid down farther into his seat and tried to get comfortable with the idea.

The bus began to slowly snake its way out of the downtown area and search out its first subdivision stop. Despite the air conditioning and the cautious lyrical promise he felt at his uncle's mention of the Thing, beads of sweat began to appear on his forehead and neck. He observed that he wasn't alone on the bus, counted seven other passengers, nervously recounted, and came up again with seven.

He's gotta be a disease, he thought again. Gotta be. Because if he's just a symptom. . . .

He let the thought trail off where it did, managing to distract himself (at first softly, and then — finding the song's pulse — more confidently, loudly) by humming what he envisioned as the mandolin line he wanted to run through a short, melodically irresistible tune he and The Paddocks had been playing around with since last summer but hadn't completely put together yet, even as an instrumental. The bunch of them a little afternoon-tipsy at the time of its composition, a late-August, mid-ninety-degree scorcher, they had decided for no good reason other than brow-soaked wishful thinking to call it "Having Snow". James hummed himself pleasantly invisible.

Trying to work out where he next wanted the fiddle part to come in, James lost all interest in trying to distinguish between disease and symptom, the ditty at hand demanding all his attention, the bus he was riding steadily moving him towards home.

13

The bus let him off a block and a half from where he wanted to be. Still humming, he hoofed the remaining distance home.

Walking across the front lawn of his grandparents' house, on his way around to the back door that directly led down into the basement, James noticed a manila envelope folded in half and slipped in behind the handle to the screened front door. He made a detour across the grass, plucked out the envelope, and held it up to the sun. A photograph, that was clear, but not as clear of what. Checking the mailbox while he was there, he found a special-delivery letter addressed to him from Willie Pee Musics. He folded the thing neatly in half and stuck it deep in the back pocket of his jeans.

At the back door, he fished for the single key in his pocket and gave the mystery envelope a final, sun-assisted inspection. Topographical, perhaps; either that, or a picture of a plate of spaghetti covered with lots of sauce. Or something.

Downstairs, James boots-off collapsed on the only comfortable chair in the room and flicked on the standing lamp beside his chair (necessary in spite of the midday beams he had just been in). He opened the envelope in his right hand by tearing off one of the ends with his teeth, pulling the picture out of its package with his left, and studying it a few inches from his face. Presently he cleared his throat, adjusted himself deeper into the stuffed chair, and brought the photo an inch or so closer.

He could have been flattered, but was sure that wasn't

the sender's intention. Shock? Was that it? He had had occasion to see one or two before (though never under such . . . excellent lighting conditions). And then there was the works-cited note on the back of it. In a word: odd.

He took a deep breath and offered another slowly back out. The inexplicability of the shot for some reason troubled him more than he knew it should have.

"And what have I done to deserve such a . . . thing?" Even (as he was) alone, he would have liked to hear the question sounding somewhere between disinterested and ironic, nothing more. Instead, an uneasy misgiving coloured his words. He lifted the picture to his eyes again and gave it another once-over.

"Really, what have I . . . ?"

A nap, he decided. The necessary manufacturing of songs and all that this — setting the photograph face down on his knee — implied, could wait.

He closed his eyes and began almost immediately to doze, an involuntary twitch of his left leg soon after unconsciousness set upon him causing to flutter to the ground a Polaroid shot of what at first would appear to be a shrieking close-up of an immoderately black-furred bat's mouth screaming with full terror and teeth his last bat squeak into an oncoming motorcycle's single white headlight — but which, upon further examination, would only reveal a woman's well-spread, black-bearded vagina illuminated by a flashlight beam.

Fluttered and fallen, settling finally on the carpeted floor anatomical-side down, the text on the back of the shot, handwritten in careful blue-pen print, read:

> *It is remarkable that the genitals themselves, the sight of which is always exciting, are hardly ever regarded as beautiful* (Freud, *Civilization and It's Discontents* 39).

He slept in his chair until the curtain-sieved yellow light

filing into the basement changed slowly but solidly to black.

14

Dream, dream, dream; secular dreams. . . .

Although, of course, never knowing these things, these were the things that he knew best:

The sad, oh-so-sad, strange animal wail of steel-guitar sounds somewhere in more than likely a very late, after-hours Nashville night. Music needing no words to say what it says; music that makes you (a little embarrassing, it's true, but still . . .) go, simply, "Wow," when it is done. And, when done — enough. The band does not play on.

Or: deep fall-season kisses of Mozart in the morning and this moment is not restless. Why, just now, a heartbeat held in the palm of your hand; and, look, a moment be-fore, the warmth from below the blanket spilling over the nape of her neck. Warm bath smells beneath clean white sheets paining you (thank you) good.

Or: tired, friendly cowboy boots to shine and polish very early in hard-wood-floor industrious mornings. Alone but full of vigour, and really, when you think about it, not all that alone. Alone not being alone when all alone with objective and plan. "I've got this and that and this and that to do today, but first I think I'll just do these boots." Bed. Chair. Window. Small bookcase (overflowing). All this with the now-coming-up sun through the curtainless win-dow the perfect post-dawn workshop. Stripped to your everything, you say to yourself, "Yeah, it's pretty early (pretty late?) and I really should grab some shut-eye, but I'm up so, what the hey, I'll just do a hell of a job on these boots just like old _____ showed me how." (Laughing a little here as you say what you say, recalling the beautiful but still tragically silly seriousness of _____ not all that patiently showing you how.)

Or: cruising in over centre ice, shaking off your man with a quick glide of speed and, just for good measure, a little leather from your glove stuck up into his face; taking the pass at the blue line (softly: black-rubber-on-taped-stick kiss) and (eyes closed, stick swung back, crazy but knowing head-in-helmet radar telling you what to do and how to do it) slap — shot — score! Five, maybe ten seconds to do; a rush like this one sticking in the brain long after the jock has been hung up for good.

Or: completely right words strung together expert-angler hook-on-line-like; words you wish you had said but didn't, and, upon not saying, cringing, and, after cringing, cursing mother, father, and ancestry in general for inarticulate speech-pattern learnings and no encyclopedia of even the cheaper sort within childhood little arm's length. And, instead of syntax fumbling and everywhere grammatical clutching, beautiful and as yet unknown oration smooth and sure-sounding, surely sounding something like this (you've heard it all before, a thousand times before, in your longing-to-be-a-hero head):

"What rain?"

"The rain against the window."

"That's not rain."

"Oh, really," she says, a little amused, raised on the bed on one elbow. "What is it then?"

"Everyone I know, wishing they were here."

"Softly tapping? Trying to get in?"

"That's right."

"And let me guess: we won't let them in?"

"No, we won't."

RAY ROBERTSON

"Not ever?"
"No."
Not long after, "No," she says, as solemn as he.
Or: the perfect, soaring, unspeaking poem; one long, lengthy alliteration, senseless and soundless (yet, at the same time, teeming with meaning, every line lifting, dancing, and finally ending in perfect, knowing, nodding brilliance.)
So yes, all of these things were the things he knew best. Without, of course, knowing these things at all.

15

Awakened from his nap, still in his chair, James — in spite of the momentary melodic respite on the bus — briefly but seriously considered showing up at his Uncle Buckly's place and simply demanding the recently recalled thing the Thing.
Might just be the thing, he mused. No sign of any sort of sign yet, and damn it, something from this supposed-to-be poetic pilgrimage must be delivered. Songs, real songs — the kind with words to them — demanded to be written. And soon, too.
He figured that no fewer than ten new tunes would suffice for the September deadline Devanchuck had given him; ten songs and he would have an album. He owed him that much. Not that Willie Pee Musics was the perfect label to work for. To begin and end with, there was its owner, Devanchuck himself.
Willie Pee Musics was a late-seventies purchase

Devanchuck's family had made on the strong recommen-
dation of several well-paid, chin-pulling mental health care
professionals; this, after a particularly tough year for all
concerned which Devanchuck had for the most part spent
in drug rehabilitation at a very private Montreal clinic serving high-level business executives, lower-level federal
politicians, and, increasingly, the nasal-broken baby-
boomed sons and daughters of the post-World War Two
Canadian mercantile much-rich (Devanchuck's family the
same Devanchucks of Devanchuck Mock-Meats and
Lunch-Spreads success).

A Bridle Path birth and rearing, Upper Canada College (and, later, University of Toronto) education, summers
in Europe — all had combined in the formation of, not a
young man destined to someday lead his country, but,
rather, a man who liked nothing more than to ingest enormous quantities of cocaine and follow around his own
country and that of the United States any number of rock-
and-roll groups. "Groupie with a gold card", the verdict
Devanchuck Senior had arrived at. Hence, at age twenty-
eight, the out-of-province rehabilitation centre; *ergo*, the
acquisition of the record label.

Eventually satisfied that, as predicted, his son's previ-
ously recalcitrant energies had begun to find a wholly ac-
ceptable means of expression ("Executing a business of
some sort, preferably one revolving around the boy's interests or hobbies," it had been suggested), Devanchuck
Senior was sufficiently relieved by his son's fairly rapid
transformation in lifestyle to make a very generous contribution to the rehabilitation centre in the way of an addition to the main building on the provision that it be named
in honour of his own mentorial father. How many formerly
stray youths have benefited from the basketball court,
snack bar, and lounge housed in the Honourable P.H.
Devanchuck (MPP — Brantford 1917–1921) Wing over the
years is incalculable.

In time, after adjusting to getting up in the morning

and going to bed at night in the same place, Devanchuck began to like the life of a music executive. Began to like it quite a lot. He still got to hang around with musicians and vicariously thrill to their assorted non-prescribed medicinal indulgences, and, much more importantly, even gradually came to inherit the family skill for making money. Lots of it. Initial plans of running the business co-operatively and stocking the label's roster with only musicians shunned by the mainstream industry were — while for publicity's sake nominally maintained — soon abandoned in practice upon Devanchuck's discovery that bringing a small business out of the red and keeping it thick in the black was almost as good a buzz as all the drugs you could score in High Park on a Saturday night.

Still, James knew he was lucky. Because Devanchuck had quickly discovered upon taking control of Willie Pee Musics that he was defined under the *Canadian Guide to Cultural Grants, Loans, and Services* as "the operator of an independent enterprise of artistic production", he applied for (and received, it seemed) every possible grant and matching grant offered by the various levels of government, each in the allegiant attempt to keep Canada's offices of culture distinctly Canadian. And because part of the government's musical mandate was "to encourage and actively promote as many distinct means of Canadian-performed or -produced musical expression as is possible", country music, despite Devanchuck's and the general public's indifference to the form itself, was as nearly a potential cash cow as even the alternative music that Devanchuck so openly promoted. Consumption of artistic goods by the public was not, here, of the greatest economic importance; production of them, and dutiful documentation and timely grant-application to the proper governmental departments, was.

For James, his music and Willie Pee Musics made a begrudgingly admitted but nearly perfect fit. The label allowed him to record and see distributed a brand of C&W

that other, more commercially minded companies would never think of touching because of its too musically pure texture (real drums and brushes; featured steel-guitar runs; dobro solos; twin steel and electric guitar parts; mostly ruined-relationship-free lyrical content). In return, James gave the organization, in the form of himself, the perfect Canadian token country bumpkin: good-looking and hip enough to conform to the label's self-consciously concocted young, beautiful, and pensive image (never a cowboy hat on his head, for instance; sideburns of just medium length; 519 Levi–legged only, no wildly flared rhinestone saddle-pants for him); necessarily altogether grant-eligible; and, most important to Devanchuck, not the least bit interested in anything other than the requisite means of publicity and promotion (speculation among James's label-mates had it that James and The Paddocks received by far the least money for their record launches and tours of any of Willie Pee's acts).

James needed — wanted — to stay with Willie Pee Musics. The trade-off of deficiency of material support for almost complete artistic control was just fine with him. More likely he would end up busking at the corner of Yonge and Bloor in a February snowstorm with a sleet-filled donation hat for his efforts before he got a deal with another label as artistically indulgent as the one he had now.

Panicking slightly at the prospect of a Willie P.-less future, No need to panic, he told himself. It's early. Very early. The Thing can wait. Thing or noThing, songs will get written. The kind with words to them, too.

When out with the band on tour and (mostly meta-phorically speaking) encountering a nasty patch of weather (hotel reservations gone missing; no time for a proper soundcheck; rubber cheques written on non-existent bank accounts by evil, dwarf-like bar owners; et cetera), the Kansas-born Webby was always fond of saying that "When she's blowing outside, fellas, there's always room for one more in the storm cellar." On the road, this usually was the signal for a hasty hedonistic retreat from all worldly concerns into a careproof, all-night protective shell of hotel room, till-dawn poker, Labatt Blue and Jim Beam boilermakers, and the greatest hits of Ferlin Husky. In any case, reversion to the immutable.

Along these very lines, then, James, caught in his own light but persistent pain-in-the-ass drizzle ever since stepping off the bus home almost forty-eight hours earlier, clung to the idea of a dry, safe place. Naturally, he thought: M.C.

16

Since high school, James had slept with a few models of the more provincial sort, put out two mildly successful albums (in a mostly critically ignored, lukewarm commercial but nonetheless still-out-there sort of way), and been on the radio a little bit. M.C. had gotten his girlfriend — Jeanie, now his wife — pregnant a couple of times over, suffered through two miscarriages, and managed a sixty-cent raise from South Western and all the work gloves he could steal in his lunchbox. Despite the inequality of worldly experience, James believed that the two had yet to feel the uncomfortable chasm that often develops between geographically distanced high-school chums who are not the letter-writing sort.

M.C. had always worked the four-to-midnight shift, even when he had first started at the plant in their last year of high school, and James could think of no good reason why it should be any different now. Having walked the half-mile or so from his grandparents' place, he would have liked to talk to Jeanie for a few minutes before M.C. got home, but thought better of likely waking her out of a sound sleep. He settled on waiting on the already lightly dewed picnic table in the back yard.

A link in a chain of several subdivisions built in the early seventies in expectation of an economic boom that did not in fact boom, M.C.'s house looked exactly like all the other two-bedroom-one-bath ranch houses that by now had surrounded Datum's older downtown section, each distinguished by how high its TV tower stood. As with most of the houses in the neighbourhood, no fence divided M.C.'s lawn from any other. Everywhere, red and blue plastic toys dotted the green-black plots, as if abandoned by their child owners in mid-use, the three-wheelers and oversized plastic baseball bats illumined by the yellow shinings of a streetful of all-night-on porchlights.

Nothing in the vicinity he particularly wanted it to hang on, James's mind naturally wandered: first to the photograph, which, but for the slight anxiety he experienced each time he contemplated it, he knew he should consider nothing more than an admittedly curious gift; then to the special-delivery letter from the record label, which he hadn't as yet opened. Still sitting, he raised his right buttock up slightly from the picnic table and pulled the envelope out of his back pocket, thankful for the diversion.

The dull yellow porchlight his only light, James opened the envelope and held the letter as close to his eyes as he could, skimming over the Willie Pee Musics letterhead and half-typed salutation (*Dear . . .*) and reading with some difficulty the beginning of the handwriting below he instantly identified as Devanchuck's nearly microscopic scrawl.

. . . James,

*Just this minute found out about your little trip
home. Wonderful idea! Glad to know that our little
talk the other day managed to help you see the light.
Anyway, here's the rub.*

*Never have told and never will tell one of the
artists on my label how to do what it is they do. Ask
anybody who knows me and they'll tell that's just
not Devanchuck's style. Nor Willie Pee Musics' for
that matter. Company policy numero uno. Period.
End of discussion. It's just that it occurred to me
after you left the office the other day that I had entirely forgotten to bring up one of the things I had
wanted to talk with you about when I asked you to
drop by in the first place, and I knew that if I just let
it go I wouldn't be able to live with my conscience
for depriving you as an artist of information that
might be beneficial to your creative welfare.*

*As you well know, I'm sure, the recent federal
election has brought to power a government pretty
serious about enforcing their new Canadian Content laws. Seems like they've discovered that the one
thing they can do right is stand tough on keeping
the True North Strong and Free. Seems like Joe and
Josephine Canuck have gotten just a little bit sick
and tired of being told one too many times what to
do by big old Uncle Sam. And of course we at Willie
Pee Musics are 110% behind any attempt (even if it
is by the government!) to preserve our eroding Canadian identity in the face of our increasingly im-
perialistic (economic and cultural) neighbour to the
south, and applaud the recent legislation that makes
it necessary now for 40% of all radio time to be given
over to Canadian-performed or -produced music. To
quote from your own label mate, Honkin' Ron Dod-
ders, "Just because the big wind blows/My star-
spangled friend/This don't mean/That the small*

grass has got to bend." *Everything we can do to keep this old land our land, right? Right.*

Okay. But the thing is, James, the word on the old vino line is saying something like just being Canadian might be enough, same as it ever was, to get you on the airwaves, but your likelihood of staying there these days wouldn't be at all hurt by being Canadian just a little bit more. Your basic difference here being that fine line between just being something and sincerely looking like it. You following me here?

All I'm really saying, James, is that maybe a mention or two of a couple Canadian cities should make it into a few of your newest songs. Or a transnational highway. Or a distinguishing, easily recognizable landmark. Just for instance. Or let's say one of the Great Lakes makes for a nice rhyme somewhere along the line. Where's the harm? You are Canadian, right? And hey, worked wonders for Lightfoot in that sunken ship song of his. Or maybe one of the old-time Maple Leafs finds his way into a tune somehow (better leave any of the old Montreal Canadiens out of things for now, at least until this separation business boils over). Anyway, you get the picture. Do yourself a favour and keep it in the back of your mind.

Anyway, have a nice vacation and see you no later than September 7 with a real record full of songs with words to them. (But not before August 15, okay? — leaving for a rain-forest tour of Southern Colombia right about then.)
Sincerely,
Devanchuck

Slowly James folded the letter back into its original three-creased form, just as slowly sliding it back into the envelope, returning it with an assertive force into his back pocket. Motionless, looking directly ahead at nothing at all, he sat on top of the picnic table as he had all along, feet flat on the part intended for the picnickers' bottoms. Creative welfare my ass, he thought.

James knew, as Devanchuck must have known he knew (bullshitting, he supposed, probably becoming as much a habit as anything else, even when there was no good reason to do it), that according to governmental guidelines, for his record to be eligible for a provincial subsidy (and hence for Willie Pee Musics to want to make and distribute it), it had to contain songs that for the most part had words, words that "preferably, though not exclusively, express and/or explore Canadian themes, perspectives, or issues." Ten songs with words to be written, recorded, and on Devanchuck's desk by early fall, or within a week after that, James knew, every drugstore cowboy in Toronto would be sleeping in Willie Pee Musics' reception room, driving Francine crazy for the chance to try their best high lonesome on the boss.

Do *yourself* a fucking favour, Devanchuck, and. . . .

Still, James knew Devanchuck wasn't acting alone; countless conspirators lay in wait for him all along Canada's grassy-knolled cultural watchtower. An unsigned review of his second album, of nearly three years before, was still capable of calling up in James genuine esthetic rage. In part:

> So although on a purely musical basis Thompson's songs are pleasant enough in and of themselves, they retain, nonetheless, a certain curious ambiguity of content; a sense, that is, that any one of the songs on the record could just as easily have taken place in any rust-belt town in the United States as they could in a distinctly Canadian milieu. There remains, then, a certain amount of cultural blindness in Thompson's work, a blindness that he surely must remedy if he wishes to be taken seriously as an artist. As an artist in this country, at any rate.

Brief adolescent Gordon Lightfoot folk-styling fetish aside, the sole Canadian contribution to James's countrified musical consciousness was small-label legend William B. Remy, a favourite of James's since discovering Remy's relatively unknown though meticulously crafted and heartfelt records at a second-hand store in Datum as a teenager. But how could it honestly be otherwise? As absurd as banana-bread-brown Californians sitting in beach clothes and eating sushi while watching with confused glee a hockey game in a heavily air-conditioned basketball stadium, almost entirely counterfeit singing cowboys on James's northern side of the border. Consequently, when for the first time truly cognizant of the near-exclusive U.S. musical stamp on his butt (and a little self-conscious about it too), James had quickly come to reason once and for all that, Hey, it's everybody's music, isn't it? The form — the husk of the harmony, and all the other wonderfully indescribable intangibles of the song that stay in the head and heart until death do you part — *this* remains the same, regardless of which coloured portion of the map you happened to be begotten. In matters musical James was henceforth an esthetic imperialist — Devanchucks, royal commissions, and provincially patriotic minor music reviewers all be damned.

With a quick start James retrieved Devanchuck's letter from his pocket and mashed it into a white paper ball, throwing it in the direction of the unlidded garbage can sitting next to M.C.'s back door. He missed. He didn't hear M.C's car pull into the driveway.

"So you're back."

"Yep."

"And?"

"And what?"

"And why exactly is it you're back?"

"Nice to see you too, you sonofabitch," James said, wanting to smile but knowing it would ruin the moment.

"Christ, I need a shower and a beer. Let's go inside,"

M.C. said.

"Exactly," James said, following his friend into the house.

James's instincts had been right; Jeanie had been asleep. Hearing beer rustling and talk in the kitchen, she came downstairs to find James sitting alone at the table. She pulled tight at the top of her housecoat and sat down across from him.

James liked to think he knew Jeanie pretty well; did, in fact, when he considered just how many women he could simply sit and shoot the shit with and not have to endure the requisite morning-after Did-her-name-rhyme-with-Sue-or-was-it-Holly? ordeal. M.C., however, being the complete madman he was when it came to Jeanie, made it difficult for anything but a bridled yet friendly formality to guide James and Jeanie's relationship. This, the consequence of his letting everyone (including his best buddy, James) know right from his and Jeanie's grade-twelve beginning that she was to be treated like Mrs. McCellar, their nearly octogenarian English teacher — a woman, yes, but at the same time somehow not — only allowable the sort of affection normally reserved for half-senile aunts bearing unappreciated Christmas gifts. Extreme, of course, not to mention absolutely unnecessary, but this was the one eccentricity James allowed M.C., a man for whom the term "meat and potatoes" might have been invented had it not already existed.

Appropriately, then, James exchanged pleasant small talk, smiled a lot, and generally soaked up the kitchen's matching wallpaper and tiled-floor tranquillity, enjoying a calm domesticity his bachelor apartment in Toronto did not possess.

"Hope it's all right that I gave the record company your phone number for emergency's sake. Can't see why they would call," he said, thinking of Devanchuck's garbaged letter and regretting having given anyone from his other world such easy access to this one. "I guess I should have asked you guys first, but I didn't want to go through all the hassle of getting a phone installed for just a couple of months."

"Don't be silly, James, of course it's all right," Jeanie said. "As a matter of fact. . . ." She got up from her chair and went to the fridge. "You've already gotten a couple messages." She pulled two yellow Post-it notes off the fridge door, sat back down, and handed them over. "Neither one of them left their names, but I don't think they're from your company." James read the first.

> *I hate fish I hate I hate fish.*
> *Written any good songs lately?*

"Any idea?" Jeanie said. "He told me to write it down just like that."

James smiled. "Apparently someone who doesn't care for fish a whole lot." He put Smitty's note in his back pocket.

He then read and reread the second note, and looked up quizzically.

"All I can tell you is that it was a woman," Jeanie said. "She didn't say any more than what I wrote down there. She asked if she could please leave a message for you, said what I put down, and said you'd understand when I asked her if there was anything else."

James looked at the note again, studied it for a long minute, then crumpled it in his hand. "Garbage pail still under the sink?" he asked.

"Uh-huh."

He rose, opened up one of the cupboard doors under the sink, lifted up the white plastic lid of the garbage pail suspended from the door, then sat back down. One-handed, free-throw style, aiming carefully — right eye shut in concentration — he tossed the tiny yellow paper ball. He missed. The thing ricocheted off the rim of the pail and landed directly in front of him. He looked at the balled note. Replaying its ten-word message, he thought: So: Rose is a Rose is a rose is a rose. Also: Why tell me? Also: I mean, really, why tell me?

"M.C.'s in the shower," he said, eager to change the mood of the moment. He pulled hard on his beer, eyes over the edge of his raised can, however, not leaving the yellow spot of paper on the floor.

"I know," Jeanie said, bending over in her chair, one hand on the throat of her housecoat, the other picking up the piece of paper. She put it in the ashtray on the table and gave James, for the first time since they had sat down, a good long look.

"Oh."

"He has a shower every night after he comes home from work," she said.

"Oh."

"James?" Jeanie said.

"Yes, Jeanie?" James answered, far too pleasant, too decorous, to be legitimately either.

"To what do we owe this surprise? I mean, what brings you back to Datum? Everything okay with your uncle? Your mother's not sick, is she?" She lit a cigarette and pushed the pack towards him. He ignored it.

"Jesus, Jeanie," he said, "between you and your husband you'd think I'd never been born here. I *can* come back home if I want to, you know."

"Oh, don't take it the wrong way. You know that if we had our way, M.C. and I would see a lot more of you than we already do. It's just that . . . well, you've got to admit you've never exactly . . . been at your best when you're in Datum, and—"

"Now, what's that supposed to mean?" James interrupted, taking one of Jeanie's cigarettes from the pack on the table. James only smoked when he was either drunk or angry. He noticed she had eleven left. That leaves her with ten, he for some reason thought.

"Oh, James, don't get mad. You're among friends here, remember? All I'm trying to say is that you usually only come back when you absolutely need to, and I just wondered—"

"I was born here, you know. I can come back. I might have come back here for a very good reason. There might just be a *very* good reason why I'm back," James said, cigarette and fingers trembling just slightly, but enough for James to wish they weren't.

"Oh, James. You see? It's starting already." She stared out the kitchen window at the neighbouring children's swing-set and took a deep drag.

"What's starting already?" M.C. said, appearing in the kitchen doorway rubbing a white bath towel over his wet hair.

"Apparently I go crazy whenever I'm in Datum," James said.

"We all do, " M.C. replied, getting two more cans of beer out of the fridge. "You just make a bigger production out of it than the rest of us. The performer in you, I've always thought."

17

Excepting a physically absent father and a predominantly psychically unoccupied mother, James had had pretty much the usual little-one, medium-one, big-one, boy-to-manhood sprouting. Then, inexplicably, at just-turned seventeen James could not stop self-consciously swallowing his spit and thinking about yesterday. And not his own days before, either, but nearly everyone else's: father's, mother's, uncle's, et cetera.

Specifically: soon after the arrival of his seventeenth birthday, his mouth began to fill up with saliva (and him having to empty it out by spitting) every five minutes or so. And naturally, him unable to sing, read, or concentrate any more, because every time he attempted to do so, his mouth would fill up with saliva and he'd have to empty it out, of course, by spitting. And how can you sing, read, or think if you're busy either spitting out spit or busy thinking about the next time you've got to spit out spit?

At about the same time, a strong desire on James's part to be a black-and-white photograph where it looked like all the fun was. A shoebox taken from his grandmother's closet his only accomplice, James on his bed in his bedroom would for hours see snapshot faces healthy with sport (his father's, for example) and honest with true sorrow (his mother's, for example) — a real emoting humanity, anyway, and not the merely sweaty and sad walking-and-talking types that present-tense filled up his house, school, and town. Life is elsewhere, he profounded, right up until, a little red-faced, he spotted an inspirational Christian prayer-book at his high school by the very same name.

This perpetual push towards yesterday tendency was not the problem the spit-swallowing was to become (the urge towards anywhere but right now and here not a half-bad place to hang around in for a while, James had found). But the fact remained that, like going to an afternoon movie, sometime or another you unfortunately have to leave the theatre and step back outside again. And after you've sat through enough afternoon movies, and really come to appreciate the healing properties of good, dim darkness, the eyes begin to hurt a little bit, then a lot, each and every time you slump back out into the dogged daylight again.

"How're you ever going to grow up to be president one day if you keep sleeping through your alarm? It's ten to eight, you know. You're gonna miss your bus."

Flat on his back, drifting somewhat adequately amid lost, clean sheets, he lifted an eyelid, no more.

"I told you, Grandma. We've got a prime minister. It's the States that have a president."

"Well, you just get up and get a move on anyway," she said. James's grandmother didn't like to hear, any more than any other Datumite, that what she had seen and heard on television — mostly Detroit signals slid over (or was it under?) the largest undefended border in the world — wasn't absolutely true and applicable to her very own life. "Your grandpa'll be outta the washroom in a minute. I want you in there getting ready pronto when he's done. Understood?"

Am I for ever fated to only be the following act to an old man's gaseous and aftershave-flavoured bathroom performance? (They were reading *Hamlet* in his grade-twelve English class; the stylistic influence was unavoidable.) James struggled to think of something else similarly intelligent, but was train of thought intruded upon by his grandmother reminding him that it was, you know, the early bird that got the worm. Instead, he found himself riveted in attention to the roof of his mouth and all that aggravatingly washed through there. Suck suck suck: the perfect neurotic soother.

I need help, he thought. I am one sick (suck suck) puppy.

Although the concept of seeing a psychiatrist wasn't completely foreign to James (in the biographical appendix to his high-school poetry anthology it was noted, for example, how his favourite non-singing poet of the moment, Allen Ginsberg, had suffered a mental breakdown and undergone psychiatric hospitalization as a young man himself), actually going to Datum Mental Health, making

RAY ROBERTSON

an appointment, and dutifully keeping it was not something his lineage had prepared him for. People in Datum
got lazy, old, and senile, but rarely, if ever, went crazy.

He went, made it, and kept it, though, and — except
for when he was scanning the file on his lap that contained
James's family history — the doctor seemed sympathetic
enough, Uh huh-ing and Yes, I see-ing throughout James's
confession. At the end of their hour together, James leaned
forward on (literally) the edge of his seat and eagerly eyed
the doctor, anticipating an explanation (optional) and so-
lution (not optional) for what the doctor had referred to as
his "inattentiveness difficulty" (James neglecting to
mention his concurrent family-history compulsion).

The psychiatrist leaned back, folded his hands on his
double-breasted belly, and suggested that James exercise
more. A hobby might not be a bad idea either. Perhaps
something that would test his stamina and general physical condition. The doctor wondered if James knew anyone who might be willing to play a little recreational ten-
nis with him now and then. Did this sound like an interesting proposition?

James rose, shook hands, and walked out of the office,
stunned by the impotence of the encounter. For the first
time since the whole swallowing thing had shown its ugly
head that spring, he was scared, really, truly scared. What,
he thought, if never again music without swallowing interruption? No more harmony plain and simple? Priorities, out of infirmity, began popping up out of nowhere.

Up until this point, he had shared his problem with no
one except the psychiatrist and his secretary. M.C., with
Jeanie along for the trip, had left town right after school
ended in May (M.C. a reserve infielder on a hand-picked
rookie squad the Wheels had put together for a summer-
long barnstorming tour), and who the hell else was there
he could talk to about what it felt like to have a head(ache)
on rewind for ever and a mouth like a frigging waterfall?
He put his grandfather's Ford Fairlane in reverse, looked

out for traffic in the rearview mirror, and without the least bit of warning felt a wash of near-relief launder up through his stomach and throat and into his anxious face. He peeled out of the parking lot and let his arm hang out of the window in the breeze. Sure. Why the hell not? Worth a try, anyway. He remembered that his Uncle Buckly was working afternoons that month — the four-till-twelve shift — and it was only quarter to two now. He could be there in ten minutes.

Sensing the seriousness of his nephew's obvious unwellness nearly immediately (Come to think of it, he *had* noticed recently that James had not been his old whistling and humming young self), Buckly secured a cold drink each from the house and, returning momentarily, open-palm offered James the empty lawnchair next to his. Eight-month-old Al, fed just a few minutes before James's arrival, dozed a dog's summer after-dinner snooze at his kind, feeding master's feet. (Buckly having seen through puppyhood to old-age backyard plot-placement three — and was now on his fourth — purebred black Lab Als.)

For testimony of earnestness, Buckly turned off the Tigers' game in mid-inning ("Sonofabitches are five and a half games out and it's only the middle of May") and, after hearing the gist of what James had already told the psychiatrist (and then some), crossed one cut-off-blue-jeaned leg over another, cracked his neck without using his hands, and took a long drink from his glass of iced tea. He spoke like a man who believed what he was saying.

"Okay, here we go: lot of bastards out there," he began, forefinger pumping/pointing sufficiently towards the neighbours' cornfield to signify just about everyone but himself and James, "believe you me. Small town in every way like Datum only makes the mix worse, believe me again." Warming up to his subject, he drained the last half of his drink in one gulp and began working on the ice cubes with his back molars as he spoke.

"Find a garden and cultivate it, son — a little pussy

every once in a while's A-okay too, for sure, and maybe, if you're lucky, one once-in-a-lifetime buddy as well, the kind of guy you'd trust the henhouse to when you the rooster are away — but mainly the main thing being finding yourself a goddamn place to hang your goddamn hat, if you know what I'm saying. A place to make your stand, so to speak.

"And," he added, and clearly not as an afterthought, either, "remember to lock your door at night. The sonofabitches like nothing better than to see somebody besides themselves unhappy for a change. Do everything they can to make it the case, in fact. Can't imagine you'll keep on with this gulping thing if you get yourself in line like I say. You're a smart boy, you'll be all right."

"You think so?" James asked, wanting affirmation, not a deliberated answer.

"Sure. I'm sure of it."

"How come?"

"Let's just say I know where you're coming from, all right?"

James smiled goodly and took a deep drink from his glass of iced tea.

"As for this other thing," his uncle continued, "this hard-on you seem to have for all sorts of things not there — I don't know what the hell to tell you, I really don't. You've always been a queer bird that way, believe me, even as a knee-higher. As a six-year-old you used to always ask me what cars looked like back when I was a kid. Were they as big as now? Smaller? Faster? Sound the same?" James laughed, hazily remembering, too, that boy. Buckly smiled wide himself, pretty much as close as he ever got to downright guffawing. "Now don't get me wrong, didn't say it wasn't cute at the time, but. . . ." His voice trailed off as he thought about what next to say. Finally:

"You say you're thinking of being a singer, a storyteller. All right. Okay. A healthy respect for all that dead stuff, I guess. A look through the old scrapbook once in a while, sure. Probably even necessary in the line of work you're fixing on entering. But you're getting — how shall I put it? — a little fucked up in the head about all sorts of stuff that just ain't there. A guy can get lost in places like that, you know that? It's happened. Don't let it happen to you, is all I'm saying." Al, awaking, shook his head violently from side to side, then yawned. Sitting up, he scratched his ear, staring unblinkingly as he did so into Buckly's eyes looking back at him. "All right," Buckly said, "there you are."

What he had to say said, the ice cubes in his drink crushed, Buckly leaned forward in his lawnchair, softly kneading Al's black dangling ears. Then, leaning back, he looked off into the trees, his trees, on all sides bordering his house. Quiet, all three of them.

A minor setback, however, when James, buoyed by his uncle's words, too literally took Buckly's advice regarding garden-variety cultivation as the path to an end of spit-sucking allrightness. Apparent, soon, that Buckly's row was not James's to hoe, a couple afternoon attempts at following his uncle's fashion of sun-soaked, small-town stoicism resulting in merely a nasty sunburn and a hatred of the common back-yard mosquito. Also, oddly, recurring closed-eye remembrance of how once, after pestering his grandparents for months one summer for a BB gun like the other boys in the neighbourhood had, he had received on his ninth birthday, by way of compromise, a Salvation Army–bought $1.99 broken Daisy 420, a wooden and steel instrument as wonderfully solid and black-metal-barrelled as it was useless. Over and over again, James remembered standing stupid in up-to-his-neck, late-May green cornstalks holding the disabled instrument at eye level, listening, spirit shrunk, at the other boys' pellets whizzing by him all through the field.

The prognosis had been right, then, but the medicine was all wrong. Before long, though — by the time James's last year of high school had wrapped up early the following May — James got it down right, humming and strumming himself right out of Datum, swallowing no more and only professionally nostalgic, his garden a garden of the movable variety. Finding for himself at about this time his very own saint, Saint Stephen Dedalus, saint of everyday commonplace savouring and celebrating, didn't hurt either; the Irishman's slim portrait of a novel was the only reading James at the end of his Datum stay found any time for, his days at this time being through and through full of musical playing with a playful high seriousness.

High-school diploma earned and boozily sentimental two-day M.C. send-off behind him; a thousand burger-flipping-earned dollars in his bank account; and yes, cliché of clichés, his Gibson in its case on the bus terminal seat beside him: on the appointed day Uncle Buckly, alone at the bus station, reassured James that for a bunch of damn good reasons he was doing the right thing by getting out of town (neither Grandma nor Grandpa feeling quite well enough to brave the day's humidity and heat, so saying their goodbyes at home with the giving of a two-pound packed lunch, bony hugs and wrinkled kisses, and a two-hundred-dollar "rainy day" cheque).

For one thing, Buckly said, you can really carry a friggin' tune, James. For another, he continued, it 's obvious to anybody and his brother that Datum is like a shoe that fit you all right at one time, but now is only a pain-in-the-ass floppy, untied thing. His own (Buckly's, that is) garden could be grown practically anywhere, even in Datum. But by the looks of it, James's would only sprout where the bigger buildings stood and the real money flowed. Nashville North: that was the place where the boy otta be: Toronto. Between the music stuck in his head and heart and this move north towards his chosen musical end, Buckly assured his nephew, he was pretty sure his swallowing days were over for good.

Like many who have gotten better after being a bit

bananas, however, James was not in any hurry to consider the hows and whys of why, for a while, he had gone slightly off the track. He only cared that right now he really, really liked to sing and make song, and that his mind these days stayed clear of the glands in his mouth, and that yesterday's people and places were only a nowadays opportunity to say about all his people — poor, ineloquent, quiet ones — the things they would say themselves if saying as he could say was a thing they could say.

But he was the one with the benefit of a high-school education, plenty of growing up playing-time leisure-time, and all the opportunities his steel-working kin had never had. So put the load right on me, people. My garden, you understand.

18

Last call at the Duke made quick work of, inevitably (in no particular order): sloshed, 24-hour bank machines, and pickled eggs to go.

Entering the empty house, tiptoeing and sshhing each other out of habit, James and M.C. settled, as had always been their way, on the floor in front of the television. It seemed not quite right to plunk down on the mildewed rug when three black vinyl stools sat un-sat-in in front of James's grandfather's wet bar, the TV supported for as long as James could remember on two nine-inch two-by-fours hanging over the bar in his grandparents' basement. Habit and the late hour being what they were, however, neither of them made much of an effort to get up off the ground.

The television itself was a survivor of the birth of the television period, the slightly bubbled screen encased in one of those really handsome wooden numbers that resembled nothing more than a mahogany baby coffin with a record player built right in on top just for the hell of it. They passed the after-midnight hour sucking on two of the three beers in the refrigerator, finishing off the take-out eggs, and playing a few of James's grandmother's scratchy Buck Owens records. Also, with the sound turned down, they watched with attempted interest a crime program that featured real cops, robbers, and victims. Every time James looked up from his egg, the cops seemed to be winning.

Once upon a time, it had become apparent to James that if the budding grade-ten relationship he and M.C. had begun was to grow into honest-to-goodness, honest Injun fellowship, his new friend would have to be brought over to his way (that is, the country-and-western way) of seeing and hearing. Country music was then, as now, typically viewed by anyone urban-born and under the age of forty-five as redneckism personified: odes to various dying farm animals; an endless parade of broken hearts; the perpetual lure of the open bottle — all recounted over hopelessly hokey melodious arrangements. James knew what he was up against.

As professional a proselytizer as any who lawfully led a flock, James had made sure to go slowly at first, introducing M.C. to the C&W genre much as he on his own had first encountered it: the odd, steel-flavoured Allman Brothers' instrumental popping up between the requisite fifteen-minute blues jams M.C. was so found of; a couple of acoustic-guitar-and-dobro-driven Neil Young songs to go along with the Crosby, Stills, Nash, and Young *Greatest Hits* album that was so popular that year; a few authentic country numbers thrown into the mix when he knew M.C. would be able to make an easy, rock-and-roll, cover-tune corollary.

In Datum (as in a thousand other North American towns north and south), a place where an early appreciation of country music is not a naturally inherited, elder-given thing but instead a searched-out and well-earned acquired taste (if at all ever tasted), rock and roll was the bridge, the everywhere-in-the-radio-air given that potentially serves as the starting point for the neophyte country listener's first-time rustic-tune exposure. Here, amidst predictably plodding 4/4 rhythms and obligatory middle-of-song guitar solos, the occasional high lonesome duet might be discovered. Or maybe a dancing steel lick. Or perhaps even a soaring fiddle line, some producer's idea of having a paid session player inject some "roots" into the mix. An introduction, anyway; an inkling, at least; a drip, drip, drip, after all was said and done, that announced in slow but sure drop-plops a conceivably incipient country and western deluge. A tonic, certainly, to five-minute drum solo infected ears and souls.

Gradually, then, M.C. jumped musical ships, though the honest metallic restlessness of pure, 100 percent squeezed-out rock and roll would always hold an untouchable (both radio-conditioned and deeply felt) place in his psyche. For who, after all, given the right time, place, and controlled substances, can sincerely say no to Hendrix or Chuck Berry or the early Clapton at their and its very best, everywhere spraying the electric-slivered poundings of a plugged-in big id-thing, the euphonious moment bursting open, finally, in a thousand melted-down trembling directions? (Certainly not James, instigator of M.C.'s and countless others' two-step country baptizing. At his most recent shows, for instance, he had been encoring with his own Chuck Berryish "Lazy Kinda Day" and a countrified but still raucous version of Elvis's "Just Because".) In the end, though, country and western — straight up, no chaser — increasingly became the place where M.C. turned for no-bullshit, pure soul-thumping kicks.

James took Buck's *Greatest Hits* record off the turntable and put the *Close-up* album on. The needle finally lost itself in the beginning grooves that led up to the album's first cut, "My Heart Skips a Beat".

"Buck still making music?" M.C. asked casually, standing now, looking down with James at the record turn turn turn. M.C. only listened to classic rock on the radio, and to a couple of milk crates full of the country and bluegrass tapes James periodically sent him for his musical sustenance. It had once taken James a forty-five-minute long-distance phone call just to convince him that Lynyrd Skynyrd wasn't still making records. ("I never heard nothing about no plane crash," M.C. had insisted. "You sure you got your bands straight? They play them about ten times a day on the radio, you know.")

"Yeah," James said, "he's still kicking his old heart around, but it's not pretty, believe me. Nothing more depressing than an overweight, sixty-year-old man singing with a bunch of underpaid session men on awards shows and sick kids' telethons about being a young fool in love for the first time."

"I hear you."

"But we always got Buck at twenty-six with the original Buckaroos, don't we?" James added, nodding at the record player and raising his beer bottle in mock honour.

"Damn straight," M.C. said. They clinked bottles and turned their attention back to the TV screen.

"What time's it?" James asked, pleased he was only slightly slurring his s's, as sure a sign as any of a man who couldn't hold his alcohol.

"About three," M.C. replied.

"No, really, c'mon. Look."

M.C. had worn the same watch for as long as James had known him; couldn't ever remember him taking it off, if he really thought of it.

M.C. pulled up his shirt-sleeve. "Five to three," he said.

"Good stuff," James said, "five more minutes."

M.C. sprinkled some salt onto the last half of the last

pickled egg, popped it into his mouth (chewing, James noticed, six times carefully), took a swallow of beer, belched once (moderately loud), cracked his knuckles, and, looking directly at James the whole time, blinked a few times for effect before finally saying, "Okay, I'll bite: five minutes to what?"

"Very funny," James said, getting up to change the record, though the first song wasn't even halfway through yet. Restless tonight, he thought. Where's that live thing Buck did in England without the Buckaroos?

M.C. tried hard to burp again, but couldn't. Frustrated, he asked once more, "No, really. Five minutes to what?"

James could tell he was serious. This he hadn't counted on. Carefully he put Buck back in his cover and closed the plastic cover to the record player. He turned around and faced M.C. slowly, as if with intense physical effort.

"You're not kidding, are you?" James asked, hoping, as they say, against hope.

"C'mon, cut the shit. And what's with the music? You think your company is enough to keep me down here all night in this stinky basement? You should open a window or something. It smells like a thousand mothballs died down here."

"J.T. Jones ring a bell, M.C.?" James asked, arms crossed, his eyes not leaving his friend's.

"Who? J.T. Jones? Um . . . ah. . . . Oh, wait a minute, yeah, it does, actually. Give me a minute. Tip of my fucking tongue. A beer might help. Any more left?"

"No," James said quickly, quickly enough for M.C. to see that he was — for whatever reason — deadly serious about the identity of the aforementioned Mr. Jones.

"He didn't open up for you at that gig in Barrie last summer, did he? The one me and Jeanie drove up for?"

"Jesus fucking Christ," James sighed, almost sneering, turning away.

"Hold on," M.C. said, running his fingers through his hair, trying hard now, "just hold on a friggin' second."

James found some consolation in the fact that M.C. was actively searching his memory, giving his brain a real workout, something he knew M.C. had tried hard his entire adult life to avoid doing. Still, to have forgotten. . . .

"Oh shit, yes."

"Yes?" James asked, ashamed, instantly, of having his doubts. M.C., he thought, I'll make it up to you, buddy.

"Fuck, yeah," M.C. answered, "J.T. Jones. Oh, sure. Little greasy guy used to go to school with us at D.C.I. Played the tuba in the band and went out I think with that fat chick, what's her name, Rita. Yeah, Rita. We used to call them Laurel and Hard-up, remember? Betcha even you didn't remember that one. Hah. Old J.T. Why the sudden interest?"

M.C. leaned back on the carpet on both hands, whistled the chorus to "Act Naturally", and belched out a good one. Although he didn't consider himself by any means an intellectual man, he felt pretty pleased with himself anyway. In spite of all those years of being bad to his body and mind, the memory not quite so gone after all.

James looked a little like a man who had lost a winning lottery ticket and then found it, only to lose it again, this time for good. He switched on the television, turned it to channel forty-seven, and looked at M.C. looking happy with himself lying on the floor, eyes closed and trying to balance the salt shaker on the middle of his forehead.

A commercial for something nobody really needed finished up, and then theme-show music followed by a lengthy and emotional introduction by a movie star who hadn't made a decent film in years. M.C. opened his eyes and the salt shaker fell away. Shit, was all he thought: Shit. Shit. Shit.

The J.T. Jones show was on the air.

The most resilient of a bunch of late-night positive-thinking gurus who burst upon the infomercial scene in the early-1980s, J.T. Jones had been — back in high school, when James didn't have a girlfriend and M.C. didn't feel like going over to Jeanie's parents' house — the one they always flopped in front of after long evenings of Saturday-night and even, occasionally, school-night debauchery. And what was the appeal? Why, finally? When James thought about it, this: the same earnest testimonies by the same fading celebrities, episode after episode; the same amazing success stories recounted by the same formerly lost housewives and small-time businessmen documented and charted ("Jonesified") night after night; the same 1-800 number flashing across the bottom of the TV screen month after month; the same smiling west-coast philosophy shakedown raking in credit card number after credit card number, year after year after year after year. For James — and M.C. too, James had up to tonight always believed without question — J.T. Jones was, quite simply, It ("It" being the antichrist for all those who didn't have a god up or out there but knew anyway that the Simpsons-Sears spring, summer, fall, and Christmas catalogues and the Home Shopping Network were the real devils, and that salvation could not be bought, at any price, on the instalment plan).

Admittedly, the majority of the programs that Datum's late-night self-helpers and television shoppers digested nightly were American-concocted and American-produced, each aimed chiefly at taking in citizens of their own. But through the power of that wonderful system of reproducing actual or recorded scenes at both small and large distances (and capable, too, of leaping national borders in a single, bouncing signal bound), the distance between J.T.'s world and Datum was — in spite of any number of governmentally commissioned and compensated cultural declarations of Canadian independence — negligible. Regardless of whether you next morning jammed down your bacon and eggs in L.A. sunshine-smog or Datum pig-shit breeze, in New York car-honking fantasia or Toronto street-bustling civility, the base impulse of your very average North American citizen for channel-surfing deliverance was the same; only where the delusion was sowed, it seemed, varied.

Spiritually speaking, then, regardless of north or south souls sullied, all of this quite the opposite of the finely crafted musical odes James, as a tuning-up teenager, was intent upon giving to the world. And if he had yet to decide upon just what his songs would actually be about, he did know how they would sound: melodies deluxe, with sweet pedal steel and churning guitars throughout. Serious medicine, he had decided early on, for a serious cultural malaise.

Now, however, not even a decade later, M.C. looking embarrassed lying on the rug. Frankly, James feared, amnesia to the Cause.

"Listen man, I'm really sorry, I . . . ," M.C. said. Sitting up, knees under his chin, he looked for something like a trace of humour on James's face. No dice. Furrows raised, eyes intent — that look, M.C. thought. For as long as he had known James. . . .

"Just let me ask you one thing," James said.

"Okay, " M.C. answered, wondering if he was going to have to lie, "go ahead."

"And don't even think about lying."

"Okay."

"All that time," James said, his line of questioning here approaching that brand of interrogation (often employed in theological argumentation) which always leads with a pleading glass chin, "it meant something to you like it did to me, didn't it? Maybe even more, if you really thought about it, right?"

M.C. looked at the TV screen, at the by now familiar blinking telephone number, searching for something like an answer. He wanted to fart, burp, anything. Instead: "I thought it was funny."

"You thought it was funny," James nearly jeered.

"Look, James, don't get all self-righteous on me, all right? I'm bigger than you, remember?"

James decided to give him a chance. He leaned his back up against the bar's soft, black-cushioned front and uncrossed his arms, only to quickly recross them over his chest.

"I saw it in you, all right?" M.C. said. "Anybody with half a brain could see what it meant to you. A sign or a symbol or some damn thing. A warning for you not to give in like everybody else in this goddamn town does. A lesson for you to do the thing you were put on earth to do — play good honest music. Okay, then. Amen. Damn straight. Fucking A. I hoped like hell all along that you'd actually get the hell out of here and do it and become Datum's very own Buck Owens, because you were my best friend. But that wasn't enough, though. You only seemed really happy thinking I was just like you. So what the hell, I was game. A friend tries to make another friend happy. No crime in that, is there? Shoot me if you want."

James looked at M.C., at J.T. doing his thing on the television screen, then back at his friend. Finally, "Wait a minute, now," he said, "c'mon now. Just hold on a damn second, all right? It *was* the same for you. I know it was. It's just that your memory's been shot through with too much Molson Golden for too long. Wet brain, I think they call it. Can't quite get that pea-sized brain of yours to think back that far." Hoping for joking confirmation of what he desperately wanted to hear, but seeing only M.C. looking in silence at an empty beer bottle lying a few inches from his right foot, James became slightly panicky, changing rhetorical gears from the comic to the plaintive.

"Look, M.C., I didn't want a clone. Not at all. I just liked sharing an obsession with an ally. You know: the two of us against all of them, that sort of romantic bullshit. Nice to know somebody was gritting his teeth along with me." Unmoved, M.C. still stared at the bottle.

Then: "Oh, wait, wait. Wait a minute. Just wait a minute. Remember? Remember this?" James stood at attention, right hand cocked to his brow in mock salute, attempting his version of a German general's accent : "'Ze enemy, he must be vatched at all times. He is, I tell you, very, very dangerous.' Remember? Hell, yes, *you* remember. You did that better than I did, for Christ's sake. Sure. You remember."

"Aw, James," M.C. said, looking at his friend with an odd combination of pity and pride, "you're beautiful, you know that? Pure as that fake white fucking snow they spray every Christmas on the windows down at the mall."

James missed this last remark, intent as he was upon hearing what he wanted to hear. He decided on another route: affirmation through elimination of alternatives.

"All right. If you were just going along with me to make me happy, what the hell could you have possibly gotten out of it besides humouring me? You never liked anybody well enough to sit up all those nights watching something you supposedly didn't believe against just for me. It had to be more than that," he said, a little too triumphantly. "It had to be."

"Like I said, it was funny," M.C. said. "All those stupid fucking people thinking their miserable little lives were gonna be changed in six easy lessons by some Yankee Doodle with a foot-long smile and a grilled-cheese tan. Man, you gotta laugh at that or you're gonna end up crying. I personally have always been of the laughing school of thinking. You used to read all that philosophy shit, James, what does that make me? One of them optimist types, or one of them pessimist types?"

M.C. lifted up his beer bottle and drained the last of it. A physical sort of man, he felt a disappointing incompleteness drinking beer out of anything but cans, missing the convincing finality a crushed beer can gives to the end of a long evening of beverage-taking.

"Besides," he continued, "you know me. I hate to go home and go right to sleep after I've been drinking a lot. Better to go somewhere and sit around for a while and wait for the buzz to wear off. Feel a whole lot better the next morning that way."

M.C. sometime soon after straggled home to warm sheets and married-man snuggles, leaving James to stare at the turned off TV and think about pulling out the fold-up bed and putting himself and the day's accumulated nothing to sleep. Four a.m., he thought: always too late or too early for anything worth anything to happen.

He began to clean up the beer-bottle mess he and M.C. had made, but spotted before long his guitar sitting in its case against the bar, untouched and for the most part unthought of since he had arrived in Datum two days earlier. He found himself sitting in the middle of the room on a hard wooden chair in just his cowboy boots and boxer shorts with the brown leather guitar strap snugly familiar around his shoulder and back and not thinking of anything else but why the damn G string wouldn't ever behave like a G string ought to. He finally got the instrument more or less in tune, and casually strummed some straightforward chord progressions.

God, that feels good, he thought, without actually thinking it. It feels good just to hold it.

He started up with "Together Again", Buck Owens all over his head from earlier in the evening. Not even halfway through the song though, he stopped.

No. Buck was Buck and that was fine, and even, usually, enough. But with sun-up not that far off and him beginning to doubt the wisdom of this most recent homecoming, something else was needed, something that packed a little more punch. Like chugging a light beer when a bourbon straight up was needed. Bring on the high octane. Okay. Early Merle Haggard. "Sing Me Back Home".

James finished up singing the chorus in the falsetto he had been using lately when doing softer, ballad-type songs, a little too dramatically bowing his head to his right knee and following through with his strumming hand nearly to the floor when playing out the final chords. "Sing Me

Back Home" always did the job, no problem there; not once never not goose bumps all the way up his forearms and on the back of his neck. The body never lies. But still, no, no release.

This often happened when a particular ill ailed him. Your average day-to-day blues? Fine; just about any three-chord acoustic number with the requisite love-lost lyrics would do the trick. But for an honest-to-goodness burr under his saddle — say this month's girlfriend making eyes at the doorman all through the second set, or some slick deciding he isn't going to pay the band because they haven't played enough "fast, you know, *up* numbers" — something had to be delivered that hit home, and hit home good.

No trucking songs, for instance, no odes in praise of the freedom of the road. He hated travelling long distances by bus, and in his experience most truckers were little more than amphetamine-fuelled professional football fanatics who had failed to find real jobs, and who played up the adventure of driving eighteen hours straight with two tons of sheep manure in the back mostly in the hope that some middle-aged truckstop waitress, twenty-five pounds over-weight herself, didn't completely hate the idea of a three-hundred-pound speed freak slobbering all over her in the women's washroom when the busy lunch crowd had slacked off.

No, too, to serious hurtin' songs, admittedly the staple of the classic country-and-western canon. To be sure, James had acted stupid for a few girls and even a few women in his time, but nothing that would classify as a genuine George Jones pain in the old ticker. It was nice in a melancholy merry sort of way to play out on stage, in front of hundreds of people, those monster heartaches that George or Hank or Loretta had suffered through, survived, and eventually sung about so well, but James simply didn't have the heartbreak resources to draw upon yet to get the right kick. Something else entirely was needed, something requiring the creation of his very own musical notes.

James had never forgotten what William B. Remy had told him once, after one of the older man's infrequent live shows in Toronto. A little weak-kneed because it was actually Remy, James had solemnly approached the one-man band, sound crew, and roadie all rolled into one, and asked him what it was that inspired him to write the deceptively simple tales of human bumbling and stumbling that made up, in brief, his wonderful music. Remy had just looked at him for a few seconds — dumbfounded, it seemed, at the nature of the question. Finally, bent over and wrapping a microphone cord around his fist and upper arm, he stood up, laughed a quiet little laugh, stroked his ragged goatee, and replied, in the tone of a man stating the obvious, "Couldn't understand what the hell was on the radio. *Had* to write my own songs. Couldn't find anything out there good enough to get me off. And you gotta get off, son. Gotta."

And at this particular moment, 4:36 a.m. in a mildewy basement in a but-for-him vacated house in a town populated by people and places who just weren't doing their duly inspirational part, a ballad in E flat got James off. Words, at first, to go along with the simple three-chord strumming — little words that really said nothing next to the pure language coming from the guitar — and then, finally, just the instrument itself, helped along, of course, by James's fretboard-travelling fingers. Some humming, too, but nothing close to information when you got right down to it.

Minutes into half-hours, half-hours into hours; music perfect in pitch and true in tone to the homesickness that comes from knowing all too well that, though weary of travelling, you are already home. Soon, dawn, and later, through the basement windows, streaks of early-morning sun. All of this barely noticed by James, however, happy as hell oblivious for the first time in, well, days.

PART TWO

19

Ding-dongs in his dreams: a doorbell from above brought James up from below.

"Hey."

"Hey," James said without thinking, thinking, when he got a good look at what Melissa was wearing, Hey, maybe this is okay. Maybe I could use some of that. A job to do, can't forget why I'm here, but still. . . . Maybe . . . just . . . a little . . . carnal . . . comfort . . . in lieu of a city seemingly set upon obscuring its true mettle from musically desperate hometown biographers. Yes. Certainly. That most certainly was probably it.

The Polaroid of yesterday, suddenly no longer ominous, screamed to mind. Present-tense appetite erased his previous apprehension.

"Should I feel privileged to wake up to you on my front doorstep?" he asked.

Melissa handed him a yellowed *Datum Daily News* and some junk mail addressed to his late grandfather. "Yep."

James stood in the doorway, barefoot, in blue jeans and a white T-shirt, trying to decide whether any girl from his high-school years could have gotten away with pedalling around Datum on a May afternoon so wonderfully frugally attired, in a blue cotton dress with white polka-dots, and green, high-top Converse. Panties? Yes, he decided; too much to ask for so little. Also, Dukes of Hazzard lunchbox, *très* kitsch-chic, hanging from her right hand.

"I locked my bicycle up out back. That okay?"

The wind caught at the edge of her dress just enough to answer the underwear question positively in the negative. She put her hand on the hem and smiled, not shyly, at James.

"They let you get away with this around here?" he said, genuinely admiringly, right palm taking in from head to toe all of her.

"This?" she asked.

"Yeah," he said, arm around her waist, drawing Melissa off the front step and through the doorway into the living room. "This."

"Damn right," she said, blue dress raised manually this time. "Who do you think I would ever let get in my way?"

20

"You gotta be kidding."

Hurried untangling, half under, half out of the bed-sheets; all of a sudden, not much made much sense all at once.

"If I was kidding, do you think I'd be brandishing a semi-automatic in the buff?" Melissa replied, pointing the pistol and everything else she possessed at James.

He thought twice, then decided to laugh aloud. Just to be safe, though, he laughed not all that loudly.

"Give me a fucking break," he said, rising from the bed.

"I'm serious, cowboy," she said, straddling him at chest level, the gun ever since *coitus completus* pointed directly at his head. He on his back, she on top, neither of them was thinking much about what was natural.

"Okay," he said, "okay."

Taking a deep inhale and a still deeper exhale to show he was serious about shutting up and hearing out whatever madness it was she was selling, he thought to himself: She fucked too good to be entirely harmless. You would have thought by now I would have learned that harmless women simply do not copulate like bad dogs in need of a cold bucket of water.

Looking to raise at least a smirk, and obscure from her his mood of real concern, James said, "What is it? Money? There's about three dollars in my pants pocket and I think about a dollar twenty in empties beside the fridge. Should make a nice haul, Bonnie." He looked up at her face but saw only the barrel of a gun with a naked woman attached to it. This definitely isn't about sex any more, he thought. The slight edge of baseless but nauseous suspicion that had dogged nearly every reflection he sent her way now returned, full force.

"James," she said, ignoring this last little bit, "I want to help you. I've wanted to help you for quite a while now, ever since the first time I heard your first album. That's why I'm sitting here on your chest pointing this weapon at you."

"I see."

"Good. I tried to make some headway on this matter the other night at my parents' house, but you weren't very receptive. Most men will do almost anything after enough beer and a nice roll in the hay, but all you could do was sleep and occasionally snore."

"Call me special."

"With certain reservations I hope to make you aware of, I do, believe me, I do."

"And let me guess: the Freudian twat-shot? That was your way of helping me too, I suppose?"

"Sure," she said, her face not at all the crimson colour James had been shooting for with his question. "And I hope you appreciate the effort put into that production. Talk about dexterity. Whew!"

She moved up on his chest, trying to make her knees a little more comfortable. James could smell the slightly acidic lingering reminder of what had been, not ten minutes before, their meeting. As she adjusted her weight on him, he slid his hands behind his head, closed his eyes shut, gave an involuntary whiff, and waited.

"Windmills, James."

"Windmills?"

"Windmills. Not always." She raised the forefinger of her non-shooting hand to note the exception. "What you've got to say in your songs about lust and dogs, respectively, is quite often on the money and good. Beautiful melodies and simple, accurate language that frequently gets right down to the heart of the matter. But unfortunately, more often than not—"

"Windmills," he said, finishing her sentence.

"Exactly. Windmills."

"I see," he said, nodding, not in the least seeing.

"Good, I'm glad. Now, specifics. Okay. Let's start with your father."

James opened his eyes wide at the ceiling, as if in some bad back-from-the-dead horror movie. Suddenly he felt just a little bit sick to his stomach. Suddenly he forgot all about the gun.

"Okay. James? James, honey?"

He managed to pull himself away from himself for a moment and look her way.

"The man who was your father was not — and I quote here directly from 'Fallen Man', the bonus track included on your first CD — which features some lovely three-part harmonies, by the way, you've never had a problem raising the flesh on this particular listener's skin with your melodies:

> *A man under a crushing wheel*
> *A man unable to feel.*
> *A man not meant to be known*
> *A man without a country or home.*

Now listen to me, James. Your father, James Thompson, Sr., was a simple autoworker free of any enigma other than the simple mystery we all share by virtue of being alive on this earth. And his death? On his wedding day? Ouch. And then some. Tough stuff for you to take as a kid, I'm sure. But time to face the facts, cowboy: the truth of the matter is that Newton's gonna have his day with all of us sooner or later. James Sr. just got it a little more literally than most people. You've gotta realize, cowboy, that there's a nobility — in art and elsewhere — in things unadorned. Are you familiar at all with the early Imagist manifestos? Specifically, Pound's dictum that—"

Too dazed to be really angry, simple acknowledgement on James's part that he had no choice but to have the conversation he was having. He croaked the first thing that came to mind.

"You didn't know my father."

"No, and neither did you, James. And I think that's a big part of the problem here. But based on what I've been able to figure out from talking to some of the people who knew him, I really don't think—"

"Jesus Christ," he said, "who have you been talking to about my father?" She still on him, he was up on his elbows now. "Better yet, why have you been talking to *anybody* about my father?"

"Calm down, cowboy," she said. "To answer your first question first: nobody special. A few of the men he worked with at South Western. Three or four guys he played hockey with. His brother, Buckly—"

"You talked to my Uncle Buckly!"

"Of course, silly. He was essential. Actually, James, Sr. always considered your uncle his best friend — not, as everybody seemed to think, Bobby Hatcher, who played left wing on his line for all those years."

Casually, Melissa scratched the underside of her left breast with the barrel of the pistol. "Your uncle's something, isn't he? Sweet in a crotchety sort of way, wouldn't you say? Not a thing like my uncle. My Uncle Albert? The one I told you about, who's dying? First it was the holistic medicine thing. Meat-eating, chain-smoking, waste-disposal slash used-car rental genius his entire life — I

mean, this is a guy who kept telling anyone who would
listen that what we needed in Canada was a real no-BS
man like Rush Limbaugh to set straight 'all those damn
Frenchies' and 'all them other whining minorities we
should've never let in here in the first damn place' — and
then all of a sudden he gets the big C and *poof!* What do
you know? Fifty-eight-year-old born-again hippie. Sensitive as all get out. Next thing you know, it's carrot juice at
five in the morning, megadoses of Vitamin C, and rhythmic chanting with finger cymbals three times a day. Chanting! Yes! Chanting! Supposed to purify his system or something, get rid of the pollutants that got him sick in the first
place. None of it made a damn difference, of course. Still
sick as a dog. Although he did develop by the end of it a
pretty decent baritone, I hear. Anyway, now, as a last-ditch
effort, he's decided to try some new wonder drug that
can only be administered at some hospital in Hamilton.
Something like a 3% chance it could maybe — maybe —
prolong his life six months, or a year if he gets lucky. Tough
luck for me, eh? Could screw up my plans for hitting Toronto by September, all because my mother's rich brother
would rather die a year later in a hospital in — yuck —
Hamilton than pass away with dignity in Oshawa, the city
he's lived in his whole adult life. But there's the bourgeoi-
sie for you. Go figure, eh?"

James closed his eyes again, tight, disbelieving all of
this. She talked to my uncle, was all he could think. She
talked about my father with my uncle.

"But we're not here to talk about me, are we, cowboy?
We're here to see if we can help you, right?"

No reply.

"Right," she continued. "Next question. Okay. Why
have I been talking to all these people who knew your
father? This troubles you a good deal, am I correct?"

James opened his eyes, but only saw the same thing
he had been seeing all along. He closed them again.

"Right again. Okay. Here we go," she said.

All right, everything in him seemed to scream out at once, that's enough. It's one thing to get me naked, hold me prisoner, then confuse the hell out of me; it's another thing entirely to talk like my goddamn uncle.

"He's *my* goddamn uncle," he roared, grabbing the gun out of her hand and knocking her off the bed and onto the floor with the same quick motion. He opened up the chamber of the gun. It was empty. Of course, he thought, it had to be empty. Otherwise she might have . . . shot me. He tossed the gun at her feet.

Risen from the carpet now, still buck naked, Melissa turned up both hands in front of her as an offering of some sort of understanding. "Cowboy, you don't understand," she said. "There are things left that absolutely must get discussed, things—"

"Go to hell," he said, picking up her dress, shoes, lunchbox, and taking her by the hand, leading them all in a rush up the stairs into the daylight, tossing her and everything else into the afternoon sun.

"And another thing," he said, breathing fairly heavily for a man who was still two days short of his twenty-fifth birthday. "I'm not a cowboy. I hate horses, hate the outdoors, and hate cows too, for that matter. My heroes have not always been cowboys. In fact, they've mostly been hockey players. Particularly big, aggressive right-wingers with soft hands around the edge of the net. I was born and raised in Datum, Ontario, not Luckenbach, Texas. I love the music. That's all. I just love the fucking music."

He slammed the back door leading downstairs to the basement, careful to lock the deadbolt behind him.

Casually pulling on her dress on the back-yard grass, Melissa just smiled. "Progress," she said. "I do believe we are making progress."

21

Why, was what he was thinking. Why? That and whether or not he should have another cup of coffee.

Sitting at the corner table by the front window of the greasy spoon that had been, aside from his music and a failed attempt to read in its entirety Will and Ariel Durant's *The Story of Civilization* (he had made it as far as the fall of Athens), his only real extracurricular activity during high school, James wondered why everything could not be as straightforward simple as this, his favourite Datum coffee shop, neon-emblazoned with the simple moniker "The Coffee Shop".

After six refills, his nerves were wound about as tight as anyone's should be, but he needed something to do with his hands. He had always envied chain smokers for this very reason. He trailed the last french fry on his plate through a cold brown gravy lake and considered whether to peruse the baseball box scores again. Baseball wasn't hockey, but still, it was somewhere to rest your brain.

In what sick way, he all of a sudden thought, mind unable to stick to the page lying in front of him, in what sick, fucking way could she possibly think she could possibly help me? And my father? *My* father? James didn't even want to consider what she had meant by all that "simple mystery" BS. Nothing simple about my father's life, he thought. Or his death, for that matter. *Simple* mystery? Simple *mystery*? *Simple mystery*? And she said she was a fan.

James's father was, to James, no Lost Father; no aching boyhood space deep-seated in James Junior for ever yearned to be replaced by never-to-be-had happy fishing trips or Hockey Night in Canada pop-and-chips Saturday nights. Naturally, he had his fair share of familial what-ifs, but James was, in the main, safeguarded against the sowing of any excessive father-fixation by the steady, older-male-buddy steering of Buckly. Which is not to say that father did not hold considerable pull on son.

For the inside and out beginning-to-bloom James, never had it been enough to simply say (as his Uncle Buckly would say whenever James would prod) that it was nothing but damn bad luck that the guts of a truck had fallen down on James Sr.'s wedding-day head. Not exactly theologically, but certainly intellectually, in matters such as killing car parts and other portentous life events, James's mind early on demanded the positing of some sort of earthly Prime Mover — because this, this; because that, that; et cetera, et cetera, for as long as the brain is wide. A comfortable reason, anyway, why stuff is, does, and was. His father's untimely honeymoon demise was, to James, exhibit number one of the way in which the obvious is, much too often, much too obvious. More to the picture than meets the eye. Never judge a book by its cover. Still waters run deep. And so on. And even if, with time, it seemed more and more (as James had all along feared) that most everything in his Datumic musical oeuvre was just straight and simple geography coloured by a sneaky shade of purple prose, the deeper, elusive meaning of his father's King Street escape remained to him essentially unchanged, untouched by even this dispiriting visit home.

He sang to himself softly the chorus to "Nothing from Something (Requiem for a Father)":

> *They can say what they want to say*
> *They can do what they want to do*
> *Nothing from something I will not believe*
> *Nothing from something is more than just you.*

Chorus sung, coffeecup-holding-hand steadied, lyrical sentiment gave way to maddening cognizance: Melissa had been snooping through his past, conversing about his father with some of the other significant players in the Thompson family drama. Next, a more horrible thought: I bet Uncle Buckly spilled the beans, the whole damn can, in fact. Probably told her everything worth mentioning about me, Mum, Dad. . . . Sonofabitch probably had a hard-on the entire time. Old fart.

Finally, a distressing if slightly consoling realization: No wonder I haven't managed to write a word since I've touched home soil; too busy dealing with this crazy woman every time I turn around. No wonder at all.

He paid the cashier, who doubled as his waitress, and went back to his table, leaving a bigger tip than he was accustomed to. No trespassing on my mythology, he told himself. Yes sir, this one is definitely off-limits. Definitely.

Datum wasn't so large he couldn't walk to his Uncle Buckly's place in under an hour, even from where he was standing downtown — probably not a bad idea given the job the caffeine was doing on his system — but he took the bus as far as it would take him, to the outskirts of town, hoping to gather up as much energy as possible for the showdown that loomed. Maybe she's paid him off, he speculated. Ten bucks an interview, and everything that's mine by birthright sold off to a spoiled rich kid who's swallowed too many books and not yet grasped the essential dictum shared amongst all creators, musicians and all the rest, which says that you don't spy on other people's visions.

As the bus (empty but for him, as only buses in small towns on Sunday afternoons can be) crawled through what seemed like a maze of nearly every subdivision in town, James in his seat at the back of the vehicle began to have a notion. And like most notions given enough time to work their way in and not enough distractions to dissuade one from them, this one began more and more to look like the truth. And frankly, the truth wasn't all that pretty. Naturally, he concluded, she is intent upon stealing my artistic

trump card, on sucking the blood of the Thompson family's noble losses for her own first shallow jab in the world
of art-making. Cowboy opus, my ass. Makes perfect sense.
No heroic failing to speak of in her own life, so she's obviously set upon using mine and my people's for her own
easy gain. He could see it all now.

Having spent most of the morning in the restaurant
doing little more than thinking about something he
couldn't quite get his mind around, James's decision to
act was a relief, the exchange of anxiety for action energiz-
ing. He almost missed his stop, so enamoured was he of
this revelation of Melissa's conspiratorial ways and simul-
taneously caught up in plans to, in more or less the following order: henceforth avoid Melissa at all costs and, as
a result, allow the inspirational flow of Datum to
unimpeded wash all over him; give his Uncle Buckly a
good scolding about the propriety of mythological family
jewels; and, finally, ask for — no, make that *demand* — the
Thing, a thing that — like a painted-up plain Jane seen
through the slightly skewed eyes of alcohol-induced last-
call deduction — had taken on an increasing significance
in his mind as the night of his visit home had steadily begun to darken.

He would have missed his stop for sure if the driver
had not yelled out at the last minute, "Hey, buddy! Wake
up! See what that sign out there says? This is the last stop
before the bus goes back downtown. You want off or not?"

James assured him he did, thanked the driver, and got
off where he was supposed to.

A fire-engine-red, pot-bellied mailbox played compan-
ion to the yellow bus-stop sign that the driver had alerted
James to. Nothing else for as far as his uncle's place a half-
mile away disturbed the landscape. He waved from his face
an upward-travelling cloud of bus exhaust and pulled out
of his back pocket a postcard he had purchased that morning at The Coffee Shop. Superimposed over a symbolically
triadic illustration of the county's principal forms of

employment — tractor, factory, field — were, in block capitals, the words DATUM, ONTARIO, CANADA, with the slightly menacing line KEEP IT CLEAN underneath. He pulled down on the mailbox's paint-chipped metal handle and quickly scanned what he had written earlier that morning, before finally letting it fall down and in.

>*Bous Stephaneforos,*
>*Behind or beyond or above my musical handiwork, invisible, refined out of existence, indifferent, paring my fingernails while the Datum parade goes by; as always, it goes just as you have all along argued it should.*
>
>*Lately though (don't be cross with me), I wonder: You absolutely sure about this? I mean, you're the guy who had the benefit of that good Irish university education, the one who knows his Latin and Aristotle and Aquinas and all that. But it's hard, I tell you, damn hard, to be as objective as you want to be and shout out those epiphanies as loud as you can when you're naked as a jaybird with your back to the mat and somebody else is telling the stories. And telling them real different.*
>*As ever, (mostly) silent, in exile, and (trying my hardest to be) cunning,*
>*Bous Jimmyeforos*

22

After readying himself to collect the Thing and, at the same time, give his uncle a good deal of hell for talking to a total stranger about things one just shouldn't discuss with strangers — not to mention enduring the fifteen-minute bus ride and the additional ten-or-so-minute walk from where the bus had let him off — James and his taste for the dramatic were more than a little bit soured when he discovered that Buckly was not home. No sign of Al, either, so he must be planning on being gone for a while, James reasoned (Buckly always Al-accompanied when anytime out for more than a few minutes).

He contemplated hiking back to the bus stop and catching up with M.C. putting in a half-day's worth of Sunday overtime at work, detailing to his friend the pistol incident, the Polaroid, and the conspiracy incident he had formulated on the bus. An actual physical aversion to even driving past South Western put a quick stop to this plan, however, the direct result of too many suppers from childhood right up through adolescence spent sitting across the dining-room table from his grandfather home on his supper break, smelling like a grease gun and looking as if he'd just gone ten tough rounds with the punch press, his workday only half over. Of course, given James's by age seventeen self-appointed status as Datum's very own cowpoke laureate, not a little disconcerting for him to have to acknowledge that the focal point of both his kin's and his hometown's life — it's very Being, he might have said in his flightier moments — was a thing that he himself, the examiner, was content to leave unexamined. He consoled himself with double-underlined-in-red passages in the library's only edition of Plato's dialogues (a paperback), reminding himself that — less philosophically put — the facts of the case aren't always right out there on the table. He was a songster, he comforted himself, a troubadour, not a sociologist. What counted was whether or not he got at the essence of his subject — Datum's soul — and not how much filthy research he managed to do.

Instead of tracking down M.C., then, James let himself into his uncle's house with the spare key that had hung for as long as he could remember underneath the gas barbecue in the back yard. He tried to give himself some cheer by whistling the melody to the tune "Having Snow", which had been stuck in his head since the day before on the bus. He whistled and waited in the living room for his uncle. No words to accompany the song emerged in the interim.

It had not been necessary for James to knock at the front door or even check around back; enough to see that all the lights were on inside the house. Although it was not even two in the afternoon, Buckly was a fervent believer in discouraging potential thieves with a fully lit, feigned full house. Once, back in Datum to visit his ailing grandmother in the hospital not long after he had left home for Toronto for the first time, James had wondered aloud to his uncle just a little too tongue-in-cheek just how much gun-wielding men intent upon robbing a home could be intimidated by four or five sixty-watt lightbulbs burning barely visible in the middle of the afternoon. His uncle, barbecuing hamburgers for the two of them at the time, had told him that, first of all, Datum wasn't Toronto, and second of all, you'd be surprised at what tiny little things tend to scare some of your biggest big shots who like to think they aren't afraid of nothing at all — things even they don't know they're scared of. Thirdly, he had told James that if he wanted to remain a dinner guest in good standing he should go into the house and get the potato salad that was in the fridge and stop saying things with his goddamn tongue stuck in the side of his goddamn cheek. James had entered the kitchen through the back door wondering whether to be insulted or awed. He had been hungry, though, just off the bus from Toronto, and his uncle's potato salad was to die for, so he had settled out of necessity on amazement.

Buckly not the coffee-table sort, James rested his boots on the end of the couch he wasn't slouching on. He noticed a package about the size of a paperback, covered in manila wrapping paper, sitting atop the record player, and smiled, a little modest colour coming to his cheeks. Old coot, he thought warmly. Can't stay mad at a man very long if he manages to remember your birthday, can you? He decided against getting up and taking a closer look on the grounds that the only gifts he could count on receiving this year were from his uncle, M.C., and Jeanie (his mother lucky if she remembered who he was). He didn't want to ruin what little suspense there was to the first birthday he was spending anywhere but Toronto since he had turned eighteen.

Of course, there was also the Thing. Whatever the hell it is, he thought. Probably just killed Uncle Buckly not giving it to me all these years, knowing the use I might have gotten out of it making the first two albums. Tenderly, James thought: Probably means more to him than it ever will to me.

The record player that his birthday gift sat on gave him the idea of listening to some of his uncle's records to pass the time, but he settled instead upon simply looking out the living-room window. Music made every kind of waiting so much easier, but it seemed like a lifetime since he had just sat alone in his uncle's house. He slumped deeper into the couch.

What a joke, he said aloud, lying flat out now. Living room, my ass. There's an oxymoron for you, Mrs. McCellar, if there ever was one: my uncle Buckly doing his living in this little room. A-minus for me, he thought, before nodding off for a fine spring-afternoon nap.

23

Most of Buckly's living occurred outside the inside of his house. As a result, most of the money he had sunk into home improvements over the years had gone towards what some might consider back-yard frivolity, and less in the line of what your average homeowner would judge as actual household priorities. So, for instance, the living room in which James at that moment slept was little more than a room with a window carved into the side of it, entered into by a door. Included in the room — almost, it seemed, as an afterthought — were a second-hand couch, a second-hand, overstuffed chair, a good to excellent stereo (phonograph player, AM/FM receiver, and speakers) supported on a two-foot-high wooden-plank-and-cement-block home-made structure, and several red milk crates crammed full of record albums, primarily of the country-and-western variety, most from Buckly's late-forties youth, or just before. Second-hand furniture was something you didn't do in Datum, second-hand anything indicating that you just didn't have enough class (something you got from your parents and they from theirs) to know that the finer things in life could in fact be bought, and bought on credit, too, if you were a little bit low on cash, both Sears and Libby's Lighting and Home Furnishings offering very attractive credit plans for just about anyone who looked like they realized the value of an honest lifetime's work.

In contrast, Buckly spared nothing when it came to the upkeep and enjoyment of his back yard. First had come the garden, of course; in place of the demolished barn, a small football field of a plot that every summer provided the starting soil point for virtually every vegetable adaptable to humid southern Ontario summers. Individual gardening tools worth nearly half a C-note each hung in the aluminum shed, cleaned and dried after use with a meticulous care that would satisfy even the most sterility-obsessed surgeon at Datum General Hospital, each instrument silver and sharp, ready whenever Buckly felt like getting his horticultural digs in. And although Al's nights were passed on a three-inch foam mattress covered with second-hand bedding on the floor at the foot of his master's bed, Buckly had handmade out of British Columbian redwood a rain-repellent, white-and-blue painted doghouse.

Later, with the years and generous portions of weekend overtime: the fourteen-foot green cedar deck; the screened-in porch later added directly onto that same deck; the red and blue and yellow patio lanterns that dangled year-round from the top of the patio's screen enclosure; the 350-watt Mister BugKiller-V6 that, like an inverted electric beehive, hung *zzzzz pshhing* and *zzzzz psh pshhing* all summer and into the fall under the weeping willow in a sort of Home Hardware Sisyphean struggle to keep at a minimum the nuisance of nature's irritating winged accompaniment; the shuffleboard court, with real steel markers and mahogany wood sidings and scoreboard for solitary playing and score-keeping; these, and numerous other items necessary for the enormous green area's upkeep: a John Deere riding lawnmower; an underground sprinkling system; a white medicine cabinet moved from the bathroom out to the tool shed, stocked full of enough lawn and weed chemicals to contaminate a small town. And finally — the only significant indoor sign of Buckly's homestead conscientiousness — a completely remodelled and re-equipped kitchen, perfect for the low-rent food preparation Buckly so delighted in (baked macaroni and cheese casserole and Frito chili pie among his specialities; every Sunday night a different meat; Al on the seventh day indulging too, the one day of the week he was allowed to eat exactly what the big guy with the can-opener ate).

For Buckly these things, among others, were not

matters of household expense; these things the things instrumental to the maintenance of the whole darn Why; the Why, that is, that kept at happy arm's length all those nasty other little whys that periodically raised their ugly little heads and whispered to him in panicked, middle-of-the-night, sweaty-sheeted thinking times (wintertime times, especially — December, January, February the worst — when the Detroit Tigers, after-dinner breezes, and conscientious gardening were only hurried spring expectations; sidewalk shovelling, white-trash gourmetism, and baseball trade rumours a starving man's snow and sleet-time ration):

Why get up out of bed on such a razor-blade cold Sunday morning at all? Why, with everything outside that matters covered by an avalanche of dirty white stuff anyway? Why, when you know, don't you (you just know), that the car won't even start the first six times you try it, and even when you do get the thing going, only insufferable AM and FM talking, talking, always talking talking? Why go in to work on such mornings, then, even for time-and-a-half, going to a job that — obvious to even an idiot like yourself — in many ways kills? Also, why not perhaps a beer? Just one or two or four, perhaps? Enough, anyway, to stop for a while all these bastard little whys.

1953.
To all eyes, including his own, the first sign that there might be a problem was Buckly's more than once waking up in the bushes: leaves over and under him, legs out and pointing, Buckly a soggy flesh star resting in a deep black August night cleverly disguised as his parents' prized shrubs. Up to this point — waking near sun-up in twigs and green — all activities revolving around alcohol consumption could be put down to good old-fashioned small-town sowing. This, however, required reflection.

Do I always must have to must end up like like this to have?

Um . . . ah . . . I, Buckly decided; for now, at least, con-clusive only in closing his eyes to the real stars (just now beginning to fade) overhead.

With time, however, and a few more repeats of the sloppy shrubbery sort, Buckly was forced to face the fact that a few cold beers with the boys after Saturday-after-noon hockey practice were no longer a pleasant tes-tosterone diversion, but the beginning of a process to be endured — *having a good time* taken to its nasty logical con-clusion.

So: calling in sick to work when he really wasn't; usu-ally sick as a dog when he did manage to make it in; every paycheque spent before the next payday was even close; Mum and Dad always wondering aloud where the old Buckly went; physically a mess, of course; even the heavier drinkers on the team shunning him when, at parties and such, deep into his cups, messing around by himself in the corner with knives and cigarette lighters on his fore-arms and palms of his hands (frankly, a wacko after about twelve beers, and only to be tolerated because he was a solid, defensive defenceman); and, to Buckly, most unset-tling of all — the selling of a brand-new pair of Cooper hockey gloves his mother had given him that Christmas (an item, he knew, she had saved for hard for nearly a year) for the pathetically low price of three dollars and change to a teammate because — South Western having given him a two-week unpaid "vacation" to get his act together — he needed cash very badly, at that very moment, for a very necessary half-pint of the cheapest sort of whisky avail-able. What was next, he shuddering thought. Rubbing-alcohol cocktails at midnight behind the train station with the rest of the town's graduated rummies? Real considera-tion when not soused as to just where this going-nowhere business was going.

Still, even after each of these sordid indications and events, no firm decision on Buckly's part to cut out the sauce and get his act in gear. After all, what was the alternative?

In a nutshell, what were the facts?

From the top:

Family? Only sibling and mother and father alike sin-
gularly sweet people but everyday strangers still, the kind
of people who, if you didn't know them, you would walk
right by on the street without ever wanting to say hello to
or ever get to know.

Love? A six-second itch occasionally scratched, and
only then if enough Coca-Cola and cherry whiskies managed to make it down the gullet of Betty or Angie or Bethie
on Friday or Saturday night, and only then if you promised to love them like your best best friend the next morning and every morning after.

Work? Gently streamed at age fourteen into the voca-
tional program (shop, auto mechanics, gym, and rudimentary arithmetic being the basic curriculum) at Victoria Park
High School with the basic idea on the guidance council-
lor's part being that the son of an auto-worker would very
likely make a good auto-worker himself.

Naturally, then, in due course, before Buckly turned
eighteen, a filthy, semi-dangerous, mind-numbing eight-
hour-a-day occupation that before too long dulls you out
more than you would have ever thought possible.

Naturally, then, in due course (even though in every
way up to this point the most average sort of baby, then
boy, then young man anyone was likely to ever meet): blue-
collar liquid mysticism; 40% suburban-basement-guzzling
sainthood; and, when enough crazy-pop flooded the system, most everything that since knee-high-hood that
seemed like a bad black and white television program
broadcast in a language you can't quite understand mi-
raculously turned into a show that, if maybe a little *too*
colourful and *too* loud, was at least never boring.

At the end of it, not for the usual reasons did Buckly
finally cease being a drunk; only looked that way to
everyone else. Now we see the hard-working Buckly
Thompson (the young man plainly discovering the value

of an honest day's work), and now we see the newly dutiful son (the boy obviously repentant over past parental pain), and now we see this and now we see that and now we see and now we see and now we see. Which was just fine with Buckly. Very fine, in fact. Keep all those nosy bastards out of your face that way. Give them an answer they want to hear and they'll leave you alone with the truth. A-fucking-men.

Formerly a pretty approachable guy, Buckly the teetotaller became an honest-to-goodness cynic. A happy scoffer, however, the kind of skeptic who views with humorous disgust the action down below because he's sitting so happily so high above.

People — they had been his (and, he figured, everybody else's) problem all along. From first breath crawling until last gasp falling, always it was somebody trying to tell you what they thought was wrong with you, the water quality, the local hockey team, women, men, the school superintendent, the government (local, provincial, and federal), softball, blacks, whites, the weather, the phone company, insurance rates, X-rays, soda pop in cans as opposed to bottles, sex, chastity, space travel, church, promiscuity, television, credit cards, the United States, Canada, Russia, cartoons, beans, children, drunkenness, Marilyn Monroe, foreign cars, rock and roll, sobriety, best friends, the Boy Scouts, newspapers, doctors, fags, butches, dentists, lawyers, dogs, cats, parakeets, kumquats, soccer, but — most of all — you. You you you. You. Everyone you'd ever known (friends and foes alike) an authority on why you were just you and not the person you really could be. Really. And — when all is said and done — all you really wanting to be was left alone with an ice-cold ginger ale and the game on the radio, the radio sitting on the kitchen table, the kitchen table near the window, the window open to a spring evening just beginning to perform its yearly magic act of winter-forgetting, and you, a part of all of it, almost forgotten too.

And this pretty close to how what happened finally happened.

As was not unusual at that time, Buckly had dropped belly-up about three a.m. a few houses down from his parents' house, in a neighbour's back yard. After an hour or so of not particularly restful shut-eye, he awoke not so drunk as not to notice — for the first time, really — morning's first soft pink and blue and white sketches splashed across the emerging skyline. The gentle gibberish of robins, private music for early risers (or, as in Buckly's case, late-nighters) was audible by this time, too, sounds surely identical to — yet so different from — the irritating chatter he had always considered the goddamn birds made in the goddamn morning-after.

Although he was managing nicely by not doing a whole lot of thinking — just lying there happily being — the few thoughts he did have said that all he was missing was a hot shower, a clean change of clothes, a comfortable chair, some solid food in his stomach to calm his nerves, and a clear head to better ease back into this smoothing-out breeze. And maybe even my own furry friend, with sharp teeth and quick claws for uninvited guests, he thought.

Soon, to employer's and parents' pleased amazement, responsible to the point of purposeful: as much overtime as possible, in pursuit of the old Swankly place outside of town, and, as best he could manage, alone with not so much his thoughts as something else entirely (and much, much better), his parents' barely passable excuse for a back yard (clothesline, garage, and other typical accompaniments barely allowing for ten square feet for breathing) having for the time being to suffice. As a simultaneous sidenote, Buckly became near-religious in following his already beloved Detroit Tigers' baseball fortunes, and prodigiously pursuant of nearly all Datum's red-headed single women. Also, owner of a two-month-old purebred black lab dubbed Al (after Al Kaline, the up-and-coming rookie Tiger right-fielder Buckly felt, not surprisingly, a deep sense of connection with — Buckly up-and-coming himself that year).

The ceasing of his alcohol intake complete, a flood of happy energy Buckly didn't know he possessed exploded into passion for outdoor aloneness, baseball, and red-haired women with lots of freckles on their necks and chests.

To everyone else in Datum, only the birth of the work-horse bachelor and confirmed baseball nut they recognized as grouchy old Buckly Thompson. To Buckly himself, however — the only recognition that really counted — a life that, thank you very much (and mind your own fucking business), smiled softly but strongly, somewhere very deeply, very deep inside.

24

When James finally awakened from his nap it was nearly half-past three in the afternoon. Crows, eagles for an insignificant town, glided and caw-cawed over as yet unplanted cornfields to the left, right, front, and back of Buckly's house. Tractors and unidentifiable farm machinery raised swirling clouds of dust, working their way through the dead afternoon heat. The faint but unmistakeable sickly-sweet smell of liquid pig manure was carried on the breeze, stirring both Buckly's living-room curtains and James's nostrils. In the distance, a radio faintly buzzed a song whose melody he could not catch.

One would never have known it by reading the lyrics

printed on the inside of his albums, but this — maybe more
than anything else — was, for James, Datum at its deep-
est: the pre-sunset onset of that almost physical heaviness
on the soul that was, for him, Sunday night in the hometown coming down ("a spiritual half-nelson, Datum style,"
he had half-jokingly tried to describe it to the metro-
politan-born Paddocks late one particularly well lubricated
night on the road).

From his reclining spot on the couch, then, a sudden
series of spirit-smothering Sunday-evening holographs in
the head, as intense as the day taken:

James's grandfather
  in the carport
  operating a four-legged stationary bandsaw
  in an after-dinner drizzle,
  sawdust disappearing up into the beginnings
  of a light, soon-to-be night-time mist;
  clearly a back-yard project gotten entirely out of hand,
  all in the name of well-earned weekend leisure;
James's grandmother
  at the kitchen table
  fully seeing but blind nonetheless
  to the Sunday *Datum Daily News* being flipped by her
  own hand
  on the table
  in front of her,
  the noise of CFPO coming from the clock radio
  on the fridge
  incessant
  yet unheard,
  the constant cup of tea at her bathrobed sleeve
  warm
  but soon to become cold;
James's mother
  mummified in her bedroom,
  door closed and the television on,
  the laugh-track to some sitcom or other on the TV

the only evidence for hours now
to the others
she is alive
and still in there.

Having had the benefit of living in Toronto for the past five and a half years, and, with it, all the pleasant distractions a three-million-and-then-some city can offer, James had been able to tone his disheartening capacity for Sabbath-day sensitivity down a notch to a liveable level through sheer frenzied activity, though never completely eliminate it. And like, say, knowing how to ride a bicycle, being back in Datum made it unavoidable to do anything but regretfully climb right back on.

Sitting up on the edge of the couch, he steadied himself for a moment, waiting for the almost nauseous after-effects of his nap to disappear. Rubbing the sleep gunk from the corners of his eyes, he looked out the living-room window and saw Melissa pedalling her bicycle up his uncle's driveway.

Showing excellent, ice-level goaltending style, James, in a panic, dropped his knees. Slowly, anxious not to be detected, he lay down with his back against the living room's cool hardwood floor, arms and legs extended like a child ready to make a snow angel; then, using his elbows and heels, he manoeuvred himself like an enormous, upside-down crab into the windowless kitchen by way of the six-foot hallway that connected the two rooms. Once there — linoleum sanctuary everywhere at eyeball level — his breathing resumed, semi-regular, if shallow.

He lay silent and still, waiting for it, wondering, How could she have known? Nobody knows I'm here.

Finally, it came.

Christ, he thought, what's she using, a ballpeen hammer? The knocking, steady and, to James's ear, thunderous, kept on until he was sure either the door would give way from its hinges or his eardrums would explode. At last it ceased. He counted out three full minutes. Then, just to be careful, another three.

As sure as he felt he could be that the danger had passed, he arose — first to his knees, then to a standing position — and walked to the end of the hallway. From there he stopped and peeked around the corner, looking from a distance out of the living-room window. He saw no Melissa in sight.

What he did see were some farm workers gathered around what appeared to be a stalled tractor in the field west of his uncle's house.

He saw (he said to himself inside his head): Six people. Five men and one woman. All of them wearing blue jeans. All but the woman and the youngest man in white work shirts. Those two wearing red. A red T-shirt and a red long-sleeved shirt. Six people, five pairs of blue jeans, four white work shirts, and two others in red. Six five four two. Six thousand five hundred and forty two. Six plus five plus four plus two equals seventeen. Seventeen divided by. . . .

He exited the house quickly, through the back door, remembering to lock the door behind him but forgetting to put the house key back underneath the barbecue. He was in a hurry. He was starting to be unable not to count. And this sort of counting not a matter of mere enumeration; this the kind of counting unnatural as certain kinds of nonstop spit-swallowing. Goddamn it, he thought, walking at a pace someone else might have called running, I'm starting to count just like the way I used to swallow spit.

He didn't notice it, but he was walking back down the same road the bus had brought him on a couple hours earlier. He didn't know. His head just said walk. Walk fast, in fact. That was all his head said.

25

The sky, to James, a vast, blue-faded dishcloth, heavy with wet, waiting to be wrung. Walking the road back to town, he wondered if it would rain, reconsidered, and decided that, no, he really didn't wonder a flying fuck if it rained. Or hailed or galed or even snowed, for that matter. What if like before, all he at that moment could think; what if never any more interference-free music? The possibility seemed absurd (he had been free of any excessively self-conscious nuttiness for years and years now), but terrifying just the same. As he made his way down the empty-but-for-him road, he tried to remember some of the Zen techniques Webby had tried to teach him during a particularly uninspiring mid-winter, five-night, five-city, northern Michigan bar tour.

One night after a show somewhere in Toledo (or was it Traverse City?), in the hotel lounge, James, with the aid of many Slim Jims (Jim Beam and Diet Coke), had tried to grasp the Zen concept of nothingness and what, Webby kept repeating over the college basketball game playing on the TV above on the bar, "it could do for you, really, and, like, today." Three nights in, the tour had thus far been a disaster (two near-empty clubs to begin with, the third cancelled outright after a virtually audienceless first set). James had tried his best to learn to be "disinterested". In the morning, however, all he had been was hung over.

The road leading back towards town was nothing more than a road; no view especially, no landmarks to speak of. Hands in pockets, James after a bit managed, without the aid of any official philosophy, not to do too much thinking for a solid five minutes. Relieved to notice, in a looking-over-his-shoulder-into-his-head sort of way, that this sudden counting business was in no way intense as had been the spit-swallowing thing years before, he felt some of his terror at the thought of a musicless near future subside. He told himself not to encourage the damn thing (the only usable slice of advice his psychiatrist had given him way back when and obviously not knowing what to tell the swallowing-too-much youth on his couch), to think about the why of it all later, to hope it would simply go away as inexplicably as the swallowing thing had done, and to right now concentrate on the troubles at hand. There were, after all, things to do and get done. Like getting ahold of the Thing, he reminded himself.

He stuck out his thumb. Transportation was approaching; a bus, it looked like. Maybe the first break I catch today, he thought.

Out of the lifting dust a brightly painted yellow schoolbus with tinted black windows idled on the left-hand side of the gravel road about twenty feet ahead of him, waiting. Red blinking lights said Do Not Pass, but with her crimson head hanging out of the driver's-side window Bertha McNaughton, a woman James knew only as one of his Uncle Buckly's "lady friends", said, "James Thompson? Buckly Thompson's nephew James? You've grown up, boy. Long time no see. You plan on hoofing it all the way into town? Well, you can forget that, mister, looks like it'll be pissing a bucketful in no time at all. Climb right up." So James stepped up, and the bus first, then seconded, forward.

Here, one must imagine a small child entering, unprepared, an amusement park's best effort at a house of horrors that truly does the trick. Had James known that Bertha was delivering twelve Thames River Community Home for the Chronologically Challenged residents (his mother second row from the front) on a mandatory field trip to see a late afternoon production of *Daniel Boone* by a group of fourth-graders over at Queen Elizabeth Public School, it is safe to say he would not have accepted Bertha's kind offer of a ride. The bus was moving, though, and, standing on the steps with one hand on the guard rail, he recovered from the pure sensory punch of so many eyes seeing so little, all those ears straining to hear but barely hearing, and a dozen sets of lips forming in grand total nothing at all, to wave a half-wave at his mother. Showing little sign of recognition, Margaret turned her attention back to whatever it was she saw through her portion of the bus's one-way mirror.

James looked down at his boots, inhaled and exhaled, then turned his head upward to quickly, unwillingly, count the number of people (himself excluded) on the bus. His enumerating was broken by a cracked voice coming from the back of the vehicle wondering when they would be there.

"When we get there," Bertha replied, smiling at James in winking-conspiratorial fashion. James scanned the vehicle for something, anything, but found only himself standing at the front of a schoolbus stuffed full of senior citizens travelling, he noticed, eight miles over the speed limit.

Bertha cleared her throat with five chain-smoker's ahems and asked him how "that old sonofagun of an uncle" of his was doing. "Been ages since I been out to the old Buckly mansion, heh, heh, heh," she continued. "He still got that old water-bed of his, heh, heh, hah, hah, hah."

Out of a combination of assumed politeness and the possibility of pure tête-à-tête escapism, James briefly considered making an honest effort at answering, but then remembered that, first, he had only met this woman a handful of times before, each time as she was leaving his uncle's place very early on the Saturday mornings James was supposed to wash his uncle's car (and, as a result, owed her nothing in the way of conversational ums and ahs), and, second, that that was his mother sitting over there, that woman in the blue track-suit with the far-away eyes. Standing on the top step, still holding onto the silver guard rail, James stared at his mother. He found it difficult to imagine

her as the source material for any new song; found it difficult, in fact, to imagine her as anything but his mother.
That's my mother, was all he could think. That's my mum.

"That's my mother," he said, surprised when he heard
himself say it.

"I beg your pardon, sweetheart?" Bertha answered,
hearing clearly what James had said, but out of plain lazi-
ness liking for people to repeat what they had just spoken.

"Where's my mother going with all these people?"

"You don't say, eh? Your mother, huh? Well, let me see.
Yeah, I guess that does ring a bell, doesn't it? Sure. Margaret
Hazel was married to Buckly's brother, James. Guess that's
your dad, huh? James like you, huh? Cute. That's real cute,
hon."

Approaching the incline on Second Street that meant
the Third Street bridge was coming right up, Bertha put
the bus in third, then checked herself out in the mirror
over the dash, giving herself a little smile when she was
through.

"I said, what is my mother doing with all these people?" He was nearly shouting now, and even his mother
had begun to take notice of the young man in the black
cowboy boots standing by himself at the front of the bus.

"Why, honey, didn't anybody ever tell you? Oh, for
goodness sake," Bertha said, tsking and shaking her head
slowly from side to side. Lowering her voice, she nodded
James closer. "Your mother was put into a nursing home
right after your grandfather died. Poor woman, she—"

"It's not a nursing home, damn it, it's a residence," he
burst out.

"Hey now." Bertha recoiled, turning away from the
road just long enough to look at him with an up-and-down,
who-do-you-think-you're-talking-to expression. "No need
to get sharp with me, now. I'm sure I'm very sorry your
mother can't manage to take care of herself any more, but
it's not my fault and I don't appreciate. . . ."

James wasn't listening.

Two seats back, on his knee, he asked, "Mum, where are you going? Where are you going with all these" (in a whisper) "old people?"

His mother looked at him with the kind of patient pity usually reserved by the very young for the very old.

"I live with these people now. Over near the river. We're going to see some thing this afternoon. Supposed to be good for us to get out and see it, they said." She turned her head to look out the window again.

He looked at her looking away, and thought, Boy, she looks old. My mother looks like an old lady who belongs in a nursing home.

He put his hand on hers and asked, "Do you want to go, Mum? Do you want to go to this thing that's supposed to be good for you?"

She looked at him and sighed. "I'd like to go back to my room. Eat something first, maybe, and then go back to my room. Have a nap. Maybe watch some TV tonight if I'm not too tired."

James as a teenager would periodically forget that his mother was just his mother. Pen in hand, sitting beside her on the bed in her room, he would patiently quiz her about life as a girl living with her stepparents, the Hazels; what had started her and his father dating; and, most of all, what his father had really been like, particularly any details of his disposition on the increasingly disturbing and seemingly teleological-proof day of his demise. His mother's response never varied: long, sad smile; smoothing of dress at the knee; and complete attention turned from James's expectant face back to the television set sitting atop the dressing bureau.

Then (empty notebook hanging; defeated; out the door and down the hall to his own room; headphones on and Flatt and Scruggs very very loud):

Mother, Father, me, no more (he would think, hard). Nothing. No more. Just . . . nothing.

Then:

Lester: Rolling rhythm guitar, punchy bass-string dreadnought G-run. Yes.

Earl: Three-finger banjo-string-snapping incorporeality. Yes Yes.

In each ear, loud: "Pike County Breakdown" ... "Foggy Mountain Breakdown" ... "Farewell Blues" ... yes yes yes. ...

Then:

Everything was lost of function, was not itself, could be anything, could be ... perfect. ...

Now:

James squeezed his mother's hand and she let him. He walked back to the front of the bus.

"Bertha, my mother wants to go home." Bertha looked at him. Then, dismissively, she looked back to the road.

"James, I think I'm done talking to you. I offer you a free ride out of simple respect for the good memories I have of sharing some wonderful times with your sweet Uncle Buckly — who, I might add, you could certainly learn a few things from in the manners department — and all you can do is sass me. I think what you should do is find a seat and sit in it until we get to the school. You can get off there."

James leaned over, lending his right hand to Bertha's two on the steering wheel. He whispered clearly in her ear, "Bertha, I want you to turn this bus around, and I want you to do it now. My mother wants to go home. I'm not going to ask you again. Do it, turn it around, or we're all going to end up going for a very quick left-hand turn into the next oncoming automobile." Looking into Bertha's hard, painted-on eyes, James tightened his grip on the wheel, happily scaring himself with an adrenalin-like shot of recognition that told him he was capable of the deed.

Bertha thought for a moment, too, but just for a moment, putting the turn signal on at the first intersection she saw. James let loose his grip on the wheel. He leaned into the standing pole next to him and put his hands in his pockets.

Making a slow, wide U-turn, the bus began to turn around. James looked at his mother again looking out the window and thought a plain, pleasant thought: About five-thirty, I would guess. She might make it home in time to catch "Wheel of Fortune". Always did like "Wheel of Fortune", he thought. That sure was something she always did like.

26

He got off with the others at the residence, saw his mother to her room, and, much to Bertha's chagrin, managed to talk the girl at the front desk out of calling the police. Like the majority of Datum's girls just this side of sweet sixteen, she was undeniably pretty without being in any way what could be called desirable. Different mould entirely from What's-her-name (although fully knowing Melissa's name), James thought, this in spite of his recently self-imposed dictum of crazy-woman non-reflection and non-entanglement. Different mould entirely.

The girl's nametag said "Miss Cumberland" but she insisted, "Oh heck, my name's Judy, for goodness' sake." And while she wasn't exactly ecstatic about having the whole geriatric gang back a full two hours before their expected arrival time, she did understand Mrs. Thompson's not feeling all that well, and (after Bertha had nose-in-the-air-indignant, calls-for-kidnapping-charges-ignored, paycheque-in-purse left) admitted that, well, she never did care all that much for that McNaughton woman anyway, and, well, "Are you the James Thompson used to live around here and are the singer now?" No, she didn't have any of his records, but yes, she had heard a few of his songs on an after-midnight country alternative show she sometimes managed to pick up on the college station out of London, and, well, she had never really ever met anyone famous before. Could she have his autograph?

James scrawled himself on the back of an enema-bag patient request form and was on his way. He walked the eight blocks to M.C.'s house refreshingly full of himself, the last hour's events inducing a feeling of well-being not unlike that of a good-deed-done Boy Scout who is reminded that he is, as well, in no way unattractive. Even forgot for a while to remember his burgeoning numerical neurosis. He whistled something he didn't at first recognize before realizing it to be "Having Snow", the instrumental he had had stuck in his head recently. Two or three minutes of this, and then: Boy, that's a nice little tune, isn't it? He whistled the chorus part again, and thought: That really *is* a nice little bit of music.

"What's up? Thought you'd be home from work by now."

"You're a popular guy today," M.C. answered. He was just finishing up washing his car in the driveway, scrubbing the whitewalls of his Cavalier and listening to, and occasionally singing along with, a classic rock station out of Detroit playing on the car stereo. The soapy doors of the vehicle were wide open, Hendrix playing his head off.

"Oh, yeah? How's that? Don't feel all that popular," James said. Everything considered, though, he didn't feel all that bad. Read his uncle the historically correct riot act, get the Thing from him, and hide out in the basement for a couple of days and get down to it. Put all the silliness of the past few days behind him and strum the hell out of that old Gibson of his. He knew of what he spoke. He had made music. He would make music again. Like an amnesiac who suddenly remembers he's somebody important, I make music, he thought. Maybe I'll write something about Mum. Something new . . . something different. . . .

"Girl name Melissa keeps calling here," M.C. said, getting up from his hubcap-high squatting position, "wanting to know if, and I'm quoting here, 'cowboy, you know, James, is there?'"

"Ah, for Christ's sake, how'd she . . . ? Ah, Jesus," James said, rocked out of his momentary contentment. Feeling a renewed attack of calculation coming on, he dived back into the conversation in the hope of avoiding it.

"What did you tell her?"

"What the hell do you think I told her?" M.C. said. "Told her you weren't here." M.C. rinsed his chamois rag in the washbucket and began winding up the hose. "Some Toronto poontang follow you all the way down here to Datum, cowboy?"

"Cut that shit out. This woman is dangerous." James looked for concern in M.C.'s face but saw only an amused smile.

"No shit."

"Yeah," James said, "no shit."

"Okay." M.C. was smiling now.

"Pulled a gun on me yesterday."

James said it for impact, to impart to his friend the seriousness of his situation, but M.C. only smiled harder, reeling in the last of his wet green line.

"Was this before or after you banged her?"

"After, actually." He watched the hose's final inches get sucked up and wrapped around their cylindrical steel resting place, and replayed in his mind the incident of his and Melissa's coming together at gunpoint. Unexpectedly, and with an embarrassed frustration, he felt himself getting a hard-on.

Suddenly: "How the hell did you know we—"

Laughing openly now, M.C. said, "Like the man says, 'I heard it through the grapevine.'"

"So she told you we slept together. Big deal. Doesn't surprise me. Doesn't surprise me at all."

"A groupie got lost down the 401 South?"

"She's from Datum," James said. "Though you wouldn't know it by looking at her. Not a groupie exactly, more like. . . ." More like what? Hard to say, actually. He told himself he didn't have the time or the interest to worry about it, though, so: "One sick, dangerous woman any way you look at it. She also mention to you she held me up? Made me a hostage in my own house?"

"Nope. Just asked me to get you to give her a call whenever I ran into you. Said it was important. Said — and I'm just repeating what I've been told, now — 'New day, different location, same old lesson.' Whatever the hell that means. Lovers' talk, I guess. Also something about the Hamilton option being ruled out and how the old man's money is as good as in the bank. Anyway, her number's in the house. On the fridge."

"Lose it. She's not right in the head." Involuntarily he began figuring out how many days remained before Devanchuck's deadline. Thirty days in June plus thirty in July plus thirty-one in August is ninety-one plus seven more days in — stop it, he reproached himself. Get a fucking grip. "Look, I really gotta get hold of my uncle. Any ideas?"

"Sounds urgent. What's up?"

"I've got something he's gotta know, and he's got something, a thing that's mine, that I gotta have."

"Sounds sensible to me. Did you check the ballpark? He likes to get there early to get a good spot for his lawnchair behind the cage behind home plate."

"The Wheels playing?"

"Double-header with Tilbury. First one starts at six-thirty, I think. If it don't rain first."

"Damn, I knew that, too. You going?" James asked, knowing he was. M.C. didn't play any more (hung up his cleats three years before — bum knee), but he never missed a home game when he could help it.

"Soon as I dry this baby off. Don't want the sun to streak her," M.C. said, beginning to work the chamois over the roof. "Probably rain before that has a chance to happen, though."

"Got another one? Another rag?"

"Right beside the pail."

"You take that side, I'll get over here. I wanna get going," James said.

"All right, but do the job right, okay? Don't work in little half-assed circles like you used to on your uncle's car. Up-and-down motion only. And put some elbow into it."

"Anything else?"

"Yeah, get that rag moving. Don't want to end up with streak marks all over it."

"Anything else?" James repeated.

"Yeah," M.C. said, answering almost in tune with the song playing on the radio, "What's a nice cowboy like you doing in a place like this?"

"Not much of a singer," James said, smiling in spite of himself.

"Not much of an answer," M.C. replied. Longer than for the car's sake, both of them just wiped, the songs on the radio, it seemed, never about ready to stop.

27

In M.C.'s car and finally moving, a slight hold-up on the way to the baseball diamond when M.C. insisted they make a detour to grab a quick bite to eat. James protested from the passenger side that there wasn't time; M.C., with a heavy-footed roar and quick smirking glance indicated that that was, in fact, all they had. They split the difference and agreed to stop at the Duke, but for no more than half an hour. The game started at six-thirty, and it was nearly six o'clock now.

"Jeanie's working tonight, right?" James asked.

"Every Monday, Wednesday, and Sunday."

"Well, at least maybe I can talk to her while you fill your face."

"Sure," M.C. said. "And who knows? Once we get there, you might even see something you like."

Back in high school, James had liked to sit in one of the booths along the wall at the Duke and listen to the same crumbling old men who had frequented the place for years complain with bitter animation about the circumstances of their day-to-day lives. Interesting in a voyeuristic sort of way, of course, but the real appeal lay in sitting and sipping his cup of coffee while waiting with nervous expectation for the talk to shift, gradually but unfailingly, from grievance to gladness — and always after the third or fourth beer; never before. Of what would ostensibly trigger the change, it varied: an Indian-summer afternoon; that So-and-so hadn't shown his sorry-ass face in a good long while; the size of the carrots and lima beans in today's soup. Not so fickle, though, was the invariable shift from appropriate disgust to cheerful gleam in the old men's mood. And then the inexplicably exploding desire on James's part to join in with the old men in glad, let-me-buy-every-stranger-here-a-beer release — impossible to realize, of course, because James was only an onlooker, and not one who had already first told or shown the truth.

After grabbing yesterday's sport section off the top of the cigarette machine, M.C. cleared a path to an empty booth near the kitchen at the back, M.C. facing the front door, James sitting down to a view that included the dark hallway that led to the restrooms and a mop sitting up in a soapy bucket of dark water. M.C. caught his wife's attention as she was setting down glasses of ice-water and menus for a table of four, giving her an exaggerated slow wink but no smile. Jeanie laughed out loud, not covering her mouth quickly enough, the table of four looking up from their menus and tinkling glasses to see what was so funny.

Jeanie got her lunches and dinners at the Duke at cost on the days she was working. On Sundays her boss, Mr. Pinnalli, didn't come into the restaurant, so it was easy for M.C. to get the discounted Sunday dinner his wife was entitled to. Jeanie didn't mind; she rarely ate dinner the days she worked, and liked it when her husband dropped by and broke up the monotony of eight hours of talking about, serving up, and cleaning up other people's food.

M.C. handed the slightly food-soiled newspaper across the table to James. "Here. Haven't forgotten how just eating when you eat isn't enough for you. It's Saturday's, but it might have something on Friday's Wheels' game. Get you caught up a bit, anyway."

"Just like old times," James answered, wanting but not quite able to forget the disappointment that had passed between them in the basement the night before.

"Better," M.C. replied, eyeing the small pyramid of stacked dinner rolls Jeanie was bringing their way. "Now I get my roast beef dinner with all the bread I can eat. And — get this — the whole thing, with beverage, coming in at less than half-price."

"Not exactly what I meant," James said, surprised at the prick of anger he felt at M.C.'s dogged literalness.

"Sorry," M.C. said, kissing the top of Jeanie's hand as she set down the basket of hot buns on their table, "sometimes I forget that you mean to mean something else when you're trying to talk about something. Out of practice, I guess."

Smiling weakly up at Jeanie, James broke open a roll, trying to decide, first, if he should use butter on his bread, and second, what the hell M.C. was talking about. Everybody so damn cryptic around here these days, he thought, suddenly irked at the proclivity his hometown seemed to have developed in his absence for the ambiguous epithet. He watched his friend knifing with surgical care the low-cal margarine pad his wife had brought, and decided for the sake of a calm dinner hour — and in the interest of the bigger fish he was set upon frying — to forgo any further enquiry along these lines.

Steam from the broken bun getting in the way of the words on the pages spread out in front of him, James bit into his bread and tried to get lost in an unsigned recap of Datum's 10-6 loss to Wallaceburg on Friday. Before either the bun in his stomach or the recounted game on the table could submerge him, however, M.C. flicked the edge of the newspaper with his non-bun-eating hand. He raised a forefinger to indicate his still-chewing condition.

"Good news and bad news," M.C. said, finally.

"Oh yeah?"

"Yeah. Good news is that your uncle is ordering what appears to be the banana cream pie. Enjoyed it many times myself. Solid choice."

"Oh yeah?" James said, swivelling around in the booth, forgetting for an instant the annoyance with his uncle that had put him where he was now sitting. "And what's the bad—"

"Well, either that's your little Miss Colt .45 with him, or I'd say your uncle's got himself the stamina of a man about thirty years his junior."

Melissa, James could see, was just going to have coffee. She crossed one black-stockinged leg over the other and put — to James's mind — a vaguely familiar manila-wrapped parcel on the stool next to her.

"It her?" M.C. asked, not knowing whether he should be entertained or concerned at James's ashen reaction.

It's her all right, James thought. Who else could it be?

For the next several minutes, nothing much in the way of anything. M.C. graduated from the rolls to the vegetable soup; Jeanie's section flooded over with an influx of eleven hungry after-mass Catholics; Melissa sipped at her coffee and talked casually with some of the old men sitting in the booths nearest the counter; Buckly attacked his pie with the same methodical preoccupation he took to most merely necessary tasks; and James, looking on at all of it (though no one, not even Melissa, looking back at him), rumbling-tummy indecisive, not knowing — both Buckly and Melissa being present — whether hard-feigned indifference or self-righteous, mythologically mongering spleen was the more appropriate stance. Also, beheld and against his will duly enumerated: twenty-two bottles of different kinds of beer (domestic and imported) on the wall, twenty-two different kinds of beer, if one of those bottles should happen to fall. . . .

Then a bark, two, then three; Al, James knew at once, letting Buckly know he wouldn't mind some sort of refreshment himself. Sitting still now, quietly digesting his pie, both hands resting palms down on the countertop in front of him, Buckly, hearing his dog's dogged command, pushed himself up and asked Jeanie for a little something to put some water in for his dog. Finding in the trash an empty aluminum pie plate, Jeanie scraped the crusty remains out, then handed it over. Buckly thanked her, took the platter, and headed towards the washroom to fill the thing up. Okay, James thought, time to get this show on the road. Here we go.

"Boys," Buckly said, nodding pleasantly at both M.C. and James. "Whadoyou know for sure?"

"Not much, Mr. Thompson," M.C. returned, looking up from his soup.

"Well, that makes two of us," Buckly said, makeshift bowl in hand, stopping beside the table. "Looks like we're in for a bit of weather this afternoon, I'd say." Buckly wasn't a man much for small talk, but he didn't mind occasionally shooting the breeze with M.C. He liked the younger man's stolid solidness, as apparent around South Western as it was around the ballpark, not to mention the fact that, thanks in no small part to Buckly's South Western supper-hour propagandizing, he was a staunch Tigers fan as well.

"Yep. And fool that I am, I just finished throwing a wash on the car, too."

"Happens every time. Let's hope we can sneak in at least the first game," Buckly said.

"Yeah. Let's hope."

Buckly again nodded at the two friends, then took his leave down the dark hall.

"For Christ's sake, do you believe that?" James asked.

"What's that?"

"I said, 'Do you believe that?'"

"I heard you the first time," M.C. said, full soupspoon at mouth level and on the brink of being slurped in. M.C., when he was eating, liked to eat. "I mean, believe what? Your uncle? What?"

James didn't answer. He got up from the table noticeably piqued and disappeared down the hallway after his uncle.

"What's the matter with James?" Jeanie said, setting down M.C.'s pot-roast dinner and side plate of creamed spinach.

"Honey, you know James. Your guess is as good as mine."

"He know his uncle's here?"

"Yeah. Somehow, I think that's part of the problem."

"I don't get it."

"And you think I do, sweetheart?"

"Anyway," Jeanie said, clearing the table of the roll basket and M.C.'s empty soupbowl, "be nice to him. You know how he gets sometimes, especially when he's here."

"Then why the hell did he bother coming back?" M.C. replied, the familiar aroma of the meat on his plate drawing his attention tableward. "Can't be just to see us. We make it up to Toronto to see him often enough. His uncle once in a while too."

"Honey," Jeanie said, blowing out of the side of her mouth a few errant, end-of-shift strands of hair, "you know I've never been able to make heads or tails of that boy's appetite for self-abuse any better than you have." She set the basket and bowl back down on the table, shifting the weight of the day's work from her left leg to her right, stretching the tired small of her back as she did so.

"I know, babe," M.C. said. "Remember that year back in high school when he made his band practise at midnight on what would have been his dad's fortieth birthday, down on King Street where his father got crushed by that engine?"

"I think it was a transmission, hon."

"Engine, transmission, whatever. What the heck was the name of that place? One of those buildings they tore down to make room for the new mall."

"Beverly's?"

"Yeah, right. Beverly's Auto Repair. Told everybody he wanted the band to play there because he was tired of only getting 'Kodak truth'. Remember?"

"Oh, sure, I remember."

"And remember how next day everybody quit on him, the whole darn bunch?" M.C. chuckled in little laughs through methodical roast-beef shovellings. "Had to do that gig at Kirby's the next night with just him and his guitar. Solo James. Old Spanky Franklin ended up paying only half what he was supposed to. Said he'd go to hell before he'd pay full price for a goddamned hippie-dippy folk act when he'd signed up for a full country-and-western band, including steel guitar — even if James did play damn near every song George Jones ever made."

"That's right," Jeanie added, on the verge of laughing herself. "I never saw James so mad. Swore he'd never play Spanky's again."

"And he didn't. Give the guy that much." M.C. picked at his spinach. He had been hoping for corn niblets. "He never did."

"No, he didn't, he sure did not."

"Nope, he sure didn't."

"Well, just be nice," Jeanie said, "that's all I'm saying. Just, you know, be the way you've always been when he gets like this."

"Of course, hon. What do you think I'm gonna do? I love the guy, for Christ's sake. He's James. But I tell you," M.C. said, looking up at Jeanie as he spoke, putting his fork down and sweeping his arm around his wife's waist, "James is one of those people you're sure glad you're friends with long distance, and not right up close."

Jeanie rested one of her hands on his shoulder, massaging the muscles slightly, staring at the closed door of the men's bathroom.

"Honey," she finally said.

"Yeah, babe?"

"You decided between the rice pudding and the Jell-O yet?"

The pie tin, filled with water, sat on top of the washroom's summer-dead radiator near the sink. James's uncle, however, was not at first glance anywhere to be seen. Soon, though, two slightly battered black dress shoes with green work pants collapsed on top of them were visible in the stall nearest to the door.

"Uncle Buckly?" James asked. In a town like Datum one just didn't go around taking chances with questions of personal identity in men's washroom stalls. The possibilities, nearly all of them tragic, were endless.

"James?"

"Yeah, it's me."

"How you doing?

"Well, to tell you the truth, not so hot."

"What's up?"

"Well, to start with, what's with the woman?"

"What woman?" Buckly asked, a sort of hollow, pig-gish snort (obviously not unrelated to the act he was set upon) punctuating his question.

"What do you mean, what do I mean? The woman you came into the Duke with."

"Oh, you mean Melissa."

"Yeah. Melissa. And what's with telling her all that stuff about Dad and the guys he worked with and the guys on his hockey team and—"

"Just hold on a minute, will you?" Less vacuous than before, even sharp in its reverberation, Buckly let go with what was, to James's ear, an elephantine wail of despair. Also, unaccountably, James picked up the not so faint hum of a harmonica and voices in song coming from the dining room. Not the ideal environment for the soul-scolding talk he had envisioned.

"You about done in there?" James said.

"How's that?"

"I said, 'You about done in there?' I wouldn't mind talking to you face to face about this."

"Sorry about that, James. Melissa made me some kinda vegetarian chili tofu deal for lunch. Know what it must sound like, but not bad actually. Not bad at all. But you know how me and pinto beans get along."

He let her cook? He doesn't even let anybody use his can-opener, James thought. "Look, Uncle Buckly, I want — I mean, I need some answers here. Let's start with why you told her all those things about our family. What could possibly make you do something like that?"

"Hell, I don't know. Because she asked me, I guess."

"Because she asked you. You guess."

"Yeah, she asked me. The acoustics bad out there or something?"

"I don't get it," James said. "Some complete stranger straight off the street comes up to you and starts asking you all sorts of intimate things about our family — things you've got no right to be sharing with anybody but family, you know — and you just go ahead and rattle on about stuff you haven't even told me? Sorry, I just don't get it."

"Well," Buckly said, still in the stall — finishing, flushing, and pulling up his pants in one clean swoop — "you don't have to get it. There ain't that much to get, in fact. She seemed like a nice kid is all, not pushy-like or anything, and what the hell, am I so busy I can't give somebody a hand once in a while when they ask for it?"

Emerging from behind door number one, Buckly ignored James's determined stare and pushed past him to the sink, where, to his frustration, the lever on the dispenser wouldn't deliver anything close to soap; dead-air clicking noises only. "Sonofabitch," he said, giving the device a final, unnecessarily violent pump. "How do they expect a guy to wash his goddamned hands properly with just hot water and elbow grease, huh? How?"

He managed, though, using a couple of brown paper towels from a stack on the sink to finish the job. Eyeing James giving him what he recognized as his serious look, he said, "Oh, quit with that holier-than-Hank Williams look, will you? Nothing I told her is so intimate she shouldn't have heard it. Christ, you'd think our people and their doings were as interesting to everybody else as they are to you."

Open-mouthed, forefinger out and ready to indict, James's intentions were interrupted by his uncle saying, "Besides, I was just trying to help you out a bit. Seems to me that, in the line of business you're in, you could use all the free publicity you can get, am I right? The way I figure it, you should be grateful to me and her both — she's doing you a favour, after all."

"A favour? A favour? How the hell can you possibly figure she's—"

"You ever in your travels, heard that line about not making a mountain out of a molehill?" Buckly asked.

"Sure. So what?" James answered.

Standing in front of the grease-smudged mirror over the sink, combing what little hair he still had straight back with a thin, black comb produced from his back pocket, "Think about it," Buckly said. He gave himself a quick final look in the mirror and returned the comb to his pocket. Looking in the mirror at James looking into the mirror looking at him looking back at him, "Think about it, is all," he repeated.

Buckly picked up the dish and carried it with both hands to the door, not asking for James's help in opening it, using, instead, one of his elbows to exit on his own.

Leaving, Buckly let in a noise — a clear melody, that much James could now recognize — that he could swear he knew but couldn't for the life of him place. The door closed slowly on its own, numbing the strands of sounds coming from the other room. James absently looked in the mirror as he tried to place the tune now wedged in his head. Knowing as a musician does when a piece of music is coming to an end, he began to feel seriously piqued, scratching ineffectually at the song's secret like an obstinate cat at a locked-tight aluminum door. He hummed the bit of melodic thread he had managed to pick out of the air. Five, maybe ten seconds of this, and then: My God, he thought: They're playing my song!

28

Entering, he saw that everything but M.C. was severely out of whack, the musicless room (just as he stepped into it) brimming with the sort of activity James could not have made up even if he had tried: the old men, eight or nine of them (most of whom James now recognized from his boyhood watchings), each with a bottle of beer, not the usual glass of draft; Jeanie and the mute short-order cook (the Catholics, the last of the dining customers, having hurriedly eaten and exited); even Buckly, wary of crowds as usual but intrigued, on the edge of the group — all of them standing around a stool at the front counter supporting the harmonica-holding sound-maker responsible for the version of his own "I've Got the Wheel (If You've Got the Wine)" he had eventually recognized in the washroom. M.C., the lone non-participant, worked on his second rice pudding, keeping a periodic eye on the proceedings from his back booth.

James zombied his way through the small crowd.

"Hey, pal, no need to get pushy, eh?" The voice belonged to one of the younger old-timers. In his late fifties, early sixties at the most, the man was an anomaly among his cronies: unsuited, for one thing (rolled-up-cuff blue jeans and white T-shirt); still carrying himself, despite his years and the sack of flesh that hung over his belt buckle and shadowed his shoes, like a real barfly, for another — not content to sit and sip and trade occasional half-truths like the others; the potential bad-ass role every bar demands to have filled still his treasured part. He wore a black Santa Claus beard (with here and there a grey streak) and, on his right forearm, a black and white tattoo that read *Wanda, R.I.P.*

"Sorry," James said.

He jostled his way through the cluster of bodies before getting a clear sight of the source of the song. Spirit stung, he ran the fingers of his left hand through his hair in a miserable attempt to keep his bearings, his elbow in the process inadvertently brushing the ear of the same oldster he had just had the run-in with.

"Hey now! I told you there was no need for that kinda thing. Lots for everybody, okay? In case you didn't hear it right the first time, buddy, that young broad over there with the harmonica said all of us here were drinking for free, okay? Nobody's money is any good here tonight? All we gotta do, as far as I can figure, is sing along with her singing a few dumb songs and then nobody has to do without. So settle down and sing what she tells you and ask the waitress for a beer and don't cause a fuss, all right?" Then, trying to lighten the mood a little, "Drinkin' in here'll sure beat standing around in what's gonna be comin' down out there," he said. "She'll be pissin' like a sonofabitch soon enough, that's for sure."

More confused (after all those watching and waiting and wanting adolescent hours, she was the one buying the old boys a round?) and embarrassed (the old man was one of the ones he had observed at the Duke time and time again) than insulted, James, in the chaos of everything that was the moment, mumbled a deferential *mea culpa*. The old man, however, wasn't buying, almost immediately regretting his earlier attempt at appeasement, eyeing James with a closer and still closer looking-over.

The old-timer finished his beer only to have an even older old boy in a Brooks Brother suit circa mid-fifties hand him another. He opened the twist-off with what was left of his rotting teeth and spat the cap to the floor. He put the fresh beer down on the counter, lit an unfiltered cigarette (sucking deeply, nearly pulling the thing down to half, James observed, in three quick but achingly deep sucks), picked up the bottle again, and, pointing at James with both smoke and drink, said, "I remember now. I've seen you before." He didn't say it like he was recounting a pleasant memory. "Yeah, I remember you. Long time ago. Five or six years. Here at the Duke. Sittin' and watchin' me and some of my friends all the time. Christ." He spat this last word as much as he spoke it. He flicked off some of the ash that had fallen onto his T-shirt from what was left of his cigarette and moved closer still, so only James could hear him. His breath was incredible, something between lighter fluid and day-old, soft-boiled eggs. "I'm on to you, boy," was all he said.

"What?" James said. This wasn't the Whitmanesque encounter he had envisioned. Why weren't boozy, saga-cious anecdotes flowing easily from the seasoned veteran of life to its youthful chronicler, the beer in each man's hand bought with James's eager money, not . . . hers.

"Don't like sissy boys around here, hear?"

"What?"

"You deaf or something? Said we don't stand for de-generate faggotism at the Duke of Connaught, okay? That means you, all right?"

Despite a musical lull as the harmonica player tried to get everyone straight on the chorus to the next song, the old man and James had been neither missed nor noticed. But at this, the old man's last exclamation, everyone turned around to see what was the excitement. Ready for a rebut-tal, happy to do what he could to protect the sanctity of the only real home he had ever known, the old man rocked back on his heels, eyeing James wildly, wiping beer froth off his moustache and beard with the back of his hand.

"It's okay, Benny," Melissa called out, "he's all right. In fact, he's more than all right. That, ladies and gentle-men — for those of you not already in the know — is James Thompson, the creator of the last little ditty we all enjoyed so much, which I'm sure I didn't do justice to, as the com-poser himself would probably agree. Wouldn't you agree, composer?"

James blinked a few times in her direction and mum-bled something about not wanting to miss the start of the baseball game.

One leg swung over each side of the stool, shoulder-length black hair tied up in a bundle of aplomb, two-inch black heels permitting her feet to touch the ground, Melissa tucked the harmonica into her right armpit and initiated a round of spirited if slightly baffled applause.

"That so?" the old man said, slowly clapping too, but scrutinizing James up and down; "that so?"

Melissa continued. "Well, folks, now that we've got the horse's mouth right here, so to speak, what do you say to hearing our music directly from the stallion himself from this point on?" A few scattered all rights and okays; one of the old men — the one who'd so quickly handed Benny his beer — starting to clap again, only to be quickly hushed by some of the others.

"James, would you honour us by doing the next number? We've decided on 'Lazy Old Home Again', but I'm sorry to say all we've got in the line of musical accompaniment is this little Hohner Special 20 harmonica, which is slightly out of tune at that. But I think most everybody knows at least the chorus by now, and that should make you feel a little less lonely up here." Someone laughed; somebody else yawned; another wondered aloud if all the free beer was gone. Others, suddenly aware of their own incipient bottom-of-bottleness, not a little anxiously echoed this same sentiment. Melissa gave a little quick nod to Jeanie, who took out a large keychain from her work apron and moved towards the locked cooler attached to the wall behind the counter. Soon, most everyone who needed to be was busy cracking open and sucking up.

Jeanie sidled up to James and placed a cold bottle of Molson Canadian in his right hand. Smiling widely, she whispered in his ear, "You sly dog, you. You should have said something."

"What?" he responded, his increasingly usual response all day.

"Oh, stop it. You don't have to be coy with me, James. You could have just come out and said that was why you came back. To tell you the truth, I'm, well, sort of relieved,

you know? I mean, you know how you used to get sometimes, and, well, you did sort of float into Datum and. . . .
Well, now that I know why you're here, let's just say I think
it's wonderful."

"What's wonderful?" he asked, sure that, whatever the
hell she was talking about, it sure as hell wasn't wonderful.

"Oh, stop it. I think it's just great. And to think she's
from right here in town. I would never in a million years
have guessed James Thompson would meet his match in
a local girl. Why, I'm almost jealous." She glanced over at
her husband busy scooping up the last of his dessert and
gave James a quick peck on the cheek.

"Jeanie, what—"

"Sorry, kiddo, gotta get back to my post. Melissa put a
hundred dollars in the cash register and she said she
doesn't want any change left over at the end of the night."
Jeanie began to laugh, looking at the revelry unfolding in
front of her.

"Some of these boys still don't know what hit them.
Had a hard time convincing half of them their money was
no good here tonight. Imagine that, with this bunch." She
began to laugh again, overhearing a nearby couple of more
than usually seasoned drinkers delicately picking through
a bowl of pretzel sticks and conjecturing how many more
free beers they could look forward to. "Probably close as
any of them will ever come to winning the lottery," she
said.

Empty brown bottles beginning to accumulate again,
Jeanie moved back towards the counter, over her shoulder saying to James, "Oh, well, drink up. Your fiancée's
putting out more than a couple bucks for all of this. The
least you can do is do her the favour of hoisting a few,
right?"

"Excuse me, my what?" he said, nervous confusion
raising his intonation an octave or so above normal.

"Sorry, James, gotta go."

"Excuse me, my what?" he said, fully shrilly now.

"All right, now," another voice — Melissa's — said, "I think we're just about ready, James. How about you? Are you just about ready yourself?" James whipped around to behold a dozen or so faces awaiting his reply with various degrees of interest. Neither James nor the crowd said a word.

Suddenly, James sprang active, calling out to M.C., "Let's go" — giving his uncle the nastiest look he could manage, Melissa not a glance, the old men a disappointed once-over — and moving with an almost convincing slow lope towards the door. He did find time along the way, though, to notice that seven booths (and not nine, as he had all along thought) sat along the left-hand wall. Seven. Seven booths. Seven.

M.C. right behind him now (shrugged shoulders and a blown kiss to Jeanie his only exiting actions), James's hand was on the door handle when he heard it.

Disbelieving at first, only the slightest standing-still-for-a-second hesitation; then, secure that what he had heard wasn't what he feared he had heard, James pushed the door open and slowly moved himself through the door-frame's open space. But before he was all the way out, he heard it again, this time for certain: laughter.

And not, either, the sort of full-belly gutted-out glee that says, in effect, "We're all in this sorry soup together, pal, and your moment of pain has been and will again be my moment of pain, and this laughter I laugh is purely the laughter of knowing it is a man's sorry lot in this more-often-than-not sorry life to either laugh as I do — and as you should too — or cry." No; this was not empathetic chuckling. This was something else entirely. This was mirth of a more common type, the kind of cackling that is nothing more than (though, to the recipient, nothing less than) contemptuous ridicule filtered through the thin screen of only seeming joviality; in short, a form of jocularity — base in origin, vile in intention — that up-turned mouth corners cannot possibly disguise. Worse, it had come from one of the old men, but not, as might have been tolerable, from Benny.

James's hand still on the handle, nose pointed towards the street, one step, two steps, almost completely out the door, James stiffened, his posture straightening. He carefully closed the door, turned around, and faced the crowd. To M.C., in a surprisingly emotionless voice, "Sit down," he said. "This'll only take a few minutes."

Looking left, behind the counter, "Jeanie," he said, "I need a double Beam, couple of cubes, lime. Just one slice should do it. Throw it right in." He picked up his unfinished beer from where he had set it on a table near the door, lifted the three-quarters-empty bottle, and downed the remains in two equal swallows. "And another one of these when you get a minute, too," he added.

He walked towards the perimeter of the crowd. "You," he said, right into Benny's ready-for-conflict face, "I need outta my fucking way." The old man's fingers were entwined, locked just above his crotch. His work-booted feet stood a solid three feet apart, ready for action.

"You want to rock and roll with me, Grandpa," James continued, "I'm easy enough to find. Just ask the waitress where I live. She'll point you the right way. And another thing," he added, this time James moving in tight so as to be perfectly understood, "how come it's always guys like you who you never for years see with a woman who are always the ones calling somebody else a fag? Huh? Why is that, you think? Think about it, Pops. Just think about, okay?"

Instinctively but (because of his relatively advanced years) with a little bit of help from his head, Benny began to flex and push out all he had, ready for whatever the situation was about to dictate, anything James had to offer. The old suits drew closer; a fight, any fight, better than television and almost as good as the whisky that, for reasons of health only, they no longer permitted themselves.

Benny licked his lips, looked at his cronies looking on with their own wet-lipped anticipation, considered James's steady figure for a moment, stared at the floor a few seconds more, and then, with a weak, back-handed wave of dismissal in James's direction, decided that he thought not after all. Benny's arms loosened, falling slack at his sides, his breathing beginning to normalize. He stepped aside, letting the younger man through the crowd.

James could have been happy with the little victory, but wasn't. He kept moving. Right to the heart of the action. Right to the source.

"And *you*," he said, addressing Melissa for the first time (in the eye or otherwise) since she had held him up in his basement and he had kicked her out, "you I want. . . ."

"Yes?"

"You, I. . . ."

"Yes?" again she said, this time with fluttering-eye mock innocence. If she had had dimples, she probably would have found a way to use them, he thought.

"Ah, just give me the fucking harmonica, would you?"

Each elbow on same-side knee, head cradled in the palm of her left hand, Melissa beamed bright and handed the instrument over. "I thought you'd never ask."

He began to reply, but managed only an under-his-breath "Yeah, right," deciding easily — unexpectedly, joyfully even — otherwise; he knew a better way of saying things. Much better. People get ready, he said inside; here's how James Jr. says what he has to say.

Everything in the restaurant was, for a change, still, the refrigeration unit behind the bar everyone's only hearing (electric purring its always job), human murmuring here and there adding to the soft quiet of it all. Melissa stood up, letting James slide into place on the counter stool.

Warm, he thought.

Comfortabling himself, he sipped at his bourbon, set the glass down between his legs, and pushed his boots hard against the floor under him until the resistance he needed began to push back. Okay, he thought; here we go. He leaned over and brought the instrument in slow inches to his mouth.

Then, out of somewhere, with feeling: "I said, 'She had a gash the size of a mayonnaise jar and it was in 1965! Not that I got a rash and something in my eye! Godohmightee, man! Are you lissening to me now? Lissen! Lissen! You might learn something if you did, you know.'" Immediately, all eyes (excepting Benny's — still staring strong at James) fell to the floor in something not unlike embarrassment, one of the old men near the very back of the pack offering himself over as every musician's right-before-esthetic-point-of-entry nightmare.

But before James had a chance to lose the push of emotion that had put him on the hot seat he was now on (the instrument so close to being blown) — or, worse, had time to find something to count — Melissa shed her nothing-but-Jekyll act and, to James's considerable surprise, showed off some serious Hyde.

"Fuckin' rummy prick bastard, I oughta . . . shhhh now, shhhh, goddamn it." The after-expletive stare she gave the old man would have been enough in itself. Admonished, the ancient offender put a knobby forefinger to his pink lips in a pathetic act of self-censorship and hunched-shouldered himself over to an abandoned booth far from the action. He pretended to read the back of his beer bottle, and clearly hoped one day to be forgiven.

Despite the oafish interruption he had caused, the sort of bar-room buffoonery James had always pet-peeve loathed as typical of your basic philistine drunk, James almost felt sorry for the old man. Poor old guy, he thought, sure got a mouthful. And then some. Boy. Without warning James giggled, then quickly covered his mouth, as if he had just belched in an elevator full of grandmothers.

He looked away from the booth to see Melissa, hands on hips, quite unnecessarily still searing the pitifully contrite old man. Watching her, he lazily scratched his cheek with the Hohner and let his eyes go where they would, from black, pointed shoe-tip to just as black, pushed-up hair-top. He swelled all over with simple appreciation of the artistically empathetic act she had just so heartfelt performed.

A lie: Biology overcame him. He simply swelled.

Directly: Okay (again), he thought: here we go.

The notes that next followed were of themselves not important (amateur musicologists would likely differ as to what exactly that melancholy but sweetly agreeable thing was that James harmonica-played as a preamble to the a cappella version of — not "Lazy Old Home Again" — but, instead, the old hillbilly gospel song "Farther Along"). The simple fact of the matter remained, however, that he had wailed his ass off on the harp (not even one of his strongest instrumental suits) and had rarely sung better. Encouraged, he continued.

Handicapped by the fact that he had only the harmonica to honk on before and after snatches of singing, James made do, the scattered requests he managed to rouse out of the old boys' collective country unconscious the foundation of his impromptu performance: Jones's "White Lightin'", the traditional "I Am a Pilgrim", Acuff's "Will the Circle be Unbroken?", Johnny C.'s "I Still Miss Someone", and, finally, letting M.C. in on the act, an abbreviated "Wild Horses" by the Stones.

Brow-beaded wet in spite of the room's three twirling ceiling fans, James emerged from the songs just discharged happily surprised by the respectful applause and even odd call for just one more that greeted the completion of his announced last number. Uniform ovation, no; but something not unlike general regard, yes. Not that at this point either really mattered much, though; sitting-up-straight polite accolades equalling out to about as much as outright gut-busting ridicule. For, times like this, the music, the playing, the plain music of the music, was the thing. The best thing. The only thing. The thing-in-itself. The thing.

Only an itch to end the evening by mouthing to the hometown crowd a new tune of indigenous sentiment — to sing, even if just for himself, an authentic song of Datum of recent making — kept him from complete musical satiation. The lyrically unstarted but all the same infectious instrumental of late, "Having Snow", came to mind, pregnant with possibility. Words, James thought (longed) . . . words. . . .

Al, his dish of refreshment done by now, bellowed from outside. Like his master (a most economical yapper himself), Buckly's dog was not a dog who barked just to hear his own bark. The rain that had been on everyone's mind all day suddenly fell down steady on a sideways wind on everything of everyone's outside. A few Sunday afterdinner strollers hand in hand on the run searched out King Street storefront canopies; others, the Duke's own M.C. included, shot through assorted shop doors up and down the street, hands on head, to put up car and pickup-truck windows.

"Jeanie?" James said. "Okay if my friend outside comes in for a while? Hears all us big people in here having such a fine time, poor little guy just wants to join in the fun." Jeanie's half-smile said yes, her as-slow shake of her head no; the two gestures put together saying, "If it was my place, James, sure, but it's not my place, you know, so. . . ."

"Tell you what," James added, clearly in his element, enjoying having the floor, "let my pal in for a while and I think you just might be able to coax another tune out of me."

Melissa, delighted just a few seconds before at seeing James's plain satisfaction at playing with himself, now looked with nervous pleading at Buckly standing hands-in-pockets at the back of the crowd.

"Aw, I don't think Mr. Pinnalli'll be coming in tonight, Jeanie," Buckly said, message from Melissa (though who knows, as is invariably the case, if identical to the one sent) received.

A parting of flesh not precipitated by any "excuse mes" or "sorry, pardons" on the parter's part gave Buckly a clear path to the door. "And if the sonofabitch *does* show up," he continued, "I'll buy the joint from him, install a frigging jukebox, and give you your damn job back at twice what you're making now, all right?" He winked at Melissa.

James thought he saw Melissa blush. Incredible.

"Besides," Buckly added, "it's the boy's birthday tomorrow. Least we can do."

Buckly's hand was on the door but, like the gentleman he was, he waited for final permission to yield entry.

Jeanie laughed.

"Oh, let that miserable mutt in, would you? And from what M.C. tells me, I suppose you'll want Garth to fry him up some liver or a pork chop, or maybe a steak with an egg on it, won't you? Spoil that dog something silly every Sunday, he tells me."

"Why, that would be fine, Jeanie," Buckly said, opening the door for his dog and nodding his prepaid thank-you to the cook at Jeanie's side, "that would be just fine."

Al, before entering, respectfully shook himself all over off of the outside elements that had gathered on him; then, as dogs are wont to do, he ambled his cold wet nose (natural) and ass (not) into the warm room like it was nobody's business, a brief sniffing inspection swiftly followed by a four-legged collapsing act beneath the table where the Melissa-chastised oldster still sat. The old man looked under the table at Al, the dog's eyelids already dropping and ready to meet, and then over to the dog's master, with near-puppydog eyes himself.

Buckly looked from animal to elder and saw nothing he didn't particularly dislike. "Hey buddy," he said, "keep an eye on my dog, would you? Don't want that beast running around loose in here. Jeanie'd have my ass in a sling if he did, you know what I mean? Thanks. Appreciate it."

The old man nodded a thousand thankful yeses and bent to pat with four (no right-hand thumb) delicate, ghost-blue, old-man fingers the peak of Al's jet-black head.

"Anybody else want another cold one?" Jeanie all around asked aloud. "Still about forty dollars left on the tab, the way I figure it."

A cheer went up, and the music continued.

29

Success-flushed, and against his better instincts, James had a wonderful idea.

"For this final number, folks, I'll sing this part right here" — he sang the part — "and you all sing together the part I tell you to sing when I say to sing it, okay? And don't be afraid to put your hands together if you feel like it, either, or maybe even bang a bottle or pot-bottom or whatever the spirit moves you to do, all right?" Sure, sure, a big voice answered; whatever you say.

This just simple saying, however, the end result of the group effort being, naturally: missed cues, wrong words carolled, lethargic mouthings, and, most especially, manic real-world re-entry for the stooled one at the front, not at all ready for the usual again so soon. Lingering, fidgeting, then finally breaking, the circle that had been around James suddenly now wasn't.

James put the harmonica in the pocket of his T-shirt, back-handed from his forehead the accumulated sweat of his moment in the fluorescent-bulb sun, picked up the beer from between the legs of the stool, and drank deeply. People, he not kindly considered; give me one real listening listener and you can have every sixteen-thousand-plus seat in every Maple Leaf or Madison Square Garden of the world. And then some.

Soon, with a shout that the regulars knew said she wasn't joking, Jeanie informed the scattering old boys that the milk train had made its final stop, about five minutes ago, in fact, and that tap water was all she was serving up. "Closing time!" she called out. "Hotel time!" Without hesitation, the old men began their way towards the door in somewhat orderly single file, swaying and tottering, weaving and wobbling, no good-nights to anyone offered, staff or other, because soon it would again be time to say, Good evening, how are you? and Wasn't that something last night? and Got a smoke? Left mine back at the room.

Benny was the only straggler, thumb-twirling, sitting by himself at the counter while the others dispersed. "Gotta go to the can, Jeanie," he announced, rising from his stool. Stuck up in his right armpit was a paper grocery bag.

"Well, hurry it up. I'm locking up as soon as I can get this sty under control."

"No sweat." James watched Benny try to contain a slight smile as he proceeded past him on the way to the bathroom.

Standing behind the counter, forking down a slice of two-day-old banana meringue pie that Jeanie was just going to have to throw out anyway, M.C. said, "What's in the bag?"

"Birthday present," Benny answered immediately. "For a friend. Had it with me when I got here tonight. On account of me seeing him later tonight and not wanting to have to go home and get it before I head on over there."

M.C. lifted his eyes from an obstinate piece of pie crust that kept breaking apart every time he attempted to spear it up. "Free country," he said. "Just asking."

"Well, I'm gonna go to the washroom and then I'll be on my way," Benny replied.

"Make it snappy, all right? We don't want to be here all night," M.C. said.

"Oh, I'll be gone before you know it."

Sucking only suds now, James put his empty beer bottle on the floor. Resting his elbows on his thighs, he hung his head deep. Subsequently: signal of shadow falling across his crossed limbs. Head up, head cleared, eyes focused: Huh?

"Sonofabitches, eh? Sonofabitches all the time everywhere, wouldn't you say?" Not in a fashion angry, as James at that moment might have said it, but more in the manner of one not happy about (but at the same time not surprised by) inefficient vending machines, idiotic motorists, dim yet surly bureaucrats, unappreciative audiences, and, generally, the more or less second-rate state of a humanity all too much at large. Melissa stood alone before James, expertly tottering softly on the back of her high black pumps, arms locked behind her head very attractively, very much unladylike.

Understandably wary, yet appreciative of the effort, not to mention the view, "Yeah, well, what can you do?" James offered, palms up and open as he said it. "Comes with the job."

"You make music, cowboy, that's your end of the bargain. And your job is done for the night. And done good, too." Swaying with authority forward, settling flat on her heeled feet, hands entwined at waist level behind her back, Melissa leaned over and kissed the surprised singer on the tip of his nose. Like a fifty-five-year-old whore blowing the nose of an orphan. Or maybe, just maybe, like a kiss on the tip of the nose.

"Let me get my stuff and we'll be out of here in a sec, okay?" she said. James nodded, okayed back without hesitation. Screen shot. One-timer. Didn't see it coming. Hundred miles an hour. Before you know it, upper right corner, bulging twine, flashing red light, roar of the crowd, no chance at all. None. Yep, there it is: goal.

Waiting for Melissa, James watched Jeanie pick up empty bottles and full ashtrays while wet-ragging all over the room, M.C. in tow right behind her in absurd, up-to-elbow yellow rubber gloves, carrying a plastic red tub of soapy water. They worked together virtually without speaking or stopping, each knowing the other's moves and what came next, the work getting done with surprising efficiency. Periodically, M.C. would lean over his wife's wiping shoulder and mouth-to-ear whisper something that without fail would make her laugh. James envied his friend his function.

"It's gone," Melissa, appearing, said.

"What's that?"

"My box. It's gone."

"Hold on. Your box?"

"Oh, for Christ's sake, cowboy, my lunchbox. Somebody took it."

"No. Who would have taken it?" James said. What a stupid thing to say, he thought; anybody could have taken it.

"Anybody could have taken it, I don't know. One of those bastards out there stumbling home down King Street at this very moment, I suppose. Typical. Why expect anything else? Spend a hundred dollars to get a roomful of men drunk and what do you get in return? Your handbag stolen. Typical."

"You wanna go look for it? I mean, most of them probably went to Tim Horton's for coffee and day-old crullers."

"Oh, let's just go. What was in it it looks like I don't need any more, anyway. And thank God they didn't get this," she said, holding up the manila-wrapped package James had earlier seen sitting on the counter. "Besides, what's a hundred blown bucks to a rich old broad like me?"

Like the old-world bride and groom read about in history books and magazine tabloids (introduced for the first time only a few hours before they are to be wed; sneaking mutual peeks soon after the knotting has been done; nervous, hand-in-hand walking down the aisle afterward),

James and Melissa, more or less in step, were on their way.

"Good-night, you two," Jeanie said, looking up from the stack of dirty ashtrays she was attacking with elbow-raised scouring tenacity behind the counter. "Drive safe."

"Yeah," M.C. added, assaulting the left-over chips and pretzels Jeanie had doggy-bagged for later at home, "don't let us hold you up, James."

James, just a little, grinned.

"C'mon, Al, let's go," Melissa said, slapping her thigh. Al stood up, stretching, a furry black hot rod, back end up, nose to the ground. After: a yawn like a bored school-girl on helium. "What's going on? Where's my Uncle Buckly?" James asked.

"While you were kind enough to entertain us all, he said that on account of what looked to be the game being rained out, he was going to call on a friend downtown instead. He said to apologize to you for slipping out a little early."

"Damn. I forgot to ask him about the. . . . Damn."

"Ask him about what?"

"Just something I need to get from him."

"Something important?

"Something that's been coming my way for a while now. Yeah, I guess you could say important. Something I need."

"Oh," Melissa said, lips spreading into an almost smile.

James gave her a quizzical look. "Say who he was going to visit?" he asked.

"Someone named Red."

Again James grinned. Just call me Chuckles tonight, he thought.

"He asked if we could save him a trip and take Al home and put him inside. He said you knew where the key was."

"Yeah, I know where it is."

"All right, then," Melissa said, scooping up James's hand in hers. "Good-night, Jeanie! Good-night, M.C.! Thanks for everything! Thanks for all your help!"

"Night, you guys," James said. He saw M.C. staring at their entwined hands. On his way out the door he could only, after due consideration, look back over his shoulder and shrug. His friend smiled back, shrugging too.

"Night," Jeanie called out. "It's still spitting a little bit out there, so drive safely!" she said, but too late, she could see, for the departing couple to hear.

30

Melissa unlatched the hinged door to the bed of her pickup truck and slapped the blue metal compartment a couple times for encouragement. "Up, Al," she said. None really needed, up Al went. She lifted the door back up, locked it, and pulled on it twice, just to be sure. "Can't say I have much experience with dogs. Think he'll be all right back here like this?"

"Oh, sure," James said, watching Al, nose to the truck-bed floor, sleuthing out the canine-choiced best spot to settle down, "he'll love it. Loves to sit in the front seat of my uncle's car and hang his head out the window and get a good breeze on him. No problem."

"Okay, well, door's unlocked. I gotta get the spare key under the hood. Damn rummies."

The slightly loony flow of one thing after another of late momentarily ceasing with only the lifted blue hood of the truck offered as a view, an unusual and obliged moment alone gave James pause. But before the unexpected, nearly funky mood of recent linked-limb moments could dissolve in the acid of self-reflection (Why am I bothering to take time to return my Uncle Judas's canine while he gets his prehistoric rocks off? Why am I not somewhere else, gathering important things — the Thing, for example — in preparation for urgent musical statements? And, more pressing still: What am I doing alone in this pickup with this crazy fucking harpy?), the hood came halfway down and a big black sky with just-starting electric flecks opened up all around him.

Involuntarily slumping, cracking with his hands and a leaning-back motion the small of his back just because it felt good, James observed, Sorta pretty, isn't it? That and, through the slightly raindrop-streaked windshield, Melissa examining by moonlight — one eye open along the shaft of the short, grease-smeared dipstick — whether or not the truck needed oil. Deciding it didn't, she plunged the rod back into place, slamming the hood in quick succession. Distractions: beautiful, beautiful distractions.

Melissa got in the cab, put the package she had carried with her from the Duke on the dash, and turned the just-fetched key in the ignition. The truck still in park, she played with the windshield wipers, looking for that just-right swipe of rubber rod on glass. Finding what she was looking for (medium speed; no fluid), sideways she said, "I guess you're probably pissed at me, right?"

"No. No, not particularly. Why?" Not waiting for a response, "Hey, what kind of tunes you got in here besides yours truly's?" Riffling through the clutter on the dashboard, James uncovered a couple of Dwight Yoakam tapes ("Positively droopy-eyed fucky," Melissa had described him as earlier in the weekend), some early k.d. lang, a slightly battered homemade cassette with the hand-printed title *Lovin' Music* on it, and something by something called The Catatonic Farmboys. He considered his options.

The lang was iffy, the latter two tapes not even alternatives; like a contented, couple-days-into-it drunk, he wanted only co-operation from his environment, nothing more, though nothing less. And although as a general rule distrustful of musicians in any genre who could be described as handsome (himself, of course, excluded), he stuffed the Yoakam in the tape deck and hoped for at least a tasteful cover tune. Just keep the ball rolling.

He got what he wanted. A duet with Buck Owens, "Streets of Bakersfield", jumped out of the truck's speakers, filling the cab with agreeably screeching steel, thumping bass guitar, and quick, snapping snare-drum shots. James harmonized along with the introductory steel guitar part, slapping simple rhythm on his thigh for accompaniment. "C'mon, let's get this show on the road," he said. "Homeward-bound animal in the back, remember?" Melissa smiled at her passenger and put it in reverse. They were moving.

In time, "Got any booze in here?" James asked.

"Didn't get your fill at the Duke?"

"As a matter of fact, no. Late start, you know."

"Right," Melissa said. "Well, no, I don't, to tell you the truth. What say we lay off the sauce for a while, anyway?" Right to left, unspoken astonishment shot through the truck.

"Oh, unfurrow thy brow, lover," she said. Crotch high, she unceremoniously back-handed dragged her non-steering hand a couple times across his thigh. "Just for the time being, I mean. Celebratory consumables will be shared this evening, that's a promise. It's just that . . . there's this thing I want to do with you first, and I don't want the moment, you know, spoiled by either of us not being capable of fully appreciating it. Okay?"

O . . . kay. Let's see what we've got here, James thought. Admittedly, yes, this teetotalling bit was a tad confusing, but, given her track record, not particularly disturbing. Paraphernalia-assisted carnal hi-jinks, perhaps? he mused, one eyebrow raised, considering the wrapped package covering the air-vent on the dash. Then again, maybe she's got something stronger than alcohol in mind for later. Do you think? And if she's holding, should I? Sure, why not? he decided at once — sooner, in fact. Why the hell not? He turned up the music slightly and slid down farther in his seat. He put his feet up on the dash. Just why the hell not?

Soon, making their one-way way down King Street on the rural route to Buckly's place. And even with the slight buzz he had accumulated at the Duke beginning to mute out, and dry mouth, he knew, forthcoming, the truck was not sitting still and the music was all right after all and . . . and, well, nothing. Nothing at all. Nothing. Go. Just go.

"Mind if I sing along with the tape? Realize, of course, nowhere near as fucky as droppy ol' Sir Dwight, but do believe I can keep up lungwise, nonetheless."

"You're the one, lover."

"All right then. Here we go."

Had it been possible for him to drop down any farther in his seat, he would have. It wasn't, though, so he just sang, closing his eyes tight, opening his mouth wide, and singing the hell out of the song at hand. Intoned in a fashion that would suggest that the words he sang actually meant something to him, had some relevance to the kind of life he led, James sweetly no-brained it all the way through. As is true in so much in love and art, knowing not being absolutely necessary, just, really, the absolute necessity of *knowing*.

Fiddle jumping, cackling, laughing (pure bow joy), the song, unavoidably, wound down. Fade-out. Tape hiss. Done.

Sensations, not one, pressed themselves upon James's ears or eyes. Bubbling silence where he sat in the truck. Just: waiting. Waiting. Any second now another song. To sing. A song. Hum? Hmm? Hum? Yass, why not? Hum. Hmmmmmmmm. . . .

"But, I mean, I *did* say some things."

Slap, whack, hack — damn! What? (Two minutes for interference! Go directly to the penalty box! No lip along the way, either!) Hey! Music! I was listening to I was singing I was waiting for I was gonna hum I was humming I — "What?" James said, jolted.

"I mean, I could understand it if you were a little bit upset."

"About what?"

"Like, oh, I don't know, telling your uncle I was doing an article on you for the Datum paper, for one. So he would tell me stuff. I had planned on making a point of bumping into you in Toronto this fall, and I thought I could use all the up-close biographical help I could get if I was going to do my best to help you out. But then he said you'd called and said you were coming back to town for a while, and, well, here we are."

"Yeah. Here we are."

"And you're not mad?"

Pronounced cotton mouth now, licking of lips, sighing, speaking (slowly), "Ah . . . well, no harm done, I guess. He said he liked you. Said . . . you made good tofu or something. Yeah. Extending his culinary dimensions. Sure. Good for you. Turn left here at the lights. First road you see is the one we're looking for."

"I've been to your uncle's house before."

"Riiiight. Right. That would make sense. Because you talked to him." As much as he tried, the now resumed music was simply not enough. "This Yoakam's okay, isn't he? Got anything else by him, or—"

"Or telling your friend Jeanie we were engaged? That kind of thing, I guess, is what I'm talking about."

Deep breath, rise and fall of chest. Leaning forward, James turned up the music and leaned back. Then, leaning forward again, he turned up the music again, the knob incapable this time of going any farther to the right. "You think you might stop talking long enough for me to listen to this goddamn tape of yours?" he snapped above the twangy blare. Yoakam. Fucking torn-jeaned poser. Hollywood fuck. Fuck.

RAY ROBERTSON

Before she could answer, however: in the headlights on the right-hand shoulder of the gravel road they were looking for, the one that led to Buckly's house, an old boy from the Duke both James and Melissa recognized but neither knew the name of. With his right hand he pulled tight to his neck the upturned lapels of his thin yellow and brown pin-striped suit jacket; with his left, in straight-arm fashion, he held out Melissa's lunchbox (in each truck-traveller's head an unspoken image of a monster-movie ghost in dead-of-night, beginning-to-rise fog, with an outstretched arm holding a cautionary lantern, the other arm protecting the spook from nature's potential doom).

"Shit, it's my box. He's got my box," Melissa said, putting on the blinker, pulling the truck over.

Wet cinders crackled and popped in egg-in-frying-pan imitation under the weight of the truck's tires. Crickets in the dark beside the road supplied the only other sound. James rolled his window all the way down, the truck slowing to a complete stop. The after-rain air was sickly clammy, warm. The old man, standing beside the truck, curved over, making his face level with James's.

In a hushed voice, "Just so you know, young man, I didn't want to have anything to do with it," he said. "He made me, you see. Simply would not take no for an answer, I tell you. After he discovered your destination, you understand."

"I beg your pardon?" James said. The old man was only a foot and a half away, but was barely audible.

"I don't know what disagreement it is you two share, and I imagine it's none of my damn business, of course (excuse my French, please), and I'm sure you two will work it out like gentlemen, naturally, but I just want you to know, regardless, that I appreciate an entertainer such as yourself. Truly, I do!"

"All right," James said, not sure what else to say.

"You wanna grab my box when you get a minute?" Melissa said. "Maybe you two can get together later for

192

coffee or something, and discuss things in depth then."

James gave her a look, then turned back to the old man, motioning with his eyes towards Melissa's box. "Did you bring that for us? I — we — really appreciate it." Slope-shouldered, the old man blinked a couple of times but didn't move.

"Yeah, well, thanks again," James said, dangling an expectant arm out of the window.

The old man gave a quick look into the black wall of bush bordering the road behind him. Then in a voice even quieter than before, almost a whisper, "Good luck, young man," he said. "I hope all goes well with you. I do, really." Another swift, over-the-shoulder glance. "I was an enter-tainer of sorts myself, you know, at one time." In spite of the muggy evening, cold fingertips rose and rested icily on James's shoulder. "Yes indeed. When I lived in Toronto, you see, in the 1940s, up there doing construction work with my older brother Peter, I used to take my violin down to Queen's Park on Saturday nights if the weather was nice and maybe if—"

In a flash, all heads turned to see a flat-footed, twig-snapping, huffing and puffing linebacker charge from the bush: hairy apparition; swelling intruder; Bigfoot in a too-tight T-shirt and discount work boots. "All right, all right. Your job is done here, Jerry. Hit the road," it said.

"Now, just hold on a second, would you, and—"

"Yeah, yeah. Go tell it to the marines."

An indignant finger straight up in the air and a sec-ond's consideration of what he wanted to say; then, re-considering, a little half-wave in James's direction and Jerry, hands deep in pockets, took the first steps of a long walk home. Just as quickly, turning around in the middle of the road ten or so feet behind the truck, he lifted Melissa's box as high as he could. "But Benny!" he said. "I forgot to give the young lady her purse back!"

"Lose it."

"But Benny, the young lady *did* spend an awful lot of

money on all of us at the Duke, and—"

"Lose it, Jerry."

"But Benny, the young lady might have valuables in—"

"Lose it, I said!" Benny yelled, just out of James's sight, jabbing an arm in Jerry's direction.

Red-spotted blotched and bony-knuckled hand to mouth, Jerry gasped, big-eyed seeing something James could not. The old man stood still for a few seconds, facing the rear end of the vehicle, staring at whatever it was. "Oh, Benny" finally all he could say, sighing as he said it. He hurled the box into the bush as far as his toothpick arm would allow. He turned around slowly in the gravel road and set out again on his way back home. This time he didn't stop. James, Melissa, and Benny watched him until he was nothing.

Taking Jerry's place beside the truck, "Get out," Benny said. James craned his neck out of the window far enough to confirm what he feared to be at the end of Benny's L-shaped arm. He slowly drew his head back into the truck and looked for more than a second or two across the front seat at Melissa.

"It's not loaded, right?" he asked.

"Well. . . . "

He looked at Benny smiling at him, then back at her.

"Well. . . ," she said.

"Well what?"

"I told you the other night there were still things we had to discuss."

"And?"

"And . . . I wasn't sure how much persuasion you might need to go into them tonight."

James looked at her again, then at Benny, then got out of the truck. Al, awakened now from his liver-dinner nap, stood, stretched, and sat most properly, lip-licking watching the two men.

"Grandpa my ass," Benny snorted, pushing by James.

He gave Al a wary little study, then stepped into the truck. "Rock and roll with you, eh?"

James looked off into the bush, his mind furious to compute so much cricketing. If one sound equalled just one insect, why, must be a million of them out there, he reasoned. Where would a guy even begin to begin?

31

Resumption of enumeration neurosis noted, James had little time for discomforting introspection, no matter how strong the impetus. Melissa, as all along, sat on the driver's side of the truck, James squeezed as tight against the passenger door as she was against hers. Benny sat between the two of them, much of the lower part of him spilled over the middle section of the seat, slabs of big blue-jeaned-butted him flowing over and onto the hard-muscled, cheek-pulling-away shore of each sequestered island on either side of the cab. Both of the outsiders looked to the one in the middle. He in turn stared a good bit at each of them. Finally, with a open-handed slap on the dash obviously intended to startle James, Benny announced, "Starterup, sweetheart! And let the good times roll!" He slid a half-pint of Canadian Club from out of his back pocket with his non-gun-holding hand and unscrewed the brown plastic cap with his teeth.

"Meaning?" Melissa said, clearly having none of this.

"Meaning, put the fucking key in the fucking ignition and start fucking driving until I tell you when to fucking stop." He tilted back his head and took a sharp pull from the bottle. Next: gargle, belch, and glare in James's face for effect. James forced himself to stare right straight back.

"And where exactly would that *fucking* be?" Melissa persisted. Pluck, James thought, succumbing to a smirking tug at the corners of his mouth. Give the girl that much. She does have, well . . . pluck.

"Well, I guess that's for me to know and for you to find out, isn't it now?"

"Oh, for Christ's sake," she said, giving her gun in Benny's hand a thoughtful once-over before inevitably, if languidly, doing as she had been directed.

Each of the three occupied thus, a solid half-hour of country-road-rambling time passed. Then, but for the one in the middle (gun-gloating satisfied to be imagined a BAD MAN), an unexpected and, to James, even oddly disappointing turn of mind: boredom.

"So. It's your birthday tomorrow," Melissa said.

"Yeah, I guess it is," James replied.

Silence.

"Twenty-five big ones, huh?"

"Sure thing. Twenty-five years old."

More silence.

"Any big plans?"

"Naw. Just get this, ah, certain thing from my uncle that I've been waiting on for a while and, you know, hang around the house a bit, I guess. Get some work done. Nothing special. You know."

"Sure."

More more silence.

"Yep," James said, "twenty-five big ones. How'd you know?"

"I know a lot about you, cowboy."

"Yeah, I guess you do, don't you?" Each looked across and around the big thing between them and gave up to the other an almost bashful grin.

More, almost pleasant (the comfortable kind of) silence.

"So, I take it you're not too mad at me then? For some of the stuff I said?"

"I don't know, you know? I was? I am? Some of the stuff you did, too, I guess. I guess I should be. . . . Should be what? I don't know."

"Understandable, cowboy, understandable. I have to admit, for being such a serious player, you're not the most reflective guy I've ever met."

"Hey now, what's—"

"Hey now your damn selves, for Christ's sake," Benny burst in. "And can the damn gibbering, all right? This ain't no frigging joy-ride." He raised the gun off his knee and made jerky motions in each passenger's direction to em-phasize his point. Too hurriedly, though, he brought the whisky up to his lips to punctuate his pistol-power play, chipping two front teeth on the lip of the bottle in the proc-ess. He tongued with a grimace the newly jagged edges, pushing the gun a couple more times in James's direction as counsel against anything other than deferential silence.

For some reason, neither was much convinced. Within minutes: "So, I'm a rich woman today," Melissa said.

"I kind of got the drift of that. Your uncle . . ."

"Albert."

"Yeah, right, your Uncle Albert. He, um, pass on?" James asked. The cab dark but for the green glow sup-plied by the instrument panel, all eyes followed the truck's headlights on the little else but darkness and dirt roads they drove.

"Early this morning, my mum said. I know I should know better, but kind of a shock, actually."

"Sounded pretty much expected from what you told me. And you know, no offence, but you didn't exactly seem choked up at the prospect of the whole thing."

"Oh yeah, I know. And you wouldn't believe how much I'm looking forward to getting out of this damn town and using the time the money is going to buy me this fall in TO. And I never really cared for the man. Not really.

Always found him kind of creepy, to tell you the truth. But after all that hullabaloo he'd raised about herbal cures, Hamilton miracle treatments, and the ultimate terror of the slow withering death, I find out today that he ends up dying in the same bed he'd been sleeping in night in, night out, for the last thirty-five years. And with the Blue Jays' pre-game show on the radio and a stack of girlie magazines at his elbow. Same as it ever was. And way before he ended up needing any of the really heavy drugs to fight off the pain, too. Nurse told my mum, 'Full control of his faculties, not much pain at all, went in his sleep, no last words.'"

Neither said anything. Then: "But isn't that always the way though, cowboy?"

"Sorry?"

"I mean, what else have I been saying and trying to show you in my own inimitable way the past couple of days, right?"

No longer looking at the unfolding late-evening road — head turned, eyes around Benny to Melissa's dark profile — "Sorry, don't follow you," James said.

"Oh, come on, cowboy, there comes a time, right? Comes a time, lover, comes a time."

"Look," James said, "I honestly don't know what you've been trying to tell me all weekend, but I've got a pretty good hunch what you've been up to. And I guess now is as good a time as any to make absolutely clear my disapproval of anyone — you included — who tries to horn in on my story-telling stake. I put in a claim to the tales of the Thompson clan a long time ago, and I have artistic, not to mention professional, reasons for being a tad protective, okay? My strike, understood? That said, you're young and pretty on the ball, and I'm sure one day soon you'll find your own—"

"No, no, look—" Melissa jumped in. James traffic-copped his hand in the air, stopping her protest at once.

"—your own individual way artistically. Title to your

own claim, so to speak. That said, I'm willing to put the incidents of recent memory down to you simply being a little esthetically inexperienced. And while that may be the case, I . . . I—"

"No, cowboy, no. Listen—" Again James with the solemn raised hand.

"No, you listen, Melissa." (The name, the first time uttered aloud out of his mouth, sounded foreign, exotic, profoundly erotic to his ear.) "What I guess I mean to say is, I guess I . . . I guess I'm not completely unamused by it all, after all, okay? I mean, it hasn't been boring with you being around these past couple of days. And . . . that's good. I kinda like that, okay?"

For several long seconds Melissa feigned concentration on her driving. James, tired of looking at the side of her head, looked down at the gun in Benny's hand instead. Benny continued to look directly out the windshield.

"I meant it as a compliment," James said.

Another country concession done, Melissa slapped on the turn signal, a little harder than was necessary. Click. Click. Click. Click. James cleared his throat. The turn signal snapped off on its own. Benny gurgled from his bottle of whisky. Another no-end-in-sight road began. This is ridiculous, James thought. "It's a good thing, okay?" he said. "I've kind of got a bad history sometimes of getting . . . sort of . . . well, distracted by things. Caught up in stuff that's dumb to think about. Like today, for instance, thinking about things I shouldn't be thinking about and not doing what I'm supposed to be doing, writing songs, making music. You've helped keep me occupied, anyway. That's good." Nothing. He grew nostalgic for the noise of the turn signal.

"Not even a little curiosity?" she said at last.

"Well, no, not particularly. Not after I realized what you were up to."

Her attention still on the road, Melissa sighed her shoulders up, then down. "I mean, I did detain you naked at gunpoint," she said. Benny's eyelashes slid in unison over to Melissa's side of the seat.

"It wasn't loaded," James answered.

"It could've been!"

"Yeah, well."

"What about the picture? Ever get one like that before?"

"Well, again, no offence, but a vagina is a vagina is a vagina, right?" Benny's lashes shifted from left to right.

Silence. Pouting. Melissa, silent, pouting.

"I'm sorry. I mean, there was the quote, I guess," James offered.

"That's right!" she said. "That's right! What about the Freud?" Benny's lashes crossed, his forehead wrinkled, eyes squinted.

"I suppose there could be some . . . deeper meaning there that I guess I could have missed."

"Okay," she said hopefully.

"Maybe some . . . metaphor or . . . "

"Yes? Yes? Keep going."

"A metaphor . . . for—"

"All right! All right! Enough!" Benny roared, resentful of the increasingly incomprehensible nature of what had started as some pretty okay smut talk. "This ain't no damn confession booth, okay?"

"Well, just what the hell is it, then, Benny?" Melissa said, anger over the unresolved ambiguity of her Jamesian intentions fuelling her kidnapped-ass fire. "Frankly, I think we're all just a little bit sick and tired of this back-road deal, and more than a little curious as to what your plans for the evening are. Out with it. We've got less than a quarter of a tank of gas left. Some decisions have to be made soon about your criminal intentions."

Spine-straightening affront; rickety gun pointing left and right; panic, like a pig wise to the slaughter, in the big man's little eyes. "Don't you be telling me what has to be done!" he said. "I'm the one holding all the cards here, ain't I?" As proof of his words, he shook the gun at Melissa, then James, then back at Melissa again, his best BAD GUY glare lost on each, neither buying, neither breaking his stare. He grabbed the bottle of whisky out of his back pocket, drank sloppily deep, stuck it about halfway back but (clearly feeling on either side of him an eye-ball vise tightening by the second) decided to keep it out after all, the gun now in one hand, the bottle (cap on, but loose) in the other.

Sensing weakness, a moment of opportunity at hand, James could only steal an anxious glance Melissa's way, and she at him. One thing to knock the gun out of the hand of a straddling, bare-bottomed teenager confused in her do-gooding ways; a whole different level of foul play altogether when the foul one with the weapon is an alcohol-punctured fat man bent on bad things not even he knows what. Soon, he and she, like the other he in the middle, peered at the road straight ahead. The indeterminacy of the moment gave James a clean, visceral rush in the pit of his stomach.

Blind to the couple's behind-his-head exchanges, Benny pecked away at the whisky, just as unconsciously running the barrel of the gun a few times back and forth across his greasy forehead, as if the answer to Now what? might somehow emerge there if he scratched at it deeply enough. He saw that there really was less than a quarter of a tank of gas left.

Then, another little swig sucked, the bottle leaving his lips, out of the corner of his eye Benny saw what he was doing, saw the head-scratching gun pointed at his head, nearly blowing his brains out in the panicked process — the gun up up and away in his fast-forward levitating hand, the thing at the end of his arm a snake, a turd, another man's dick, a thing, anyway, that he couldn't in that instant believe was actually there.

The end of the barrel thudded against the metal roof top. Long metallic waves of *pah-nnnnnnggg* sounded throughout the otherwise silent cab. Two hands on the weapon now, Benny slowly pulled the pistol down and pointed it at a space of floormat between his legs. A single bead of perspiration escalated down his three chins, hanging for a second on the last one, dropping at last in a tiny splash of salty maturity onto the blue vinyl seatcover. Faint, dying threads of *pah-nnnnnnggg* provided the only background sound to the stares of disbelief all around. A few long seconds of this and then, all together now:

"For Christ's sake would you—"

"Hey! Hey! Hey! Hey!"

"Watch that thing or—"

"For fuck's sake be—"

(Two wheels of the truck on the edge of the drainage ditch on the right-hand side of the road; next, wildly out of the ditch; next, on the wrong-hand side of the road; next, smack dab in the middle; next, back almost in the ditch again; next, numerous frenzied et ceteras).

Awhooooooo!

"Shut the damn dog up or—"

"Al? Al!"

Awhoooooo! Awhoooooooooooooo!

"Hey, I said! Hey! Hey!"

"You—"

"I—"

"She—"

"Dog—"

"All right! All right! Allll-riiight!" Benny shouted above the others. Gun out from down below and breast-level high in front of him (but still held in both hands), Benny was desperate to steady everything down, slow the pace, get back to life like before (quiet cruising, bottle sucking, BAD MAN–glaring). His eyes wildly scanned the cab. "What's this?" he snarled, pointing the pistol at the manila-wrapped package on the dashboard.

"None of your business," Melissa snapped.

A smile drifted up his bearded cheeks. The creases in

his forehead slightly smoothed out. "Well, well, well," he said. "Hit a bit of a sore spot, have we?"

"Don't, Benny."

"Don't you don't me, missy. What's in the package?"

"Look, if she doesn't want to tell you what's in the—"

"Oh, standing up for your lady friend now, are you? B-you-t-full. Brings a tear to my eye. Really." He took a big gulp of whisky, lifted his head coyote-like (eyes and pistol all the while on James), and gargled the beginning notes to "O Canada." Done, he gulped. "Awwhh, the pause that refreshes." James shook his head a slow couple of times, then stretched across Benny for the package on the middle of the dash.

Not with the gun, but with his other hand clamped onto the wrist of James's grabbing hand, Benny stopped the younger man in mid-reach. James's face grew tight, sharp bones sprouting underneath his flesh, the veins in his neck miniature blue rivers. Not moving, matching Benny eye for an eye, "Take your hand off me, fat man," he said. Back on familiar territory now, Benny squeezed at the other man's wrist harder, comfortable enough to even bring the gun up to James's temple with confidence.

"Takes a bit to get you angry, doesn't it, Mr. Singerman? Hard to get your goat. But you're quite the man of action when somebody finally lights a fire underya, ain't ya? Eh? Eh?" He pressed the gun into James's skull like he was grinding out a cigarette. "Eh?" For the first time since the three of them had first sat where they were sitting, James (and Melissa too) felt more than simply inconvenienced; a drunk with a gun was clearly running the show.

The open end of the gun barrel turning slowly clockwise, then counter-clockwise, in the soft skin of the side of his head, James could feel a faint indentation being made there, about the size of a dime. He could also feel his scrotum tighten, and feared (for he had seen such things happen in the movies) that he would at any moment wet himself (or worse), and right in front of Melissa, too.

In a low, flat voice, Melissa said, "It's a video, all right, Benny? Just a video. That's all." Pluckless, James thought. Never heard her so, well . . . pluckless. He constricted each of his waste-making orifices, growing suddenly interested — intensely so — in the question of cinematic verisimilitude.

Gleamingly pleased with the fear he was clearly putting into James, Benny turned his head towards Melissa. "Okay," he said, "now we're getting somewhere. A video of what?" James looked at the package on the dash and wondered, despite the weapon at his temple, the same thing.

"If I tell you, will you put the gun down?"

"Sure, sure."

Melissa looked hard at the road unfolding in front of her, and then briefly at James held hostage on the other side of the cab. "Okay," she said, "it's a video. Of me. Now put the gun down, all right?"

"Not so fast now. What kind of video of you?" He took a quick gulp from the bottle.

Looking at her captor, then at James, she answered, "It's James's birthday tomorrow, and I. . . ."

"Yeah, yeah, go on, go on, and you what?" Without breaking his watch over Melissa, and more out of simple excitement than as an act of intimidation, Benny ground the gun a little deeper into James's forehead, raising the bottle to his mouth at the same time.

Alarmed at the effect Melissa's tale was having on his would-be executioner, James was ready to offer appropriate protest when he saw Melissa shoot him (in the two or three seconds Benny's eyes shut tight for a long gulp of whisky) the time-honoured, accomplice-in-shenanigans wink and knowing slow nod of head. NO (his mouth a perfect three-minute egg), he mouthed. YES, she head-bobbed back. Brief consideration of the grinding gun at his head, and the soused gun-holder's increasingly slip-shod manner, and YES, James finally thought. At least worth a shot, anyway. He could feel the adrenalin pumping through his veins.

Eyes open now and trying to focus, "Whew!" Benny blew, a sordid athlete's way to say that a second wind appearance must soon be made, unrealized as of yet stamina positively necessary if the booze was going to keep going down and the eyelids were going to remain open. Alcohol sweat began to form on his forehead and below the beard-line jowl. Gun and bottle loose-limbed dripped from left and right hand. Like a sparring partner tired of dipsy-doodling for too many rounds, the whisky out of nowhere had landed him one hell of a good one, a clear shot directly to the brain pan.

"And, um. . . . Oh yeah, okay, yeah," Benny said, finding the slender thread of logic he had been clutching for. "And you what? Yeah, you what? You what then?"

"I told you," Melissa said. "I made him a movie . . . of me."

"Yeah yeah yeah?"

"This isn't easy for me, I. . . ."

"Go on, go on, you're doing all right. Doing all right. So you made a movie of you doing what then, huh? Maybe something that ol' Mr. Singer-man over here could have a little look-see at when he's out on the road with the boys?" Nestling the gun (barrel pointing downward) between his legs, Benny slapped hard James's left thigh without looking at him, retrieving the weapon from between his thighs swiftly after doing so. "For them long nights alone out there with just him and the boys on the bus?" Rubbing the red sting out of his upper thigh, James knew he could have (probably should have) chanced it right there. As best he could, peripherally (eyes ostensibly straight ahead on the road) James watched and waited.

"Maybe something like that," Melissa answered.

"Oh, I bet, sweetheart, I just bet it's something like that." Bringing the whisky to his lips, Benny nearly missed his mouth, the bottle saved from colliding with his face by a last-second, wrist-flicking manoeuvre. Pleased, he pursued his line.

"Maybe we should have a little look at this little this little thing here, huh? What you say to that, huh?" James's body tensed, teased by opportunity.

"Oh, no, Benny, please, it's all too personal to just—"

"Personal-shmersonal. Which one of you two little fucks' got one of them there outfits that plays these tape things?"

"My parents do, Benny, but—"

"Then that's the place you're gonna take us to, missie, that's just the place." Then louder, with — finally — purpose: "'Cause it's show time, kiddies!"

A thousand-pound bumble-bee buzz now in residence between his ears, Benny, like many a drunk before him fallen as deep into his cups as he, had become sloppily touchy-feely. After Melissa turned the truck around in the empty road and started off at twenty miles below the speed limit in the general direction of her parents' house, he announced afresh, "Yes, indeed! Show time!" and, slap-happy, tucked the gun between his legs, again whacking James on the thigh with an open-handed slap. But this time, instead of right away retrieving the pistol, he paused with his right hand on James's thigh to kill with his upraised other arm the last shot or two in the whisky bottle.

Sideways-eyed, James saw a door, if not exactly open, at least there for the kicking-in. Hesitating only slightly, he braced himself for the more than theoretical possibility of one heck of a big bang.

32

The wound was superficial and could be treated at home. More like a bad burn than an actual bullet wound, the doctor pulling night duty at the hospital informed James and Melissa more than once.

Bad hand medicated and bandaged, but before the doctor had a chance to write out a prescription for the medication that would be necessary for a safe and speedy recovery, a very large woman with an irregular heartbeat, a failed, fallen black permanent, running mascara, and an enormous DON'T WORRY, BE HAPPY nightgown burst through the emergency-room doors and demanded the entire night shift's attention. Acquiescing to medical urgency, James and Melissa allowed themselves to be shuffled off by one of the nurses to the magazine-splattered waiting-room.

Soon, unsated by one-handed flipping through two-year-old *Golf Digest*s and even older *Women's World*s (all the good quizzes already filled in), James excused himself in the name of having to take a leak.

"Do you need a hand?" Melissa, yawning, too pooped to pun, said. "I mean, because of your hand?"

Yawning himself, standing up swaying-tired, James said no. Leaving the room, then stopping and turning around in the waiting-room doorway, he added, "But thanks for offering." Slid deep into a yellow plastic-cushioned seat, one arm draped over her eyes, Melissa sent him away without looking, with a lazy, congenial wave. "No problem."

He wandered the length of the hospital's first floor, finding, at the end of the hall by the closed gift shop, a postcard machine. He fed in fifty cents, picked his post-card out of the silver metal slot (mid-seventies shot of the hospital with bordering flowerbeds blooming surreally brightly, and a DATUM GENERAL HOSPITAL: 1958–? logo on all four sides of the card), and returned to the waiting-room.

He sat back down beside the now sleeping Melissa, who now leaned against him, head on his bicep, as she continued to sleep. Using a pen he had borrowed from one of the nurses, with his unhurt hand he wrote:

> *St. S.,*
> *Well, it isn't (as you say) faint, but it is sometimes very sour, and it sure does seem to sometimes stink, too. But like the song says, two out of three ain't bad.*
>
> *And out of this disorder that surrounds me, the confusion of my father's house, of this, you tell me repeatedly, I am to win the day in my soul, celebrate the common, honour the everyday, wring the sacred from the banal. (How often over the years have you told me this? And I have! I have!) But is it possible (perhaps) that a rose is a rose is a rose? I mean, in your experience, have you ever had reason to call a spade a spade? Eh?*
> *Your silent, exiled, and cunning Canadian friend,*
> *J.T.*

He returned the pen to the nurse and pushed the card through a mailslot at the nurses' desk marked OUT OF TOWN ONLY.

Fully awakened by the departure of her pillow, Melissa bleary-eyed greeted James's return with a quizzical look first at him, and then at the mailslot.

"A postcard. To a friend," he said.

She looked him up and down, then back at the nurses' station.

"Just thought I'd make use of the moment. You know."

"'I see,' said the blind man," she said.

The nurse James had borrowed the pen from stuck her head in the doorway to apologize for the wait, and to say that the doctor would now see them back in the examining room. James thanked her and moved towards the door.

Melissa, following, motioned to the nurse with her chin towards the back of James's head. "Wrote a postcard — to a friend — at two a.m. in a hospital waiting-room. Decided to make use of the moment, you know." The woman smiled weakly Melissa's way, and then at James, who had by now stopped and turned around in the doorway. He took Melissa by the hand.

"Don't mind us," he said to the nurse, "we've had a very long night."

Flashing them both a professional grin, "Who hasn't?" she said.

They drove in silence. James rested the elbow of his hurt hand out of the truck window, the speed-limit breeze deflecting off his arm and into his face nearly refreshing, the empty downtown and for-no-one-but-them streetlights almost calming; each of these only almost, however, as in: in a half-second of swinging overhead red light changing to green light (that, and the acceleration of a size seven — woman's — pump to the pedal), a mosquito-bite twitch on the back of James's neck led him to shift his head slightly to the right to reveal (in a flash of splintered sudden sight) a round man in uniform in the moonlight in front of the locked front door of the brand-new mall puffing his head nearly imperceptible in swelling billows of blue gloomy cigar smoke, the entirety of his suck suck suck sucking person at that precise instant existing on the exact pre-mall spot where, once upon a tune-told time, an orange-lacquered transmission on a shiny steel chain had stirred in the wind on more than one slightly windy Datum day.

In another half-second it was gone. He looked back over his shoulder and: gone. Nothing. James slapped the same back-for-more-blood mosquito biteless evermore. The closing refrain to his own "King Street Cataclysm" ("Sacred spot of leaving place/Holy time and hallowed space") did not come to mind.

Nearing their destination, Melissa pulled the truck into the parking lot of a twenty-four-hour convenience store and asked James if he had any particular problem with microwave popcorn and whether he wanted regular or diet Coke. He gave her a little look before returning his stare to the bandaged hand resting in his lap. "I understand completely," she said solemnly, answering her own question. "It's been quite a weekend for you, I know." She stepped out of the truck and closed the door. Looking at James through the rolled-down window, "My hero," she said, and departed towards the store.

He lifted and inspected his bandaged hand, considered its weaponed injury. Whimpering — definitely — he thought. No, never with a bang, big or not. Never.

Then, a temptation — weak and for the most part unconscious, but a temptation still; sickening in scope, yet appealing to an extent all the same — to obliterate his weekend-accumulated bewilderment in one easy obsession, by counting the hell out of how-many-who-knows bags of fertilizer stacked four across and six high on wooden crates five wide in front of the store. He surprised himself, however, by managing to ride out a first wave of tallying enticement without too much effort by following Melissa's skirt-sweeping way through the aisles of the store.

Melissa came back with a bulging white plastic bag with the store's name emblazoned across it, and, after giving Al a quick rub between the ears, had them on their way again.

"Been busy while I was gone?" she said, white sack sitting between them, quick, fortifying kneading of James's thigh performed on her part entirely without strategy.

"I was tempted," he replied.

Pulling out of the parking lot and looking first for traffic and then James's way, "Hang in there, lover," she said. "'Farther along', right? Just like the song."

"I wonder sometimes," he said.

"Well, that's not entirely a bad thing either."

33

Soon, where from the beginning roughly four hours earlier they had set out to be all along: Buckly's place.

Ignition off, crickets and hissing tree creatures everyone a hundred times has heard before (yet no one knows
the name of) the only everywhere sound, James and
Melissa walked around to the back of the house by the
light of a slight moon and generous sidewalk-sliced an-
gles of windowed house light (Al already bounded out of
the truck bed and busy lost in nose-to-ground sniffing).
The day and night's humidity, in the hour or so they had
spent in the hospital, had been sucked up almost entirely
into the sky's dark overhead, a slight after-rain breeze dancing some white sheets and towels Buckly had not pru-
dently put out to dry before leaving home earlier that
evening. James managed a slight smile in noticing the
house all ablaze with inside light.

"Looks like your uncle's home after all," Melissa said.

"No, he's not home, but he'd love to be here right now
to hear you say that."

"I don't—"

"Forget it."

"Are all dogs as good as Al is, cowboy? I mean, we
didn't exactly take him on the short route home, did we?"

Laughing a little, "No, we did not, that's true," James
said.

"And when the gun went off and I slammed on the
brakes and Benny jumped over you out of the truck and

took off running through that cornfield? I thought Al would never let go of his pant-leg."

"He had ahold of him for a while, that's for sure."

"But he came back, though."

"Oh yeah, he came back — after he got his two cents in. Yeah, Al's a good boy," James said, crouching low to the ground to give the settled-down, belly-down dog a few nice kneads inside and behind his ears. "Oh yeah, Al's a good boy," he repeated, inspired in his stroking by the age-old mutt-master symbiosis of dog-tail going wag wag when the word "Good" (in the right tone told) gets spoken.

"C'mon, let's go inside," James said, rising, letting the almost sleeping dog lie. He knew where his uncle kept what Buckly referred to as "the good stuff" — Buckly's canned-food cache for the normally dry-food-eating Al — and wanted to compensate his uncle's dog for the rough road he and Melissa had brought upon him; that and the sheared mess he had made of their captor's pant-leg. He made his way across the darkened patio to the gas barbecue near the screened back door.

But:

"Ah, for Christ's sake, if it's not one thing it's—"

"What what what?" Melissa said.

"The key. The spare key. It's gone."

"It's gone?"

"I thought I just said that."

"It's been a long night for both of us, lover, so save the sarcasm for when I'm better rested, all right? Believe me, I didn't expect to be kidnapped when I put these on." One at a time, lifting one leg up and keeping her balance on the other, Melissa took off her black pumps. Holding them both in one hand, she felt with her free hand up and under the gas barbecue as James had just done.

"I already looked," he said.

"Don't pout, dear. Nobody's questioning your masculine ability to perform practical duties. It's just that it's dark as hell and maybe you. . . . You're sure it's supposed to be under here and not somewhere else?"

"Been there for the past fifteen years."

"Okay then. No need to get upset. Let's just have a good look underneath here and" — sightless fingers rushing over already explored territory — "we'll deal with . . . whatever . . . has to . . . be. . . . Damn it!"

"What?"

Silence.

"What what what?"

"If it's not one thing it's another, isn't it?" she said.

"It's not there," James said.

"It's not there."

They stood where they were, looking as best they could through the darkness at the barren barbecue, each waiting for the other to say what was next. Neither was next to say anything, though, as Al, lying on his side and seeming to sense that, at least for the time being, nobody was going anywhere, pushed off invisible earth with long Labrador limbs onto his back, four-legged-in-the-air dog dozing almost immediately ensuing. Quick tongue snap lick of lips and old-man gum-suck soon followed, the faintest black-snouted wheeze song clearly eared by James and Melissa over assorted nature noises what not. Canine calmed, they both stood and gawked a good bit in a not unpleasant fashion at the upturned Al's resting. James's good hand and Melissa's shoeless hand somehow found each other in the dark. They gawked a little while longer. They gawked.

Eventually: "Dogs sure aren't tragic, are they?"

"Nope," James replied, not knowing exactly what Melissa meant, but saying so anyway. "They sure as heck are not."

"Maybe the Buddha was a dog. What do you think about that, huh? Maybe way back when, a big old bulldog, just by doing whatever it is big old bulldogs do, showed everybody just about everything anybody needed to know about anything to do with living. The right way of living, I mean. *The Way*, I guess is what you'd call it. Except that, being the smug bastards we are, people had to make it up and write it down that a fat man in a thong and sandals with a perma-grin stuck on his face said all those deep things, and a plain old puppydog is just man's best friend and not so wise at all." They lingered in their hand-holding and looking down together at the dozing dog, chirping backyard theatre asteroid lit a thousand times redundant.

"I hear you," James said, "I hear you." Quite possibly he did.

"How late does your uncle usually stay out when he's visiting this 'Red' person?" Melissa asked, suddenly her pragmatic self again.

"Never the entire night. Besides, he's working afternoons tomorrow and he'd kick himself if he slept away the chance to work his garden the day after a good rain. No later than sun-up, anyway."

"All right then," she said, "wait here." Al instantly rolled over, upright attentive at her stockinged-feet movement along the stone sidewalk that led to the front of the house. "You too," she added, calling behind her, "stay where you are." Dog and man exchanged puzzled glances.

"You get used to it," James, to Al, said. The dog rested his head, chin leading the way, on a patch of cool grass between his earth-flat front paws.

Presently Melissa appeared around the side of the house with a large bag of wavy dip chips in one hand and her pumps still in the other. "Well, it's not much and, like I said, I don't know dogs all that well and I can't imagine this is good for him, but. . . ."

"Well, just don't give him too many," James said, conspiratorially smiling at the sight of the bag of snacks. He patted the sitting-up Al on the crown of his head as Melissa gingerly poured five or six chips onto the ground in front of the dog. Sniff sniff, then: gone; disappeared; vanished.

In a word: inhaled. "Well, more than that — that's just a tease, for Pete's sake," said James.

"I told you I didn't know anything about dogs."

"Here." He took the bag from her. He spilled out without any attempt at measurement a good third of its weighed-before-shipping contents onto the ground, gave the consumed-for-the-moment-in-consuming Al another pat on the top of the head, and took Melissa by the hand again, the chip bag cradled in his other, bandaged arm. Al crunched away.

"Where to now? The dog has been fed, the night is still young, and I've still got one good hand, you know."

"Sometimes I'd swear you actually know what you're doing," Melissa said, moving close, her shoe-filled hand wrapping around the small of his back, drawing her closer to him still.

"You should see me when I'm working with a full band behind me."

"I'd like to see that."

"You will, you will."

"I will?"

"You will. You'll like Toronto. Got its silly side, of course. Best and worst of what the entire country's got to offer." James thought of Devanchuck and his patriotically pleading letter. "But I think you'll like it. Person almost feels like they've got half a chance there. I'll show you the side of town the Ministry of Tourism doesn't want you to know about."

"I'd like that," Melissa said. Kissing, groping, closed eyes, et cetera.

A break in the amorous action. "What's next?" James said.

"Well, it is technically your birthday this morning, you know. Today, I mean."

"My birthday," he said. "I almost forgot."

"Well, I didn't."

"You didn't?"

"No."

"Meaning?"

"Meaning, as the fat man said, 'Show time.'"

"Come again?"

"Show time. You know: lights, camera, action. At my house. The VCR is ready and waiting."

"You mean . . . ?"

"Exactly," she said.

"Huh. Isn't that something?" he said. "And all along I thought it was just part of some plan you had."

34

Melissa left James waiting under the porchlight of her parents' front step. Numerous head-banging moths kamikaze'd and collided above his head. She opened up the garage door manually and carefully parked the truck inside. Hers was the only vehicle in the garage; her parents and the Corvette had already left for Oshawa on Sunday afternoon. Melissa's uncle's funeral not taking place until Tuesday, they were going to spend the next couple of days in Toronto frequenting some good restaurants, doing a little shopping, and using some lower-level first-base seats her father had been given by a client for Monday night's Blue Jays–Oakland A's game.

She emerged from the garage with the bag from the store under one arm (pumps heels-up stuck in and sticking out) and the manila package in her other hand, and on the front step asked James to hold the foodstuffs while with both hands she up and down interrogated a baby spruce tree for the spare house key. She found it, used it, returned it, and they went inside.

A blast of air-conditioned air met James like a cold embrace; right from the muggy no more but still warm night into well-chilled this, he desired nothing more than the overstuffed white couch he nearly bumped into on the way in. That, and perhaps a pillow and blanket if they happened to be handy. Or not. Either way, oblivion.

Not a chance of this, though, as Melissa marched him directly into the family room. There she flicked on a couple of table lamps, took a two-litre bottle of pop out of the plastic bag, spilled the remaining potato chips onto the coffee table, and switched on the TV, with the sound turned down, before heading into the kitchen for glasses and ice. No tour of the house was offered or asked for. James could hear the *beep* of the microwave timer being set, and the heated hum of the machine set into action.

"I'd offer to make your Coke high octane, but we killed my whole supply of bourbon the other night in the truck and my parents don't touch the stuff," Melissa called out from the other room. "Strictly gin-and-tonic people, as I'm sure you can imagine. Besides, I guess this is one movie you should definitely see through a glass clearly, isn't it?" Sporadic, then regular, almost rhythmic pop-popping sounded from the kitchen. "Get a little more comfortable out there if you want," she said. "I am. Is it as humid up in Toronto as it is in Datum? God, I hope not. Need to take two showers a day just to feel halfway normal down here."

James couldn't quite hear what Melissa was saying— something about what kind of glass he would feel comfortable with for his pop and did he want some humus she had gotten from Toronto this past year — but, already nicely part of the reclining chair she had sat him down in, he didn't request any clarification. Within seconds he was asleep, only to be awoken a few moments later, however,

RAY ROBERTSON

by a glass of fizzling cola on the rocks patiently being held underneath his twitching-awake nose, the television screen blue alive the room's only light.

He sat up, took the offered glass, sipped, and blinked a few times at the source of the room's sudden azure. Melissa, feet up on the coffee table, leaned back on the couch in her bikini-panties and bra, remote control in one hand, her own glass of pop in the other. A large white bowl of popcorn balanced on her lap. James looked on (particularly at the black-stocking-free unpainted ten toes), trying to get in the mood, running through in his head amorous acts already accomplished that weekend in the hope that an enlivened brain might help to inflate his mostly exhausted body.

But the effort was too much. The dreaded wet noodle, he knew almost at once. In the morning I'll—

"I'm touched, really — and surprised, too," he said, "believe me" — looking at the manila package sitting on top of the television set, then back at Melissa — "but really, I'm not in the right state right now, physically or mentally, to appreciate like I really want to whatever it is you've managed to put together. So why don't we call it a night, and in the morning I'll—"

"You comfortable?" Melissa said, getting up from the couch, setting the bowl of popcorn and her glass on the clear glass coffee table (wet ring forming immediately in spite of the room's coolness).

"Sure, sure, fine, but like I said, I think we'd be better off waiting until the morning and then take it from there, okay?"

Melissa padded across the room's white-shagged floor to the television, pressed the channel changer on the bottom of the unit to channel three, and picked the package up off the top. "Your birthday, I know, but I'll save you the trouble, okay? Besides, I absolutely love opening presents, even somebody else's."

Not waiting for an answer, she tore off the wrapping

paper with one sharp, artless, two-fisted tear down the middle, letting the result fall to the floor in two crumpled Scotch-taped piles. "Your uncle isn't all that big on appearances, is he?"

"My uncle?"

Holding up the plain black, manila-free video, "From your uncle," she said. "For your twenty-fifth birthday. Something he said he promised he'd give you a long time ago. Said you'd know all about it."

James, silent, slowly blinked. He sipped without thirst at his by now nearly fizzless drink. He stared at the videotape, and then at Melissa.

"Don't look at me," she said, "I was hoping you could fill me in. He made it sound so important to you and all."

Blinking, sipping, blinking.

"Well, I guess we're both in for a surprise then," she said. "He gave it to me about a week before you got here, a few days after I stopped by his place and told him I was doing that story on you for the paper. Guess he thought he and I got along okay. Anyway, since I told him I'd be looking you up in Toronto before too long, he asked me if I could give you this thing he was keeping for you, since he thought you'd make a bigger deal out of it than he wanted to deal with. And here we are."

"It's the Thing," James said.

"What do you mean? What thing?"

"The Thing," he said — all, really, he could after all this time say.

"So you know what this . . . this thing is, then? You know what's on the tape?" She sounded slightly disappointed.

"No, I, uh . . . I didn't even know it was a tape. I mean, the past little while I've wondered what it might be and . . . sometimes thought it might help with. . . . But no, no, my uncle never said. . . . I don't know what's on it. I have no idea."

"News that stays news for both of us, then," Melissa

said. "Good. I like surprises almost as much as I like opening presents." Then, before James could even begin to think of a good reason why she shouldn't, Melissa pushed the power button on the VCR and nudged the cassette a quarter of the way into the machine's same-sized slot, the tape sucking in on its own the rest of the way, tape and tapehead coming together in grinding-gear clicking confirmation.

Deep in his seat, James could only clutch at the red leather arms of the chair he sat in (a good portion of his ice-cube-sloshing drink spilling onto the rug in the process). Lunging head-first forward, his body getting nowhere, he sputtered, "Hey now, maybe we, uh, let's maybe just slow down a little bit here and uh, I mean, I think maybe first we should. . . ."

For: the screen was blue (the room was blue). The screen went white (and the room went white). Words (small, black, typographically unimpressive) out of the bright-nothing shine of the television screen began to take shape. James sat back (the muscles in his arms, neck, and buttocks, if not relaxing, at least untensing), reading what was there.

Video Transfer from 8mm Reel
by T. Baughman Video Services Inc.
For All Your Video Servicing Needs
264 Park St. East
Datum, Ontario
(516) 354-7291

Up, up off the screen with the words; a pica a second upward, and words no more. Blue screen again. Bright orange, then. Sunday-afternoon yellow, sick-fruit red, and, finally, many-coloured kaleidoscope poof flash.

Then clearing. Unclouding. Focused (though the camera at times unsteady). Then white again. White again, but scraped and scratchy, burned at the edges: just like some poor old someone's old home movie. In colour. Beginning. But not at the beginning. Still, walk-talkers alive and living, altogether all of them quiet to the viewer but with lips moving, throats laughing, ears cupped and heads leaned, heads knowing and nodding. Alive there, then, them, look. Alive.

A Canadian flag tacked to the wall over the bar slumping a little in the middle. The flag of the legion hall that this place is. A framed portrait of Queen Elizabeth. Two PLEASE DO NOT THROW CONFETTI INSIDE THE HALL signs, slightly tattered. Flowers. Streamers. More flowers. A red EXIT sign alert over the back door. A bouquet of roses in a vase half full of rose-thorned water. Long wooden tables of cheap, knotted wood. On several, where the people sit, white linen with blue embroidered flowers covering the surface and falling over the edges. On each, clothed or not, things and more things. Things like: beer bottles and cigarette packages — store-bought and individual smokes rolled. Overflowing ashtrays. Purses left unattended. Unclipped clip-on ties. Handkerchiefs. Red-lipstick-kissed balls of white toilet paper. A single can of ginger ale for the room's sole non-drinker. And this, and that, and, naturally, that most necessary thing of all of these things: the ones whose things these things are.

So the bride (back, for the most part, to the viewer), pushing a silver platter of sweets in among the sitters at each and every table, empty mouths over their shoulders smiling, mouthing thank you but no, no, no thank you, I'm fine, no, but thank you. And then relenting, smiling, giving thanks and taking one anyway, smiling, the platter moving on to the next and the next.

So the bride, of course, in white. Distinguishing features? None. Absolutely none. Like a bride, the bride wears white.

So the other, the groom, in best rented black-tie tux that can be Datum-got. A little stiff in the shoulders (manly-embarrassed looking so fine), but there. There and helping.

Helping in pushing his own sweets-stacked platter. And everyone a little hand-to-mouth laughing at him just a big unwieldy new husband he, he not even half-way as successful in emptying his plate as his just-as-new wife she.

(Scene cut here. Crazy-coloured splash of light. New scene up on the screen in a few broken-reel, whipping-by-but-soon-repaired seconds.) Showing: one arm of the groom gently resting on top of one arm of the bride's, the two of them together pushing through easily the wedding cake's delicate first piece. Mystery in any manner is nowhere to be seen; a man and woman cut a cake. James's mother and father cut the cake.

Soundless clapping.

And the bride and groom kiss.

The bride and groom kiss.

James watches his mother and father kiss.

Harder now, more hands together (old hands, young hands, work-coarsened hands: quiet hands).

And together (she with plates and forks, he alone now with knife) the cake gets cut and given out, piece by piece by piece by piece, every incredible plain white piece of it, one plain piece at a time.

No credits or acknowledgements follow the film. Simply blue screen again. Blue room.

Over an air-conditioned murmur James plucked out a medium-pitched clucking sound with the collaborative aid of his tongue, the roof of his mouth, and his back right molar. He looked up from the dead blue screen to Melissa on the couch looking right back at him — Melissa, like everything else in the room, softened by the television set's soaking blue glow. From air-conditioned chill or what not, James could not tell, across her chest she hugged herself with both arms.

"How long, you think?" he asked at last.

"Three or four minutes. Maybe four and a half, tops," Melissa answered.

He nodded his head a few times, slowly, then resumed,

if in a slightly more measured metre, his clucking.

Subsequently, "There are songs about as long as that, you know," he said.

She looked his way but didn't answer.

"I mean, it would have to be nothing special. Just a song, I mean. Nothing special."

Melissa said nothing.

"Actually, I've had this tune stuck in my head for a while now that I think it might go with. Real pretty tune. It's just music right now. But real pretty."

"I can just imagine," Melissa answered.

"Yeah?" he said.

"Yes," she said. She rose from the couch, arms at her sides now. Standing before him still sitting there in his chair, "Yes."

35

Not much was said, but things did manage to get done.

First stop, a twenty-minute hiatus at James's grandparents' place, this followed up by a quick trip to the all-night pharmacy. Then, not a dawdling but not a particularly hurried, either, tea-and-toast breakfast at The Coffee Shop. So early still, no new papers sat in the newspaper boxes, the sky's vast black crust just beginning to show signs of cracking in lightness open. Simple nourishment their only intention, the unavailability of today's new and improved information was neither noted nor lamented. One hot-water refill to their shared tin teapot later, James pushed three quarters under his crumbed-up toast plate and let Melissa pay the bill at the counter.

Unlocking the driver's door to the pickup in the res-taurant parking lot (James waiting by his door for the same), "You feel like driving a bit?" Melissa asked. "I guess you know it's about a three-and-a-half-hour drive, and I sure could use a little time on the passenger's side. Done a lot of driving tonight. I mean last night. Today? Whatever, I'm beat."

"Sure," James said, "but not right away, okay? How about when we get near London?"

"Sounds good to me," she said. "Let's get going."

"Just let me get something out of my knapsack and let's go."

"Get it."

Got it; they got.

Easily Highway 401 (officially, though not by any tongue spoken, the Macdonald Cartier Freeway) is driven; one straight line directly where, going, you want to end up. As exhausted-calm as her passenger, the truck cab musicless but for two winding air vents, Melissa, one hand on the wheel, pushed the truck steadily north. With any luck they would be in Toronto well before noon.

Twenty minutes outside Datum city limits, out of the top pocket of his red-and-black-striped work shirt, James produced a pen and one of the postcards he had packed away for his trip home four days before. The card placed flat on the dash, without a word he began to write. And hum.

"Pretty song," Melissa said.

He stopped writing. "It is all right, isn't it?" he replied.

"Hmmm. A new song?"

"An old tune that's been on my mind recently. An old tune looking to become a new song."

"*Will* it be a song?"

"You mean a real song?" he said. "A song with words to it?"

"I wouldn't have put it like that," she said, "but okay, will it be a real song? A song with words to it?"

"It's going to be a real song," he said. "And not only that, it's going to be a real song, too. At least I hope it will be. Either way, I'll let you know by no later than the first week of September." He returned to his postcard.

For a good bit, her driving, him writing.

Then: "Same friend as before?" Melissa said, motioning with her chin in the direction of the card on the dash.

"Just a sec, I'm almost . . . Okay. What's that again?" He stuck the completed postcard in his shirt pocket and leaned back in his seat, stretched. It was only a quarter to seven in the morning, but he allowed himself the feeling of a decent day's work done already. Further: fully cognizant for the first time that it was Monday morning, that the Stanley Cup Playoffs began tonight. The possibilities of the day filled up easily the empty landscape he watched from his window pass by behind him.

Then, Melissa: "I said—" Hand over and in his pocket and out quicker than he could have imagined possible without putting both them and the truck in a ditch.

"Hey, that's—"

"Just—" Quick scan, peek up at the road, quick scan; finished. "This isn't to a woman," she said, handing the card back, both hands on the wheel now.

"Who the hell said it was?" Shaking his head, he tucked the card back into his pocket, thinking, I'll have to get used to this kind of thing.

"No one. No one said it was, I just. . . . Hey, you know there's no postage on that thing. Never get to where you want it to go the way it is now."

"It'll get there. Always has before. In fact," he said, his eye on the road up ahead, "turn off at the next exit there, will you? Says there's a service station. Gotta be a mailbox there."

"They probably don't even sell stamps. And we're making such good time."

"Come on, humour the birthday boy."

"Oh, well," she said, slowing the truck down, turning onto the off-ramp, "maybe just this one time."

He took the card out of his pocket and read what he had written.

Stevie,
Dogs are not tragic. Make of this what you will. I, for one, plan to make the most of it; wedded, naturally, to lovely melodies deluxe, as per usual.

I have met a girl. Not a bit like yours. But then maybe she is. The wonder of mortal beauty. A wild angel. On and on and on. You know the sort. Maybe you don't. Tough luck for you if not.

Brother: To live, to err, to fall, to triumph, to re-create life out of life. And don't you dare forget that to everything there is a season. That's in the Bible and on a Byrds album, too.

JJ.

P.S. My mother (you've never known my mother — don't pretend like you ever did) is an old woman who has had a hell of a life for most of her life and likes to watch TV a lot and eat and sleep and that's about the whole ballgame right there.

Never knew the old man. All reports would seem to indicate that he was an all-right kinda guy. Cut quite a figure in a tux, I've been led to believe. Fatal flaw seems to have been never being able to pass up a good deal when it came to automotive parts. Transmissions, I mean. Whatever. Oh well, just thought I should set you straight. For the record.

Melissa waiting in the idling truck, James made his way across the service station parking lot. He found a mailbox in front of the Tim Horton's and threw the unstamped postcard in. Looking up and realizing where he was, Why not? he thought. He pushed the door to the doughnut shop open and fingered in his jeans pocket for enough change for a couple of mediums to go.

He stood in line behind an elderly couple in matching red track-suits and baseball caps examining the speciality doughnuts through the glass counter. He found he had enough for the coffees, as well as the spare key to his uncle's house. Now how the . . . ?

The old pair finally decided on two éclairs, no cherries, and two hot chocolates, extra-whipped. James held the key out in front of him between his right thumb and forefinger and tried to remember. Soon, the couple paying, receiving their change, and carefully placing the contents of their order in a cardboard carry-out tray, it came to him:

Forgot to put it back at Uncle Buckly's place yesterday afternoon when I started to count like. . . . To count? Yesterday? Seems more like . . . years.

The specific number of years it seemed, he didn't bother to estimate. He shrugged and put the key back in his pocket. No big deal, he thought. Just mail the thing off to him first chance I get when we get home. No big deal at all.

The room empty but for him and the girl behind the counter, it was now his turn.

"Welcome to Tim Horton's can I take your order please?"

"Yeah," James said, "two coffees, please. Two medium coffees."

"And how would you like them, sir?"

"Plain," he said. "Black, I mean."

"Both of them?"

"Both of them," he said.

"And will that be for here, or to go?"

"To go," he said.

"Anything else to go with that?"

"No," he said, "nothing."

36

Sun up. Sole-slapping along the pathway.
Head raised. Tail curled. Reflex *grrr*.
Familiar steps. Wag. Rise. Stretch. Scratch. Wag wag.
Wait.
Here.
Hand on head, ears. Rub. Lick in return. Rub, lick, rub.
"Whadoyou know for sure, pal?"
Wag wag wag.
"Well, that makes two of us."